Praise for CORPUS CHRISTMAS

"One of the pleasures of *Corpus Christmas* is . . .
its well-drawn cast of art-world characters, as
colorful a bunch of pompous types as ever enlivened
a Daumier caricature."
—*The Wall Street Journal*

"Strongest on characterization and atmosphere, this
[is an] impressive novel."
—*Ellery Queen's Mystery Magazine*

"An old-fashioned mystery . . . and I intend to return
for more."
—*Boston Sunday Globe*

"One of the field's sharpest writers. Her spare,
elegant prose and flair for characterization are
showcased in *Corpus*. . . . A fine read."
—*Greensboro News & Record*

"A Christmas gift for mystery fans, as full of surprises
and as satisfying as a rich holiday dessert."
—*The Pilot*, Southern Pines, North Carolina

"It does what a good mystery novel must—keep you
guessing to the end."
—*The News and Observer*, Raleigh, North Carolina

By Margaret Maron

CORPUS CHRISTMAS

Margaret Maron

BANTAM BOOKS
NEW YORK • TORONTO • LONDON • SYDNEY • AUCKLAND

All of the characters in this book are fictitious,
and any resemblance to actual persons, living or
dead, is purely coincidental.

*This edition contains the complete text
of the original hardcover edition.*
NOT ONE WORD HAS BEEN OMITTED.

CORPUS CHRISTMAS

*A Bantam Crime Line Book / published by arrangement with
Doubleday*

PRINTING HISTORY
Doubleday edition published November 1989
Bantam edition / December 1991

ISBN 0-553-27410-4

Published simultaneously in the United States and Canada

*Bantam Books are published by Bantam Books, a division of Bantam
Doubleday Dell Publishing Group, Inc. Its trademark, consisting
of the words "Bantam Books" and the portrayal of a rooster,
is Registered in U.S. Patent and Trademark Office and in other
countries. Marca Registrada. Bantam Books, 666 Fifth Avenue,
New York, New York 10103.*

PRINTED IN THE UNITED STATES OF AMERICA

RAD   0 9 8 7 6 5 4 3 2 1

CORPUS
CHRISTMAS

Prologue

In the mid-1820's Erich Breul's grandfather parlayed three leaky river barges and the opening of the Erie Canal into a modest fortune. During the Civil War, Erich Breul's father added a second fortune running blockades. Erich Breul himself was the first of his family to be sent to Harvard—primarily to learn the art of managing money—and his postgraduate trip to Europe was meant to complete the family's transformation from flannel cap to silk hat in three generations.

Like many young scions whose lives were destined for the administration of settled wealth, Erich had developed a taste for fine art during his college years and Europe provided an ideal opportunity to pursue that interest.

To the elder Breul's dismay, young Erich's proposed year stretched to eight. Fortunately, Mr. Breul was healthy and vigorous at the time and he was prepared, within reason, to indulge his son's acquisition of culture. Times were changing and Mr. Breul was shrewd enough to change, too.

In Europe Erich immediately grasped what his freebooter father only dimly sensed: Culture could purify and legitimize the crude and occasionally bloody foundations that too often underlay even modest financial empires.

Yet it was more than that.

Young Erich Breul genuinely liked pictures and he made a substantial effort to cultivate an eye for adventurous art, especially since his allowance did not stretch to safely pedigreed old masters. He disdained the stuffy salon painters and also avoided the impressionists, thinking them too superficial. Instead, he was instinctively attracted by that mixture of dignity and daring found in the work of expatriate Americans

1

like Whistler and Sargent. He had his portrait painted that first winter by the young Italian virtuoso, Giovanni Boldini; and although a sympathy for noble sentiment drew him to intimist painters like Tranquillo Cremona and Arcangelo Guidini, his passion for bravura technique led him as far afield as Adolphe Monticelli.

In later years he liked to think he would have bought a Van Gogh had he seen that artist's work.

For eight years, crates of pictures arrived on the piers of New York with predictable regularity. A bewildered Mr. Breul paid the freight. He might not understand his son's preoccupation with collecting art but he continued to underwrite the expense since young Erich had, while collecting Ferdinand Hodler in Switzerland, also collected Fraulein Sophie Fürst, a distant cousin with a sizable dowry and trim ankles that flashed beneath her proper skirts.

When the newlyweds finally followed their treasures to America in 1887, Mr. Breul established them at 7 Sussex Square. Sophie decorated with late-Victorian opulence and Erich turned the cavernous ballroom into a personal art gallery.

As was the fashion in those days, pictures were hung in the salon style popular in Europe. In frames monumentally carved and gilded, they were stacked on the walls from chair rail to ceiling, one above the other, with little consideration for size or shape and with almost no space between each frame.

The collection spilled into the formal drawing room, leaped the great hall to the library and dining room, and still continued to grow: George Inness; Henry Creswell; William Carver Ewing; and Walter Sickert, a student of Whistler's with whom Erich had caroused in London before his marriage to Sophie. Almost by accident he acquired a decent Chandler Grooms and a better than average John La Farge.

Old Mr. Breul thought it a deplorable waste of money but he loved his son and for Christmas one year even gave him a set of Winslow Homer's marine drawings which had caught his eye and reminded him of his blockade-running days.

Despite Erich Breul's continued passion for pictures, he did not disappoint his father's hopes once he was home. He may have lacked his grandfather's gritty pioneer spirit and his father's ruthless zest and acumen but he eventually shaped himself into a dutiful businessman and, after the crash of 1893, even managed to recoup most of the losses.

Only one child was born of his happy union with Sophie Fürst. In due time Erich Junior grew to manhood, attended Harvard like his father, and departed for his own *wander jahr* in Europe, where he was struck and killed by a team of runaway horses in a narrow Paris street two days before his twenty-second birthday.

Three months later, still dazed by his death, Sophie stumbled in front of the electric trolley that ran along the bottom of Sussex Square.

When his son's effects arrived from Europe, Erich Breul was touched to find a few crude pictures in his steamer trunks. It didn't matter that the pictures were dreadful—Erich could remember some mistakes he himself had made when he first began collecting—the tragedy was that the boy's life had been cut short before his eye could mature.

Heartbroken, he'd stored his son's possessions next to the trunk which held his memorial to Sophie: her nightdress, her autograph album, a lace handkerchief that still breathed the faint trace of her toilet water, along with a hundred other intimate bits and scraps that he couldn't bear to give away.

There was no question of another marriage for him, another child. He drew up a will that would turn 7 Sussex Square into a museum to house in perpetuity the pictures he'd collected; and although he continued to function—to work, to dine with friends at his club, to refine his collection—when the great influenza epidemic of 1918 struck, he succumbed almost gratefully.

"... August and my cycling tour up the Rhône (along with that amusing adventure in Sorgues-sur-l'Ouvèze with those bohemian chaps) was, until now, my favorite month, although the autumn lectures at Lyons's Palais des Arts were as edifying as you had hoped, Papa, and my French is much improved. But now I am in Paris, the queen of cities! I still cannot believe I am here, here in the cultural center of the universe with my own snug rooms in Montparnasse. Notre-Dame! Montmartre! *Dites-moi, mes parents,* however did you force yourselves to leave? And yet, as the days shorten, shall I confess one small misgiving? Will you laugh at your grown-up son for his weakness? How I shall miss our jolly Christmas this year! Should I live to be a hundred, dear Papa and Mama, I shall never forget the roaring fires in every hearth, every room bedecked with garlands of holly and ivy, the smell of cinnamon and ginger and roasted goose wafting from the kitchen below to the nursery on high, and in the main hall, such a tree that to a little lad seemed to tower up to the heavens, each branch a-blaze with candles and bejeweled with Mama's glass angels. . . ."

Letter from Erich Breul Jr., dated 11.5.1912.
(From the Erich Breul House Collection)

I

Thursday, December 10

Snow was predicted by Sunday and a chill morning rain had drenched the city streets but it had stopped by ten A.M. when Rick Evans arrived at Sussex Square, that little gem of urban felicity down in the East Twenties. He paused a moment, propped his tripod on the wrought-iron fence which enclosed the tiny park, uncapped the lens of the camera slung around his neck, and slowly panned the area.

Unlike the broad avenues of commerce where New York's glamorous stores were bedizened with tinsel and glitter, Christmas down here approached in a resolutely nineteenth-century fashion that was less intimidating to someone born and reared in a small college town in Louisiana. The solid townhouses that ringed Sussex Square were built of stone, not wood; but most wore heavy wreaths of fresh evergreens, waxed fruits, and lacquered nuts that gleamed in the weak winter sunlight with a homelike familiarity.

Number 7 was twice as wide as any of its neighbors and bore a small brass plaque that informed passersby that this was the Erich Breul House, built in 1868 and open to the public since 1920.

Rick Evans focused carefully on the brass plaque, then retrieved his tripod and walked up the broad marble stoop to the recessed doorway, a doorway so imposing that he automatically wiped his boots on the outer mat before entering the marbled hall.

Black velvet ropes, looped through brass stanchions, formed a walkway to a long Queen Anne tavern table where a middle-aged docent sat with a cash register on one side and a selection of brochures, books and postcards on the other. The docent looked up from her knitting and peered at him in nearsighted hopefulness; but when the young man's camera case and folded tripod came into focus, her smile faltered with disappointment. Only that photographer she'd been told to expect; not a paying sightseer wishing a tour of the house.

From an alcove at the rear of the vaulted entrance hall, a young black woman saluted him with a friendly wave of her steno pad as her high-heeled boots clicked through a doorway that had once led to the butler's pantry but was now the director's office.

On the left, midway the depth of the hall, stood a bushy fir tree, at least ten feet tall, but dwarfed by the massive proportion of the carved marble fireplace. The tree was surrounded by open boxes of ornaments, a tall aluminum stepladder, tangles of candle-shaped tree lights, and three women dressed in urban-casual woolens. As Rick Evans approached them, the light floral scent of their perfumes mingled with the fir's woodsy aroma and for a moment he felt himself unaccountably, profoundly homesick for Louisiana and Christmas in his mother's house.

He propped his tripod against the opposite side of the fireplace and smiled diffidently at a kind-looking brunette whose graying hair was tied back with a red silk scarf. "Is Mrs. Beardsley here?" he asked.

"Is God in his heaven?" the woman replied in an unexpectedly deep voice.

"Oh Helen, you're awful!" giggled a shorter, round-faced woman.

"Shh!" a third woman warned.

Sensible leather heels tapped down the wide marble staircase at the right of the hall as Mrs. Gawthrop Wallace Beardsley, senior docent at the Breul House, descended triumphantly, followed by a man in dark green coveralls whose face was obscured by the boxes he carried.

"We found them," she said, bustling over to the group. "I *knew* we had more decorations than these." Her all-seeing gaze fell upon Rick Evans and she halted to consult the old-fashioned gold watch on her wrist. "Mr. Evans. Surely I told you the tree would not be ready to be photographed until *after* lunch?"

Rick fiddled with the lens cap on the camera still slung

round his neck. "Yes, ma'am," he admitted, "but I had some free time and I thought maybe I could shoot some of the ornaments individually or something? I mean, aren't some of them pretty special?"

His voice trailed off in uncertainty.

The deep-voiced woman with the kind face took pity on him. "Yes, they certainly *are* special. Melissa, show him one of Mrs. Breul's glass angels."

Melissa, the widow of Dr. Higgins Highsmith Jr., whose many trusteeships had once included the Erich Breul House, plucked an ornament almost as delicate as she herself from its nest of tissue. From girlhood, Sophie Fürst Breul had collected dozens of fragile glass Christmas tree ornaments, charming souvenirs of carefree winter visits to relatives in Germany and Austria.

This particular angel had been blown from a pearly, opalescent glass and its features then hand-painted in soft pastels. Its robe was pale green and, incredible after so many years, fragile glass hands still held to those rosebud lips a gilt paper trumpet stamped with stars.

"Over a hundred years old!" marveled Melissa Highsmith. "And it's only frayed a bit here." Her wrinkled fingers sketched a circle around the trumpet's flare without actually touching the tattered edge.

"Do be careful," Mrs. Beardsley warned.

Her words were meant for the man, who was trying to set down his load of boxes without tipping them, but Mrs. Highsmith guiltily replaced the angel in its tissue as the deep-voiced woman stepped forward to help Pascal Grant.

Carefully, the workman straightened the boxes until each right corner was square with the one below, then turned to Mrs. Beardsley for approval with such innocent expectation that Rick automatically lifted his camera to his face to shield himself from so much physical beauty.

He knew that the Breul House contained basement quarters for a live-in handyman, but had not yet met him. In listing the people who worked there, his grandfather had hesitated at Pascal Grant's name and murmured something about a lamb of God, one of His poor unfortunates, which had led Rick to expect someone defeated or with an obvious physical handicap. A crippled alcoholic, perhaps.

Instead, now that the boxes no longer hid the man's face, Rick saw someone who looked like one of Sophie Breul's angels stepped down from a Christmas tree.

Pascal Grant was slender and finely built—even the coarse green coveralls he wore could not disguise that—with eyes as blue as the Virgin's robes and golden hair like spun glass. He had a thin, well-shaped nose, a rounded chin, and an upper lip so short that his mouth was seldom fully closed.

It must be those parted lips that made him look so innocent and young, thought Rick, twisting the barrel of his portrait lens until Grant's seraphic features filled the viewer. Too, the janitor seemed to keep his head tilted down so that when he spoke to anyone he had to look up from beneath level sandy brows like a child looking up at an adult.

He was looking now at Rick. "Hello," he said in a voice as light and sunny as his smile, and held out his right hand as if they were at a formal dinner. "You're Mr. Munson's grandson. You're going to take new pictures of everything. I'm Pascal Grant."

Puzzled, Rick lowered the camera and extended his own hand. "Rick Evans."

He was surprised by the unexpected strength of the janitor's grip, and noted that Grant's hand was calloused and that his fingertips were grease-stained beneath the ragged nails.

The women smiled approvingly at Rick. Even the patrician Mrs. Beardsley softened. "This is Helen Aldershott," she said, gesturing to the tall, deep-voiced woman. "And Melissa Highsmith, whom you've just met."

"So pleased," murmured Mrs. Highsmith, taking his hand between both of hers.

Her thin, arthritic fingers flashed with accumulated diamonds and he sensed that several of the rings were too loose, as if fashioned for younger, less gnarled hands. He wondered briefly how many generations of Highsmith fingers those rings had adorned.

The round-faced giggler and her shusher were Mrs. Dahl and Mrs. Quinones.

"Now then, Mr. Evans," Mrs. Beardsley said briskly. "Perhaps you can help Pascal bring down the last load? I don't possess quite the stamina I once had."

"You're amazing and you know it, Eloise," said Mrs. Aldershott. "You must have been from the basement to the attic a dozen times this morning. It's enough to tire anyone."

"I'll be glad to help," Rick said politely.

He hung his fleece jacket on the tripod, piled his camera and case next to them, then followed Pascal Grant up the broad marble staircase, which turned back on itself at a landing halfway up the height of the hall.

At the left of the stairs, eight thick red candles filled a freestanding fourteenth-century bronze candelabrum, and Mrs. Beardsley and her troops had garlanded the white stone balustrade in evergreen swags and tied them with red velvet ribbons.

On the wide landing, out of the way of passing traffic, stood the dummy figure of a woman, dressed in a ruffled, high-necked blouse and green serge skirt and buttoned shoes. Looking up at her from the curve of the balustrade on the floor below was her male counterpart, clothed as if on his way out for a stroll around Sussex Square on a December morning in 1905.

Thrifty Sophie Breul had seldom discarded anything, so the attic held trunks and boxes full of period clothes. When Gimbels closed its Broadway store, someone had salvaged several fashion mannequins for use at the Breul House.

It was almost like having a Ken and Barbie set for adults, and the docents enjoyed dressing the figures to suit the changing seasons.

Today, the gray-haired male figure wore a top hat, white silk muffler, and long black overcoat, and he carried a gold-headed cane.

The second floor was also open to the public, and it consisted of a wide central hall that was richly somber with a coved wooden ceiling and walls covered in dark burgundy silk. Two tall windows overlooked the park at one end and a carpeted mahogany staircase rose majestically at the other.

Narrow marble-topped tables hugged the walls beneath sumptuously framed oil paintings. The more important pieces of the Breul collection were displayed in the gallery downstairs. These were some of Erich Breul's less discerning purchases and the massive frames, each with its own small lamp, only mocked shrunken reputations. Here was a seascape by

Henry Babbage, once praised as "the American Turner"; there, a landscape by Everett Winstanley, "our Constable"; plus a pair of heroic battle scenes with heavily muscled horses, plunging and rearing about with flared nostrils, the work of Genevieve Carlton, whom the late scholar, Riley Quinn, had called the Rosa Bonheur of central New Jersey.

Between the paintings, every door stood wide to reveal bedrooms and dressing rooms, Erich Breul's oak-paneled study and Sophie Breul's sitting room. The latter was elaborately carpeted, draped, and cluttered with fringed shawls, tasseled cushions, gilt mirrors, cut-glass lamps and other ornate bric-a-brac that passed for tasteful decor in the late 1890's.

Halfway down the hall, they had to press themselves against the wall as a docent exited from the main bathroom with eight German tourists and their tour guide in tow. To judge by the laughter and bright chatter as they passed, the Victorian bathroom had been a great hit. Rick Evans had never seen a bathroom quite that large himself, nor one that lavish: walnut commode, a walnut-enclosed tub deep enough to float in, a wide marble lavatory, and all the brass fixtures fitted out with china knobs and handles.

At the end of the hall, the gloominess of the stair landing was relieved by an oval Tiffany window which Erich had ordered as a tenth anniversary present for Sophie. Even on this gray December day, its stained-glass leaves and flowers glowed with jewellike intensity.

Pascal Grant paused beneath it and smiled at Rick shyly.

"This is my second favorite window in the whole house," he said. "You should take a picture of it."

"I'm going to," Rick agreed. He had noticed it when Benjamin Peake, the director, had given him a hurried tour of the public rooms the previous week, but he planned to wait for a sunny day when the window would be more brilliantly backlighted.

"So," Rick said as they moved on up the steps to the third floor, "what's your first favorite window?"

"The front door downstairs," the other answered promptly over his shoulder. "Not the big door. *My* door."

Rick remembered seeing steps that apparently led down

to a doorway recessed beneath the stoop of the main entrance. "The service entrance?"

Pascal Grant paused at the top of the stairs and nodded. "That's mine. I'm service. I have a key and everything." He pulled a tangle of keys from his coverall pocket. "See?"

Even though he stood a step or two higher than Rick, his head was tilted so low that he seemed to be looking up at someone taller as he returned the keys to his pocket.

The third floor was as solidly built as the second, but the hall was narrower and the ceiling was simple plaster except for the cast moldings. Benjamin Peake had made a point about them, but at the moment Rick couldn't remember if the director had said they were special because of the oak-leaf-and-acorn design or because of the process by which they had been cast. Whichever the reason, Rick decided he'd better borrow Grant's stepladder, rig some lights, and take a couple of close-ups.

The front rooms had belonged to Erich Jr. before he went off to France; but in 1948, an imaginative curator had removed the young man's personal effects to a bedroom on the second floor and restored these rooms to their original state as a nursery and playroom. Like so much else, Sophie had naturally saved everything her only child ever used, so the public now saw baby Erich's cradle, his crib, his nursemaid's narrow bed, and, in the connecting playroom, his horsehide rocking horse with its genuine mane and tail, the mane sadly reduced to stubble by much hard riding.

There were also wind-up toys, books, blocks, even a handful of wax crayons which were now scattered beside a childish drawing of stick figures labeled *Papa and Mama and Erich* in straggling letters across the picture. Another Gimbels mannequin, this one resembling a four-year-old boy, sat at the table with a crayon fastened in its hand. It was dressed in short pants and a jacket of gray serge, a white batiste shirt, a black silk bow, long black lisle stockings, and high-top, button-up shoes.

Here again were more visitors. Watched by a woman whose apprehensive air immediately identified her as a docent, seven young day-care kids and their teacher were getting a first hand look at how one privileged child had lived a hundred years earlier.

"Where's his telebision?" demanded a tot as Rick and Pascal Grant passed the doorway.

"*I* have a television," Pascal whispered to Rick. "Mrs. Beardsley and her ladies gave it to me. For my birthday."

"That's nice," Rick answered, a shade too heartily. Never before had he been required to interact with someone mentally handicapped and his natural compassion was jumbled with both embarrassment and uneasiness.

Physically, Pascal Grant could be any age from sixteen to twenty-six.

Mentally, he probably wasn't too much older than those children.

A damn shame, Rick thought soberly. The guy was so good-looking. Of course, there were no rules that said it had to be otherwise, but still—

They passed through an open set of frosted glass doors that bisected the third floor. At the far end of the hall stood a mannequin dressed as a housemaid in a long black cotton dress and white bib apron, with her hair neatly pinned up under a starched white cap.

On this half of the third floor lay bedrooms for the servants, their one small bath, and a back stairs that ran from the basement kitchen to the attic. In the old days, the glass doors were normally kept shut, but after touring the spacious quarters of the master and mistress, modern visitors always wanted to see where the live-in staff slept when they weren't cooking and cleaning or fetching and carrying for the Breul family.

The docents might loyally insist that the Breuls were enlightened and considerate employers, but most visitors gleefully picked up on how even the floor coverings defined class lines. On the nursery side of that translucent glass, the carpet was a thick wool Axminster; on the servants' side, woven hemp matting.

At the rear stairwell, black velvet ropes barred the public from further passage. From kitchen to attic, the steps were wide enough to accommodate wicker laundry baskets, cleaning equipment, or storage chests, but they rose much more steeply than the wider public staircases and they were uncarpeted. Pascal Grant unclipped one of the ropes from its brass wall hook, waited for Rick Evans to pass, then carefully clipped it back again before leading the way up to the fourth-floor attic.

The huge attic was warm and smelled almost like a hayloft—a clean, dry mustiness compounded of old cardboard, lavender, and mothballs. Odds and ends crowded the space in an orderly fashion: wooden wardrobe boxes, storage cartons of all sizes, trunks, spare furniture, and, to Rick's surprise, a makeshift office of sorts.

At the far end of the attic, extension cords had been strung for lights and a typewriter, and three old tables formed a U-shaped desk for a man who sat reading intently, half hidden from their view by tall metal file cabinets in which were stored a hundred years of Breul papers.

He did not look their way.

"Who's that?" Rick murmured.

"Dr. Shambley." Pascal put his finger to his lips. "Shh."

He pointed to the remaining boxes of Christmas decorations, gave half of them to Rick and started back down. Not until they were at the bottom of the attic steps did he speak again. "Dr. Shambley's new. Mrs. Beardsley doesn't like him."

Rick remembered that his grandfather had mentioned a new trustee who was an art historian or something. "Why doesn't she like him?"

"I don't know," answered the young handyman, but his manner was uneasy and Rick wondered if it were only Mrs. Beardsley who didn't like the new trustee.

On the third floor, they had to edge around the tourists who blocked the hall's frosted glass doors as flash cameras and video minicams recorded the turn-of-the-century housemaid from the toe of her lace-up boots to the tip of her starched cap.

There was no sign of the day-care group until the two men descended past the final turn on the stairs and saw the children being herded across the wide entry hall like a flock of pigeons. The teacher's voice echoed off the marble walls as she called, "Now who has to use the bathroom before we put our coats back on?"

"I do! I do!" they all cried and streamed for the cloakrooms on either side of the main entrance.

Mrs. Beardsley wore a determined smile on her face, a

smile that became genuine as Pascal Grant set down his load of boxes and said, "We got them all, Mrs. Beardsley."

"Wonderful, Pascal. Now if you'll set up the ladder and if Mr. Evans will help you with the lights—though why we can't have real candles just once, I'll never understand," she fretted, half to herself. It was Mrs. Beardsley's annual regret that the insurance company and the New York City Fire Marshall were both so stuffy about using real candles on the tree.

Helen Aldershott rolled her eyes at the others and continued to untangle the tiny electric candles that would light the tree safely, if anachronistically.

It was a little past one and the docents were beginning to murmur of missed lunches before the last glass angel was fastened to the last bare twig. After one final inspection, Mrs. Beardsley nodded imperiously to Miss Ruffton, who tapped on the director's door and summoned him to preside at the lighting ceremony.

Every hair was sleekly in place and a festive red tie was knotted beneath his pointed chin as Benjamin Peake emerged from his office, more urbanely than the butler who had once occupied that corner of the mansion. He acknowledged the hours the women had worked to transform the mansion's formality to a Dickensian festiveness, and he assured them that he spoke on behalf of the trustees when he expressed their appreciation—his, too, of course—for their artistry and dedication.

Benjamin Peake possessed a rolling baritone that filled the marbled hall and floated up the stairwell. Alerted by his formal tones, a small crowd soon gathered around the tree and even spread themselves along the staircase for a better view.

When he was sure of everyone's attention, the director drew his remarks to a close and smiled graciously at his audience. "A very merry Christmas to you all," he said and clicked the switch Pascal Grant had rigged.

"Ah!" everyone exclaimed, as the tree blazed forth in all its Victorian glory.

Fourteen senior suburbanites, in from Connecticut for the day and fresh from touring the Theodore Roosevelt birthplace a short walk away, had gathered in the entry hall for a guided tour. Several began taking pictures of each other in front of the Christmas tree.

"Your tree is much prettier than Teddy's," one of the women told Mrs. Beardsley.

Pascal Grant paused in the act of carting away the ladder and storage boxes. "Hey, Rick," he said. "Want to see my window now?"

Rick Evans made a show of looking at his watch. "Sorry, Pascal, but I'd better finish taking pictures of the tree."

Yet when he saw the open disappointment on the other's face, he relented. "Tell you what, though. Why don't I come a little early tomorrow, around four? You can show me then, okay?"

"Okay!" Grant nodded happily.

At the top of the house, Roger Shambley lifted his massive head from a letter which had been misfiled in a cabinet with some of Erich Breul's business papers.

"*Sorgues?*" he muttered to himself, remembering that name from a biography he'd once read. "August of 1912? Hmm . . . now wouldn't that be something?"

He looked past the circle of bright light in which he sat, out to the dim stretches of attic crammed with boxes and trunks, and wild surmises filled his head.

"*Silent, upon a peak in Darien,*" he jeered at himself. And yet—!

In another attic several blocks southeast of the Breul House, a different discovery had just been made.

While renovating their old, but newly purchased, red brick row house in the East Village, Daniel and Gigi DeLucca had found a rusty tin footlocker pushed up under the eaves of the fourth-floor attic behind stacks of *National Geographics*.

"Old books?" he'd wondered.

"Old clothes," she'd guessed.

The hasp was rusted tight.

"Blackbeard's treasure," they decided and, lustily chanting, "Fifteen men on a dead man's chest, Yo-ho! Yo-ho!" they had hauled it downstairs and pried it open with a crowbar.

Inside they found an unpleasant musty odor and four little bundles wrapped in stained newspapers.

"Pigeon bones?" she asked as she finished unwrapping the first bundle.

"I don't think so," he said and carefully laid the second bundle back in the chest as if afraid it would explode.

It was a tiny mummified figure, entwined in what looked to the man like a shriveled grapevine but which the woman instantly recognized as an umbilical cord.

They left the last two bundles for the police.

Lieutenant Sigrid Harald arrived shortly after an assistant from the medical examiner's office. "I'm no Dr. Oliver when it comes to bones," said Cohen, referring to one of the country's leading experts on human skeletal remains, "but off the top of my head, I'd say all four are human and all died within hours of their births."

"When?" asked the tall, gray-eyed lieutenant.

"How the hell do I know?" Cohen answered testily.

They looked at the dates on the yellowed newspapers in which the four pathetic remains had been wrapped. The earliest was March 4, 1935; the latest was April 1, 1947.

"Look there, Lieutenant," said Detective Jim Lowry.

He showed her a flaking page of newsprint that head-lined the allied invasion of North Africa. Overlaying a map with arrows pointing to Algiers were four faded brown ovals that looked very much like old fingerprints made by bloody adult fingers.

Their Christmas card that year depicted Father Christmas in his long red robes and furred hood as he warmed himself before a roaring fire. Inside was a verse from Sir Walter Scott, one of Mr. Breul's favorite authors:

Heap on more wood!—the wind is chill:
But let it whistle as it will,
We'll keep our Christmas merry still.

from *Welcome to the Breul House!—An Informal Tour*, by Mrs. Hamilton Johnstone III, Senior Docent. (Copyright 1956)

II

Friday, December 11

Thanks to the Sussex Square Preservation Society which had successfully fought to retain them, six of the city's last original gas streetlights survived in working order, and here in the early December twilight their soft flickers gleamed upon polished brass door handles and kick plates.

A through street for cars and taxis passed along the bottom of the square, but when vehicular traffic was banned from the northern three sides around the small park, the original cobblestone carriageway was repaved in smooth brick, a substitution Mrs. Beardsley regretted anew as she stood in the doorway of number 7 and watched the last visitors descend the broad marble steps.

Mrs. Beardsley lived diagonally across the park at number 35. As senior docent, however, she spent almost as much time at the Breul House as she did in her own. She had hoped for the seat on the board of trustees which had recently gone to Dr. Shambley, but until that prize dropped into her lap, she would continue to conduct tours of the house, arrange seasonal decorations, and intimidate the reduced staff.

Mrs. Beardsley's officiousness might weary Benjamin Peake—especially when he was called upon to calm the ruffled waters she left in her wake—but the director revenged himself with the secret knowledge that the woman would never become a trustee as long as he had a say in the matter. Otherwise, he had no intention of discouraging her interest in the place. After all, she deferred to his position, she was capable of surprisingly shrewd promotional ideas, and she worked tirelessly without a salary, of itself no small consider-

18

ation, given the Erich Breul House's current financial difficulties.

Although a discreet sign inside the vestibule suggested donations of three dollars per person to view the house and its contents, at least a third of those who came either donated less or brazenly ignored the sign altogether. This wouldn't have mattered if hundreds daily thronged the house. Sadly, the two who had just departed were the forty-first and forty-second of the day.

An average day these days.

Mrs. Beardsley sighed and lingered for a moment in the chill twilight. She considered herself a closet romantic and the square was at its wintertime loveliest tonight. The very sight of it restored her good spirits because she could, she thought, take credit for its beauty—not only for the gaslights but even for the tiny colored lights that twinkled upon a tall evergreen at the center of the square's handkerchief-size park.

The tree represented compromise. Every year the question of decorative Christmas lights came before the Sussex Square Preservation Society and every year Mrs. Beardsley had managed to block their use. This year a younger, more vulgar contingent from numbers 9, 14 and 31 had rammed the motion through. Mrs. Beardsley had then rallied her forces and carried a vote which limited the lights to a single tree.

With predictable incompetence, the arrivistes had underestimated how many strings it would take to bedizen every twig, so the evergreen emerged more tasteful than Mrs. Beardsley had dared hope. In fact, it was even rather festive but Mrs. Beardsley had no intention of admitting that to a soul. Give them an inch and they'd string every bush next year.

One electrified tree was anachronism enough.

An icy gust of wind made the tall spruce dip and sway and Mrs. Beardsley shivered with a sudden chill that had nothing to do with the plummeting temperature.

"Somebody just walked over my grave," she thought and hurried inside.

Footsteps sounded on the marble stoop behind her and she held the tall door open a crack.

"I'm sorry but we're just closing and—oh! Mr. Munson. I didn't realize it was you. Do come in."

With a thin gray beard that hung down over his woolly muffler, Jacob Munson was small and spry enough to remind a more fanciful imagination than Mrs. Beardsley's of an elf escaped from Santa's workshop. Adding to the illusion was the perennial cloud of peppermint fumes in which he had moved ever since his doctors forbade cigarettes, and his eyes danced with merriment and goodwill beneath his wide-brimmed black fedora.

"Mrs. Beardsley, is it not?" A slight German accent underlay his friendly tone. "The others are here?"

"I believe so." She started to escort him toward the director's office at the far end of the vaulted marble hall where the others were gathered when she suddenly found her outstretched arm draped with Mr. Munson's muffler and overcoat. His hat and gloves followed in rapid order and he himself was speeding across the polished tiles before Mrs. Beardsley could make it clear that she was not some sort of resident butler or hatcheck girl.

Miffed, she carried the art dealer's outer garments over to a bench near Miss Ruffton's desk and dumped them there, grateful that the secretary had not been required to attend tonight's informal meeting and had therefore missed this minor humiliation. Miss Ruffton was an enigmatic young black woman who never talked back or argued, yet Mrs. Beardsley suspected that she secretly enjoyed any affronts to the older woman's dignity.

As she put on her own coat and gloves to leave, Mrs. Beardsley subconsciously tried to fault Miss Ruffton but found nothing to seize upon. The secretary's gleaming desktop was bare except for an appointment calendar, a pot of red poinsettias in gold foil, and one of those stodgy brochures which outlined the history of the Erich Breul House.

And that reminded Mrs. Beardsley: Where was young Mr. Evans? Didn't Mr. Munson expect him to join them? She pushed back the cuff of her cashmere glove and glanced at her watch. Everyone else was there except him.

"Boys!" she murmured to herself. With her children hundreds of miles away and occupied by families of their own, she had unconsciously transferred her maternal interest to Pascal Grant, who would never completely grow up. And she'd be quite surprised if Rick Evans were a day past twenty. Now what sort of mischief, she wondered, could be keeping those two so long in the basement?

Officiously, Mrs. Beardsley opened a door concealed beneath the marble stairwell, passed along a short hall that led back to what was left of the butler's pantry, turned right, and descended the stairs to the basement.

An hour earlier, Rick Evans had followed Pascal Grant down those steps into the kitchen. It was enormous, but the stamped-tin ceiling was surprisingly low and the room's dry snugness made Rick think of *Wind in the Willows* and of Mr. Badger's home and Mole's cosy tunnels. Blue rag rugs were scattered over brown floor tiles, a massive cookstove resplendent with nickel-plate ornamentation dominated the room, and one wall was lined with shallow open shelves that held the blue willowware Sophie Breul had provided for her servants' daily use.

Rick had wanted to open the doors of the huge chestnut ice box, to lift the lids of painted tin canisters and peer into the built-in storage bins, but Pascal Grant had tugged at his sleeve.

"They're all empty. Come and see my window before it gets dark, okay?"

As he trailed Pascal through the cavernous basement passages, Rick was reminded of explorations he used to take with his best friend through abandoned barns and farmhouses back home in Louisiana's bayou country. There was that same sense of sadness, of human artifacts abandoned to their own devices.

On the other side of the scullery were empty coal bins, made redundant by an oil furnace that was itself in need of replacement. Beyond the kitchen lay rooms no longer needed for their original purposes: cold closets with sharp hooks for hanging meat and poultry, bins for food supplies, a laundry room with deep stone sinks and tall drying racks. These were now lumbered with bulky storage crates, trunks, rolled-up carpets, and odds and ends too good to throw away, yet no longer needed for the day-to-day business of the museum. The hall wound past a room that held racks of pictures an earlier curator had weeded out of the main collection as too hopelessly banal; another room stored the folding chairs that were brought up whenever the main hall was used for lectures or recitals.

At the street end of the basement was a sturdy wooden service door that opened onto a shallow areaway beneath the grandeur of the high marble stoop with its elaborate railings. Echoing the rounded door top was one of those whimsicalities to which Victorians were so often given: a lacy wrought-iron spider web set into the upper third of the door, each interstice of the web fitted with clear beveled glass. At the center of the web was a tiny brass garden spider which Pascal kept polished till it shone like gold.

The window was uniquely decorative, yet city-smart as well. Callers could be identified without opening the door and the strong iron cobweb was fine enough that no burglar could smash a tiny pane of glass and reach through to unbolt the latch. Rick had no formal grounding in aesthetics but it occurred to him that Pascal's sense of beauty might be more sophisticated than he'd realized.

The young janitor was looking up at him through long golden lashes. "It's my first favorite window," he said shyly.

"It's beautiful," Rick told him. "I definitely want a picture of this." He tilted the strobe on his camera to bounce light off the ceiling and took a couple of experimental shots before switching lenses for a close-up of the spider.

As he worked, he began to consider the potentials the house offered.

"My grandfather wants me do a new brochure and perhaps some new souvenir postcards," he said, "and Dr. Peake wants me to photograph all the paintings, but I bet I could do a whole series of slides on just architectural details, another on furniture, perhaps one on Victorian clothes or dishes."

"*All* the paintings?" Pascal interrupted. "Dr. Peake said for you to take pictures of all of them?"

"Yeah, he said they've never done a photographic record of the whole collection." Rick finished with the window and recapped the lens.

"I've got some pictures in my room," Pascal said proudly. "Dr. Peake said I could. Come see."

He led Rick back down the passageway and through the

kitchen. Beyond the service stairs was what had once been the downstairs butler's pantry, connected to the one above by a large dumbwaiter. This was where the Breul maids had put the finishing touches on meals before sending them aloft. Now the space was outfitted for the only live-in help left. On the counter beside the small sink was a new microwave oven, a coffee maker and a hot-air popcorn popper; below, a half-size refrigerator.

Although the kitchenette was for Pascal Grant's use, it was open to the stairs and kitchen and to the casual inspection of anyone passing through. Perhaps that was why it looked as impersonal as any laboratory, thought Rick.

As if he could read thoughts, Pascal paused before a closed door at the rear of the alcove and looked up at him with another of those seraphic smiles. "Mrs. Beardsley says everything has to be neat out here."

He opened the door and clicked on a wall switch. "I can do what I want to in here."

The room was astonishing. Everywhere Rick looked he saw patterns upon figures upon designs—paisleys and florals beside stripes and basketweave and geometrics. It was like a private retreat designed by some mad Victorian decorator and it should have overwhelmed Rick's visual senses; yet, the colors were so rich and dark that lamplight was soaked up until the whole room coalesced into a mellow warmth that made him think again of a small anthropomorphic animal's cosy den. A human hobbit hole.

Originally the servants' sitting room, the ceiling and windowless walls were papered in a faded turkey red and the floor was layered with odd-size throw rugs, all threadbare but of oriental design. A couple of shabby easy chairs stood on either side of an open hearth that sported a handsome overmantel of carved walnut. For sleeping, Pascal had pushed a double bed mattress and box springs up against a cluttered sideboard and covered it with embroidered shawls and thickly fringed pillows so that it looked more like a Persian divan than a bed.

The lower doors of the sideboard had been folded open to store his clock radio, tape player, and stacks of tapes within easy reach, while a nearby Moroccan brass coffee table held a miniature television.

Pascal unzipped his coverall and stepped out of it. Beneath, he wore jeans and a thin knitted jersey that molded every line of his slender torso. He hung the coverall inside a tall wooden wardrobe and pulled on a blue Fair Isle sweater, a castoff from one of Mrs. Beardsley's sons that echoed his clear blue eyes. Smoothing his tousled golden hair, he looked up at Rick happily.

"See my pictures?"

It was impossible not to since every wall was covered so closely that the red wallpaper beneath was almost hidden.

A large sentimental farmyard scene hung above the fireplace. It pictured baby ducks and chicks, rosy-cheeked children, and other young animals and was doubtless meant to inspire wholesome thoughts among the servants.

But that was the only properly framed picture in the room and the only one that clearly belonged to the nineteenth century. Everything else was thumbtacked to the walls and was vigorously modern: Kandinsky, Klee, Rothko, Pollock, Picasso, Dali, Ernst—all the twentieth-century icons. None were smaller than twenty-four by thirty-six inches and, looking closer, Rick saw that they all seemed to have begun as high-quality art posters. Some were so beautifully reproduced on such heavy stock that, with the subdued lighting, he had to touch the surface of a Dali dreamscape to reassure himself that it wasn't real.

"I cut off all that writing stuff," said Pascal.

"Writing stuff?"

"Museum names and numbers and stuff like that," the young handyman explained earnestly. "I don't read so good, but I know real pictures don't have that stuff on the bottom, so I cut it off."

"Where did you find so many posters, though?" asked Rick, curious.

"Dr. Kimmelshue—he was here before Dr. Peake. He died. He had a bunch of them in his office and lots more down here." He gestured in the direction of the storage rooms. "Dr. Peake told me to throw them all out and I told him I could take them if he didn't want them so he said I could have anything there I wanted."

Pascal paused and caught his short upper lip with his lower teeth. "Well, he didn't mean *anything* I wanted. There's some trunks with clothes and stuff. I didn't take those. He just meant the pictures. And you can take pictures of them, too."

There was such innocent generosity in his voice that Rick hesitated, looking for tactful words. "They're wonderful pictures, Pascal, but I think Dr. Peake's mainly interested in the real old stuff. Like that one over the fireplace. It's a terrific room, though, and you've fixed it up great."

To change the subject, he walked around the bed, sat down on the edge, and began reading the titles on the other youth's stack of cassette tapes. "Hey, what kind of music do you like, Pasc?"

Happiness suffused Grant's beautiful features. "Pasc. That's what my friend called me, my friend at the training center. That's where I learned how to fix things. Are you going to be my friend?"

"Sure," Rick said automatically.

"I'll get us some soda," Pascal decided. He fetched two cans from the kitchenette, and upon returning, stretched across the bed to hand one to his new friend.

Rick continued to read the titles of the tapes as he sipped from the can. "Basie, Lionel Hampton, Cootie Williams, Gene Krupa—you're really into classic jazz, aren't you?"

Pascal Grant sat down on the other side of the bed and began pulling out his favorite tapes. "I like it," he said simply. "It makes me feel good. Like the pictures do. Sometimes they—they get all mixed up together sometimes, the jazz and the pictures."

"You have Benny Goodman's Carnegie Hall concert?"

" 'Sing, Sing, Sing'!" Pascal exclaimed. "It's on the player. That's my very first favorite."

Balancing his soda, he pulled himself over the billowing cushions and punched buttons until Krupa's hypnotic drums filled the room.

"Hey, yeah!" breathed Rick. He pushed a couple of cushions into a stack and leaned back on them. Pascal did the same at the opposite end of the bed so that they sprawled heel to head, facing each other as they drank and listened to the pounding intensity of one of the greatest outpourings of spontaneous jazz ever recorded.

The music, the warmth, the rich reds and golds and purples of the room, the vibrant posters—Pasc was right, he thought, somehow they *did* look like jazz would look if you could paint jazz themes—everything about this moment combined to make him feel safe and unthreatened for the first time since coming to New York.

And there was Pasc himself, his angelic face in shadows, his tangled curls turned into a golden halo by the lamp behind him. A rush of love and pity welled up inside of Rick.

Then, as Jess Stacy's piano explored the outer reaches of the melody, he felt Pascal touch his shoe, heard his low voice say, "I'm glad you're going to be my friend, Rick," and was wrenched by something deeper and terrifyingly primal.

Startled, he sat upright and saw Mrs. Beardsley's disapproving face at the door.

"I knocked," she said in a stern voice, "but the music's so loud—"

Pascal Grant eeled across the end of the bed to lower the volume, then turned to smile at the woman. "I'm sorry, Mrs. Beardsley. I was showing Rick my tapes. He's going to be my friend."

"That's very nice, Pascal," said Mrs. Beardsley, "but right now, I think Mr. Evans is expected upstairs."

"Oh, gosh!" Rick groaned. Embarrassed and guilty, he left his soda on the sideboard and bolted past the stern-faced docent.

Benjamin Peak had, on his own initiative, called this special meeting to explore—informally, he assured them archly—various ways of stemming the Erich Breul House's rapidly growing deficit, and he was prepared to be gracious about Rick Evans' tardy entry for dear old Jacob's sake.

Not that Jacob had turned into a doting grandfather. A respected dealer and now senior partner at Kohn and Munson Gallery, Jacob Munson admitted to seventy although it was generally believed that he was much nearer eighty. His fierce, explosive temper had been tamed somewhat since the death of his son several years earlier, but his devotion to art and to the business of art remained strong, and his friendship had occasionally smoothed Peake's progress in the art world.

Beside him sat Hester Kohn, daughter of his late partner, a trim and smartly dressed brunette of thirty-four, with quizzical hazel eyes and a small mouth that smiled easily. She wore gray boots and slacks, a high-collared red silk shirt, and a wide flat necklace of gold enameled in colorful Chinese chrysanthemums. She was addicted to gardenias and her heady perfume fought Munson's cloud of peppermint to a draw.

Munson had been apprehensive when young Hester Kohn inherited her father's half interest in the gallery, but these past two years had gone smoothly. She handled the financial side of the business as efficiently as her father had and seemed equally content to leave final artistic judgments to him.

Jacob Munson considered himself less fortunate than Horace Kohn in his offspring. His only son, the son he'd groomed to come into the gallery, the son who painted like an angel, had been killed in a plane crash before the lad was twenty-five. His two older daughters, resentful because he'd never encouraged their participation until after the tragedy, resisted his tardy attempts to interest them in art. One was now a doctor in Seattle, the other taught economics at a small college in Louisiana. Although the doctor had remained willfully unmaternal, the professor had eventually managed one child, Richard.

Aware of his grandfather's reservations, Rick Evans found himself a chair just inside the director's door and now fiddled with his camera lens.

He focused on Munson's narrow foot, twisting the lens until his shoelaces came into sharp detail. Rick would have liked to point his camera directly at Munson's face but knew that would annoy. He wished that he pleased his grandfather better.

As Dr. Peake spoke of the Breul House's financial problems, Rick unobtrusively moved his camera toward Francesca Leeds. Lady Francesca had turned thirty-seven that year, but there was nothing in her clean-lined profile to suggest it. Her golden complexion was as clear as a girl's, her dark red hair glossy and natural, her slender body at the peak of its physical powers, with a lithe sensuousness that was the birthright of certain fortunate women.

Her companion was five years older and if one looked closely at his straw-colored hair one could see gray at his temples. He had an outdoorsman's face, yet it took expensive tailoring to disguise the fact that his muscular body had perhaps spent too much time behind a desk instead of at the helm of his racing yacht.

Søren Thorvaldsen was a Danish entrepreneur who had parlayed a boyhood romance with the sea into great wealth by refurbishing aging transatlantic liners into luxurious West Indian cruise ships. After years of hard work, he was ready to start playing again and Lady Francesca's proposal had amused him and appealed to both his financial and aesthetic appetites.

"Why don't you explain your idea to Mr. Munson and Miss Kohn?" Peake said smoothly, turning the floor over to Francesca Leeds.

She smiled. "It's really very simple. The Erich Breul House has a serious image problem. Is it a historical house or is it an art museum? Some of the pictures in this collection are first-rate. No one questions that. The others—"

A graceful half-humorous shrug of her shoulder indicated that she did not intend to speak uncharitably about the bulk of the founder's collection unless pressed.

"The Breul Collection is highly regarded by scholars world wide," said Jacob Munson, who chaired the board of trustees. "Even now, Dr. Roger Shambley is writing a new book using examples from the house."

"But is it the general public who'll be reading it?" There was a charming hint of Celtic lilt to the lady's British accent. Her father supposedly owed his title to one of those tumble-down Irish castles.

"Jacob, it's imperative that we find new sources of revenue," reminded Benjamin Peake.

"*Ja, ja.* This is why we have lent you Richard." He unwrapped another piece of hard candy and popped it into his mouth. The fragrance of peppermint wafted through the office anew.

"And we appreciate the loan," said the director, smiling at young Evans, who looked back at him through the camera's range finder. "But there's no point in taking photographs for a new brochure or a larger collection of souvenir postcards if no one comes in to buy them."

"We think people have forgotten what serendipitous treasures the Breul House owns," Lady Francesca said coaxingly. "We must remind them—bring back not just the true art lovers but potential donors, too—the people who support what is chic to support."

Francesca Leeds described herself as a free-lance publicist but she was actually a matchmaker between money and the arts. She maintained a small one-room office in her suite at the Hotel Maintenon and new business came through personal recommendations of satisfied clients. As one of the four most highly regarded party planners in the city, she had a flair for matching corporate donors with charitable fundraising events.

An importer of Italian shoes, for example, could be persuaded to help support a fashion show to benefit a convent founded by a Sicilian nun. The importer's shoes would be featured throughout the show while the Santa Caterina Sisters of Charity would net several thousands to further their good works.

The parent company of an expensive line of camera equipment might sponsor a movie premiere to help fund further research in retinitis pigmentosa.

For every worthy cause, Lady Francesca Leeds seemed to find a moneyed patron.

Her dark red hair glinted like polished mahogany as she tilted her head toward the heretofore silent Dane. "As a ship owner, Mr. Thorvaldsen recognizes a natural affinity for the Erich Breul House."

Rich Evans' camera followed her eyes, then swept the group as Hester Kohn gave a muffled snort.

Hester was puzzled by her inclusion in this informal planning session. She was not a trustee and she was much less interested in Benjamin Peake's career than Jacob was.

She regarded her partner with fond uneasiness. He couldn't possibly last more than another year or two and then what would happen to the gallery? She had grown up speaking the specialized jargon of the art world and she was quite comfortable managing the gallery's finances. But Hester Kohn knew her limitations, knew that she was no judge of artistic merit. One could be cynical and say that given the current state of visual arts in this city artistic merit hardly mattered; yet ultimately, she knew, it *did* matter.

Although Jacob spoke halfheartedly of educating his slow-talking grandson, who had suddenly appeared full-blown from the Louisiana bayous this past September, Hester soon realized that the boy—he was only twenty—was even less intuitive about art than she herself. Her eyes lingered on him thoughtfully. Momentarily unshielded by his camera, he caught her gaze and turned away in self-conscious confusion. A tractable lad and willing enough to follow—she knew *that* better than anyone else in the room. Yet anything that couldn't be captured through a camera lens seemed difficult for him to grasp.

Jacob must see this, she thought, but would the ties of blood outweigh his devotion to Kohn and Munson's impeccable reputation? Or would he leave his share of the gallery to one of his protégés, someone like Benjamin Peake for instance?

She could keep Peake in line if she had to, she knew, shrewdly measuring his familiar, well-proportioned body with her hazel eyes. Despite his Ph.D. in modern art, she doubted that he was as sharp as Jacob wanted to believe, but allowances were made because Peake had been a close friend of Jacob's son. They had met as fellow students at one of Meyer Schapiro's seminars on modern art at Columbia, and after Paul Munson's plane crashed, Jacob had transferred his paternal interest to Peake's career. Indeed, Ben Peake owed his present position here at the Breul House to Jacob, who had persuaded the other trustees to hire him after that fiasco up at the Friedinger left him out on his ear. Jacob would not stand idly by and watch this place go down while under Ben Peake's direction if there was something he could do to help.

But what?

In accent-free English, Søren Thorvaldsen leaned forward to explain the similarities between his acquisition of a fleet of cruise ships and the first Breul's fleet of canal barges. They were kindred spirits, it would seem, and like called to like even after a century and a half.

"As I understand it, your endowment has been much eroded by inflation and maintenance," said Thorvaldsen, his keen eyes flicking from Benjamin Peake to Jacob Munson.

"*Und?*" asked the older man.

"*Und* I would like to help. If Dr. Peake and your board agree, I could underwrite the expense of mounting a major retrospective of an important artist."

"The Breul House doesn't do that sort of thing," Jacob Munson snapped, yet curiosity piqued him. "Who?"

"Oscar Nauman."

The old man smoothed his thin gray beard and shook his head. "He will not do it."

"He might if *you* asked him," said Lady Francesca.

"My dear lady, I *haf* asked him. Many times."

"Miss Kohn?"

"Don't look at me," said Hester Kohn. "I'd love to mount a comprehensive retrospective of Nauman's work, but Jacob's right. He won't even discuss it seriously."

"But why?" asked Thorvaldsen.

Munson gave a palms-out gesture.

"I think he's superstitious," said Hester Kohn. "Some artists are. They think a retrospective's the kiss of death, the beginning of the end, an official assumption that they have nothing more to say."

"Nothing more to say?" exclaimed Thorvaldsen. "But this is a man who has found a dozen new voices in his lifetime."

Hester Kohn uncrossed her trousered legs and sat more erectly in her chair. "Are you by any chance represented by Dansksambler in Copenhagen?"

Thorvaldsen hesitated, then nodded.

" 'Autumnal' and 'Topaz Two,' " she told her elderly partner.

"So, Mr. Thorvaldsen, you own two pictures by Nauman?" asked Jacob Munson.

"Actually, I own eleven of his works and I'm told there are things in his studio that have never been exhibited." It was not quite a question and there was a touch of wistfulness in the big Dane's voice.

"What do you think, Jacob?" asked Benjamin Peake and he, too, sounded wistful.

"Hester is right," Munson told them with Teutonic finality. "Oscar will not agree to this."

Lady Francesca stretched an appealing hand toward him and her soft brown eyes melted into his. "Dear Mr. Munson!

31

Have you not been Oscar Nauman's dealer for over thirty years? And if you were to explain to him the situation here at the Breul House and entreat him for old time's sake—?"

Munson considered and Peake rushed into the lull. "If you approached him, too, Lady Francesca," he said gallantly. "I'm sure you could make him agree. I've always heard that Oscar Nauman responds to beautiful women, right, Jacob?"

Her smile did not falter, thought Jacob Munson, and the old man gave her full marks for self-control. Nauman tried to keep his personal life private, but the artist was a public figure and rumors did get around. Jacob was under the impression that Oscar's affair with Lady Francesca Leeds had ended more than a year ago. He seemed to recall that there was a fresh rumor making the rounds now. A lady fireman, was it?

Or dog catcher?

Something unusual anyhow. Leave it to Oscar.

Mr. Breul had arrived in Europe in the summer of 1879, but nearly three years were to elapse before he presented his compliments to the Swiss branch of his grandfather's family in Zurich, where the Fürsts had been burghers since 1336.

In later years, Mr. Breul enjoyed speaking of that first encounter with his fair cousin, Sophie. Fresh snow had begun to fall as the young American crossed the park to the Fürst villa on the right bank of the lake. As he approached the gate, a small white dog darted through the railings, heedless of a girlish voice that called in vain. Though hardly dressed for the bitter weather, the impetuous girl had rushed from the house to rescue her wayward pet, undaunted by her thin shoes and indoor dress.

With the instant acumen which later marked his business dealings, Mr. Breul immediately grasped the situation and hastily captured the little dog by its collar before it could hurl itself beneath an oncoming carriage.

His quick action secured the young woman's gratitude, but when he insisted that she take his coat as protection against the falling snow, he won her heart from that moment forward.

Erich Breul—The Man and His Dream, privately published 1924 by the Friends and Trustees of the Erich Breul House.

III

Even before she was fully awake, Sigrid sensed a difference in the December morning light. And it wasn't just the difference between rural Connecticut and urban Manhattan either. She snuggled beneath a down comforter with her eyes half focused on one of Nauman's early oil paintings and drowsily noted a new clarity in the shifting planes of color, a new vibrancy.

A part of her brain cataloged the variance. The other part was still too drugged by sleep to care or analyze.

She yawned, turned over in the king-size bed, and abruptly caught her breath at what lay outside.

Oscar Nauman's house sprawled along the edge of a steep, thickly wooded hillside. With no near neighbors on that side, he had replaced his bedroom wall with sheets of clear glass so that nothing blocked her view of a tree-filled ravine that had transformed itself into a Currier and Ives print.

Yesterday's heavy gray sky was clear blue now and last night's thin flakes must have thickened sometime during the early morning hours because snow capped each twig and limb, softened the craggy rocks, and shone with such dazzling purity that sunlight was reflected inside to intensify Nauman's paintings and light up the room from unfamiliar angles.

A thoroughly urban creature, Lieutenant Sigrid Harald, NYPD, knew almost nothing about nature in the raw and, on the whole, rather mistrusted unpaved lanes and trackless forests. She cared little for wildflowers or for knowing the identity of birds hopping mindlessly around in treetops. An occasional National Geographic special on Channel 13 was her nearest link to wild animals.

Moreover, snow was usually an annoyance, dirty slushy stuff that got inside her boots or lay too long in messy heaps and, by alternately melting and refreezing, made city sidewalks treacherous for walking.

But to gaze out for the first time in years upon a virgin snowfall unsullied by any footsteps filled her with unexpected wonder.

She pushed herself upright in bed with Nauman's down comforter wrapped around her bare shoulders and watched a small black-capped bird try to perch on an ice-crusted twig just outside the window. It misjudged the ice's slickness and seemed startled when its feet slid out from under its first attempt at perching; but it recovered, settled onto the twig, and hunched into its gray feathers much as Sigrid hunched into the bedcovers.

Her breath puffed in visible little clouds and she felt a momentary twinge of solidarity with the bird. If it was cold in here, what must it be out there? And how did birds keep their unfeathered feet from freezing anyhow?

On the end wall opposite the bed, the stone hearth was black and lifeless. Nauman liked to sleep in an unheated room and last night's fire had already burned down to glowing embers before they fell asleep. She shivered and sank a bit deeper into the covers.

No sign of Nauman, of course. He was an early riser and had probably been up for hours.

According to the clock on the mantel, it was a quarter past eleven. Were she in her own apartment, Sigrid would have stretched contentedly and gone back to sleep. A weekend's greatest luxury was her freedom to drift in and out of sleep for several hours and she seldom rose before noon.

Nauman's Connecticut retreat offered better incentives to rise; nevertheless, it took all the willpower she could muster to leave the warm bed and snatch up jeans and sweater.

Happily, the man's Spartan attitude toward cold bedrooms did not extend to his bath. The tiled floor felt pleasantly warm to her bare feet and the hot water was a benediction.

She showered, toweled the mirror free of fog, then ran a comb through her dark hair and pushed it into shape with her hands. Until October, her hair had been long and she'd worn it pulled straight back and pinned into a tight bun at the nape of her neck. Now ragged bangs swept over her strong forehead and the back was clipped short.

Smoothing moisturizer over her face, she hesitated over the other small bottles and tubes in her toiletry bag. Cosmetics were something else new in her life, and even though she enjoyed the sexual sizzle they sent through her body, she still lacked expertise with the intricacies of technique.

She would never be very pleased with her reflection—her face was too thin, her cheeks had never dimpled, her mouth was too wide—but she was starting to be satisfied with her eyes and the way her new bangs softened the former austerity. Cutting her hair seemed to have cut away some inhibitions as well, made her less reserved and awkward.

At least with Nauman.

Suddenly impatient to find him, she smudged on eye shadow and lip gloss and quickly dressed.

An aroma of coffee hung in the air and she followed it out to the kitchen, but that utilitarian room was empty save for the tantalizing smell of onions, herbs and well-browned chicken now rising from the oven. Nauman cooked as instinctively as he painted and had evidently felt creative this morning. Sigrid poured herself a cup of strong dark liquid, pulled the plug on the coffee maker, and backtracked through the house to the end wing formed by the studio and its decks.

The lyrical intensity of a Martinu symphony was muffled by the double glass doors that led to Nauman's studio.

Essentially a huge sun porch, it was lined on both long walls with French windows that led to wide decks on either side. A high ceiling followed the pitch of the roof, accommodating two ten-foot easels; and with the snow outside today, the room was awash in brilliant natural light.

At the far end of the studio, beyond the thrift-shop assortment of tables and cabinets that held his painting supplies, was a huge stone fireplace flanked by floor-to-ceiling bookcases. Oscar Nauman sat in one of the comfortable chairs pulled up before the blazing log fire and Sigrid paused to watch him relight his pipe.

He was half a head taller than she and a generation older, with a lean hard body, piercing blue eyes, and thick silver hair that had finished turning white before he was thirty. They had sparred for six months, been lovers for six weeks, yet Sigrid was still unsure of her feelings for him—how much was sexual, how much emotional, and whether the two added up to that irrational state called love.

By nature and by training, she was cool and analytical, but Oscar Nauman was the one element in her life that she consciously refused to analyze. Clearly he was too old, too quixotic, too opinionated, too self-centered. Why was she not heeding the logic of this?

Then Nauman's head came up, he smiled in her direction, and Sigrid's heart turned over. She smiled back and started to open the door before abruptly realizing that he was not alone, that his smile had been for a red-haired woman who now walked into Sigrid's view holding one of Nauman's pictures. Specific words were indistinct but her voice held a musical lilt.

With the snow reflecting so much dazzling sunlight into the studio, Sigrid knew she would not be seen if she retreated back down the shadowed hall and read the morning paper till the woman was gone. Two months ago, she might have done just that. She was still self-conscious with Nauman when around others but she was trying to overcome it. So she told herself that she lingered here only because she was uncertain if the woman had come for business or if her Sunday morning visit were purely social. Perhaps this was something neighbors did in the country?

There was only one way to find out.

Steadying the coffee cup in her left hand, she opened one of the glass doors. The others looked up as she entered.

This time, Nauman's smile *was* for her. "Come and meet Francesca," he said.

The visitor wore brown corduroy knickers crammed inside knee-length high-heeled brown boots and a loose pullover knitted in tones of russet and amber. Windswept auburn hair tangled itself around her fair face and her classic features appeared almost flawless as she put down the painting she'd been inspecting and came to Sigrid with her hand outstretched.

"I'm Francesca Leeds, and I'm so pleased to meet you at last," she said with a smile in her warm Irish voice. "Oscar's told me all about you."

"Has he?" Sigrid mumbled.

"Have I?" asked Nauman, frowning at a picture Lady Francesca had unearthed from earlier years.

"Well, somebody did, *acushla*. If not you, perhaps Hester Kohn or Doris Quinn." She turned back to Sigrid. "Anyhow, I know you're a police officer in the city. A detective, right?"

Sigrid nodded.

"And I'm an old friend of Oscar's come to talk him into saving one of New York's landmarks. You must help me persuade him."

There was something curiously familiar about the woman but Sigrid couldn't quite decide why. As Francesca Leeds described the Breul House's near destitution and the benefits an Oscar Nauman retrospective could provide, Sigrid had an opportunity to study her features more closely.

The bright glare of snowlight was not kind to the woman's skin. It washed out the golden tones and made her seem too pale. It also revealed tiny lines around her eyes and nose so that Sigrid revised her estimate of age upward. Instead of thirty, Francesca Leeds was probably closer to forty. Nevertheless, she remained a stunning creature with the sort of poised assurance that often destroyed Sigrid's.

Not this time, she told herself, making a conscious effort not to tighten up. But it was difficult. Despite the other woman's friendly smile and easy conversation, Sigrid knew that she, too, was being studied and catalogued. She should have been used to it by now. Most of Nauman's friends fell into two camps: those who were amused by their relationship and those who were patently puzzled. Very few accepted her without question.

Lady Francesca appeared to have both amusement and curiosity well in hand and seemed bent on making Sigrid her ally as she pulled a small picture down from one of the racks.

"Think of it, Sigrid: Would you not love to see Oscar's whole career in one well-chosen show?"

"Pinned to the wall like a bunch of dead butterflies?" Nauman asked sardonically. "Forget it. Anyhow, you're talking to the wrong person. She doesn't like my work."

Francesca Leeds started to laugh, realized Oscar wasn't

entirely joking, and looked at the thin brunette with fresh interest. "Really?"

Sigrid shrugged as she studied the small purple-and-black abstract Francesca had held out to her. "He exaggerates."

The implication not lost upon her ladyship, who knew something must exist before it can be exaggerated. How perfectly ironic that Oscar should be snared by someone indifferent to his artistic achievements, someone who could see him as a fallible man standing unclothed in fame and accomplishment. Francesca deliberately turned her mind away from the memory of Oscar's lean hard frame unclothed in anything, but there was veiled mirth in her brown eyes as she delicately probed, "Then your interests will be lying in music or literature, rather than the visual?"

"She's visual," Oscar said.

His rangy body continued to lounge in the deep chair, but his tone was sharper than necessary, defensive even?

Still holding the small oil from one of Oscar's middle periods, Sigrid glanced from one to the other, aware of a sudden tension in the air. She handed the violent abstract back to Francesca Leeds. "Even if I don't completely understand them, I do like some of Nauman's pictures."

Oscar abruptly leaned forward to poke the fire and add another log to the blaze. "Ask her anything about the late Gothic, though."

"Late Gothic? You mean Dürer? Baldung? Holbein?"

"And Lucas Cranach," Sigrid nodded. "Mabuse, too. And earlier, Jan van Eyck, of course."

"Ah," said Francesca, enlightened now. "The Flemish. Precision. Order." She waved her hand to encompass Oscar's cluttered studio, the vibrant abstractions, the large canvases slashed with color and free-flowing lines. "Anarchy repels you?"

"I *am* a police officer," Sigrid said lightly. "And I do know enough about modern art to know there's structure lurking in there somewhere."

Oscar laughed and stood up. "Stay for lunch, Francesca? I'm making my famous *coq au vin*."

Francesca Leeds pushed back the heavy auburn hair from her face and turned her wrist to consult the small gold watch. "Can't, *acushla*. My hosts are expecting me back with their vehicle."

She smiled up at him as she reached for her brown suede jacket. "I'm not giving up, though. A retrospective's nothing like a ninth symphony, Oscar, and the Breul House really does need you."

She turned to Sigrid, who echoed the formulas of "so nice to meet you; perhaps we'll see each other again," and both were pleased to realize the formalities weren't totally insincere.

Exchanging comments on road conditions, icy patches, and the infrequency of snowplows through these back roads, Oscar and Sigrid followed Francesca out onto the deck. Oscar had cleared it earlier, as well as the steps leading down to the drive; but except for Francesca's single line of boot prints curving up from a borrowed van parked beside the road, the crusted snow around the house was unbroken.

"Driving's not bad," said Francesca. "The van has chains and four-wheel drive."

Even with all identifying landmarks blanketed by the snow, she seemed to know exactly how the drive curved, and walked confidently out to the van without tripping or putting a foot wrong. It was something Sigrid noted without actually considering as Francesca waved good-bye and called back, "At least you didn't say no."

"No!" Oscar grinned.

"Too late," she laughed and drove away in a flurry of snow.

Circling his studio to the rear deck, Oscar thoughtfully contemplated the ravine, where snow lay deep and crisp beneath tall pines and hardwoods so thickly branched that winter sunlight barely penetrated.

"The surface is too soft for conventional sleds," he observed.

Over the years, various visiting children had left plastic sliding sheets behind in the garage, and Oscar had discovered them while searching for a snow shovel.

His assertion that their appetites needed building sounded ridiculous to Sigrid even as Nauman bundled her into a jacket and boots. Minutes later, she found herself alone upon a sheet of plastic, careening downhill on her stomach, half terrified and wholly exhilarated.

It was like being eight years old again—pushing off, oaring herself along with mittened hands, that slow gathering of speed, crashing through ice-coated grasses, dodging tree roots and low-lying branches, a belly-dropping sense of doom as she crested a small ridge and became briefly airborne before thudding back to cushioned earth again. Another straight shoot down the hillside and she hurtled toward a creek bank lined with dormant blackberry bushes and huge granite boulders, trying to judge exactly when she should come down hard with a braking foot to land in a laughing, tangled heap beside her companion.

Delighted by the sheer physicality of the experience, Sigrid unhooked her leg from Nauman's elbow and kissed him exuberantly.

By their fourth trip down, Oscar had a long briar scratch across his forehead and Sigrid had jammed her right index finger. Climbing back to the top of the ravine each time left them winded, wet, and red-cheeked, yet both were somehow reluctant to end this brief return to childhood pleasures and go inside.

On the other hand, warmth and the expectation of good food did offer certain inducements. Not to mention the adult pleasures of stripping off their wet clothes and rediscovering other physical joys.

"What are you smiling about?" Nauman asked suspiciously.

"I was thinking about raw clams on the half-shell."

"You want to eat first?"

"No." Her slender fingers touched the red scratch on his forehead, caressed his left ear, then slipped to his bare shoulder. "I was remembering my cousin Carl. One of my Southern cousins. He bought a cottage down on Harker's Island and it took him more than ten years before he'd even taste a raw clam. He's been trying to make up for lost time ever since."

"I don't know that I like being compared to raw clams," Nauman grumbled.

"But they're so delicious," she murmured wickedly, running her hand down his muscular flank.

* * *

Lunch was just as leisurely, and afterwards, Sigrid curled up in one of the large chairs before the fire in Nauman's studio and opened the *Times* to the puzzle page. The large crossword appeared to contain a humorous yuletide limerick, and she became so absorbed in penning in the answers that she didn't notice when Nauman, perched on a tall stool at his drawing table, began to sketch her, his pencil moving rapidly across the pages of his notebook.

He hadn't done a figurative portrait in years, not since his student days, probably, but there was something about her eyes, the line of her long neck, the angularity of the way she sat that intrigued him. If he could catch her on paper—

Sigrid glanced up. Nauman's eyes were a clear deep blue and the intelligence which usually blazed there had become remote and fathomless. She moved uneasily and saw the remoteness disappear as his eyes softened.

"What did Francesca Leeds mean when she said a retrospective isn't a ninth symphony?" she asked, abandoning her puzzle.

Nauman closed the notebook before she could become self-conscious and began to relight his pipe. "It's something that seemed to start with the composer Gustav Mahler."

He looked down at the elaborately carved pipe in his hand as if he'd never before seen it. Today's was shaped like a dragon's head and fragrant smoke curled from the bowl.

"Mahler noticed that Beethoven and Bruckner had both died after composing ninth symphonies, so he decided nine was a jinx. Tried to cheat—*Das Lied von der Erde* after his eighth. Said it wasn't a symphony—was, though. Decided he was being silly, wrote his ninth. Died before he finished tenth. Dvořák and Vaughan Williams, too."

"But surely that's a coincidence?" From the way Nauman's speech had suddenly become telegraphic, Sigrid knew he was absorbed by parallel lines of thought. "By the time a composer reaches his ninth symphony, wouldn't he be old and near the end of his life anyhow?"

"Like an artist with a retrospective," Nauman said bleakly.

"Then you *are* superstitious?"

"And you're avoiding the issue. I'll be sixty goddamned years old next July, old enough to be your—"

"How many symphonies did Mozart compose?" she interrupted.

"Hell, I don't know. Forty or fifty."

"And he was thirty-five when he died. How many retrospectives do you think Picasso had before he kicked off at the tender age of—what was it? Ninety? Ninety-one?"

"Okay, okay." Nauman smiled, holding up his hands in surrender. "I'll do it."

"Only if you want to," Sigrid murmured demurely, and suddenly they were no longer talking about art exhibits.

BURRIS BROTHERS DRY GOODS
806 Broadway

To Acct. of: Mr. Erich Breul   Aug. 25th, 1900
           7 Sussex Square
           New York City

Parasol, blue silk	$1.25
Hamburg edging, 2″ wide	
20 yds. @ $0.06 per yd	1.20
2 silk glove cases @ $0.55 ea	1.10
Linen napkins,	
3 doz. @ $0.50 per doz	1.50
	$5.05

"We allow 3 per cent. discount for cash."

May 6, 1901, from Wm. Fenton & Co.,
    Agents for Genevieve Carlton:

"Maeve's Gallop"	$200.
Frame	12.50
	$212.50

July 22, 1901, from Atwater & Sons:

Babbage engr., "Running Sea"	$22.
Frame	6.
	$28.

Miscellaneous bills and memoranda.
(From the Erich Breul House Collection)

IV

Benjamin Peake arrived at the Erich Breul House shortly after ten to find his office invaded by Roger Shambley, Ph.D., scholar, newest trustee, and all-around bastard.

Shambley was shorter than his own five eleven by a good six inches and ugly as a mud fence with a dark, shaggy head that was two sizes too large for his small, stooped figure. As far as Benjamin Peake was concerned, expensive hairstyling and custom-tailored clothes were probably what kept children from throwing rocks whenever Shambley passed them in the street.

"Can I help you with something?" Peake asked sarcastically as Shambley ignored his arrival and continued to paw through the filing cabinets at the end of his long L-shaped office. He had to stand on tiptoe to read the files at the back of the top drawer.

"I doubt it." Shambley paused beside the open drawer and made a show of checking his watch against the clock over the director's beautiful mahogany desk. "I've only been here two weeks to your two years but I probably know more about what's in these files than you do."

"Now let me think," Peake responded urbanely as he hung his topcoat in a concealed closet and smoothed his brown hair. "I believe it was William Buckley who spoke of the scholar-squirrel mentality, busily gathering every little stray nut that's fallen from the tree of knowledge."

"Actually, it was Gore Vidal," said Shambley, "but don't let facts spoil your pleasure in someone else's well-turned phrases. I'm sure Buckley's said something equally clever about academic endeavor."

Annoyed, Benjamin Peake retreated through an inner door that led to the butler's pantry.

Hope Ruffton was pouring herself a cup of freshly brewed coffee and she greeted him with a pleasant smile.

When Peake took over the directorship and was introduced to her two years ago, he'd returned that first smile with condescending friendliness. "Hope, isn't it?"

"Only if it's Ben," she'd replied with equally friendly condescension.

"Oh. Well. Excuse *me*, Ms. Ruffton."

"Miss will do," she'd said pleasantly.

If he'd had the authority and if old Jacob Munson hadn't been standing by, twinkling and beaming at them like some sort of Munchkin matchmaker, Peake would have fired her then and there.

He still did not completely understand how foolish that would have been although there were times when he uneasily suspected it. But he did soon realize that professionalism was more than semantics to Miss Ruffton. She had ignored his sulks and, with cool efficiency and tact, had deflected him from stupid blunders as he settled into the directorship. The irony of being trained for his position by a nominal subordinate went right over Peake's head and Hope Ruffton was too subtle by far to let him see her own amusement.

These days, with Roger Shambley poking his nose into every cranny and making veiled allusions to certain lapses of competence, Miss Ruffton's efficiency gave Peake a sort of Dutch courage. He might not always have a clear grasp of details, but Miss Ruffton did; and without articulating it, not even to himself, Peake trusted her not to let him make a total ass of himself in front of Shambley.

So he smiled at her gratefully, accepted the coffee she poured for him, and said, "You look like a Christmas card this morning."

A Victorian card, he would have added, straightening his own red-and-green striped tie, except that he was afraid she might tartly remind him that most Victorian cards pictured only blond, blue-eyed Caucasian maidens. Her white silk blouse was tucked into a flowing skirt of dark green wool and it featured a high tight collar and cuffs, all daintily edged in lace. Her thick black hair was brushed into a smooth chignon and tied with a red grosgrain ribbon that echoed a red belt at her waist and clear red nails on her small brown fingers. She wore a simple gold locket and her drop earrings were old-fashioned garnets set in gold filigree that caught the light as she returned Peake's greeting.

"Too bad about the MacAndrews Foundation," she said.

"They turned us down *again?*"

Miss Ruffton nodded, her dark eyes sympathetic. "I left the letter on your desk."

"Oh well," he said, trying to make the best of it, "we weren't really counting on their support."

She gazed into her coffee cup with detachment. There was no way to break bad news gently. "But we *were* counting on Tybault Industries."

His thinly handsome face grew anxious. "They've withdrawn their annual donation?"

"Cut it," she said succinctly. "By a third. With a hint that it may be cut by another third next year."

"Oh, God!" Peake moaned, pacing back and forth from his office door on one side of the room to the dining room door on the far side. "Whatever happened to good old-fashioned altruism?"

"At least the projection figures look good on the Friends membership drive," she said, but Peake refused to be comforted.

"Penny-ante. We've got to find a way to raise more real money or the Erich Breul House is going right down the slop chute," he predicted gloomily.

He started back to his office and hesitated, remembering that Shambley was probably still there.

"What is Dr. Shambley really looking for?" asked Miss Ruffton, with that uncanny knack she had of reading his thoughts.

"God knows," he muttered drearily. "Fresh material for his new book on late nineteenth-century American artists, I suppose." And then, although Peake seldom consciously picked up on Miss Ruffton's subtle inflections, her last words sank in and triggered an automatic alert. "What did you mean 'really'?"

"We've allowed other historians access to the Breul papers," she said slowly. "Dr. Kimmelshue always granted permission. And not just artists or art historians. We've had antique dealers, students of interior design—"

"Well?" Peake asked impatiently.

Miss Ruffton looked at him coldly. "Perhaps it was only my imagination," she said and turned away.

"I'm sorry," he apologized. "Please go on."

But already she had opened the door to the service hall beneath the main stairs, the quickest route to her own desk, and she did not look back.

"Merde!" Peake muttered beneath his breath and charged back into his office.

"Listen, Shambley," he said to the historian's slender back, "what are you really looking for?"

"Mi scusi?" Whenever he wished to insult, obfuscate, or stall until he'd chosen his next words, Roger Shambley always affected Italian. He lifted his oversized shaggy head from a low file drawer. "Why should you think I'm looking for something special?"

"You've spent the last few days quartering this house like a bird dog," said Peake, abruptly realizing that this was true. "All the Breul papers are up in the attic. What do you expect to find in old Kimmelshue's files?"

"Merely fulfilling my duties as a trustee," Shambley said smoothly. "Familiarizing myself with past routine. And present. Which reminds me: Why are there no current inventory sheets? I find nothing later than 1972."

"The inventory hasn't changed enough to justify a new one," Peake snapped. "All the corrections have been notated on our master copy."

He strode over to the file cabinet nearest his desk and extracted the inventory folder. "I can have Miss Ruffton make you a copy, if you wish."

"You checked it thoroughly against the contents of the house when you took over?" asked Shambley.

"Well, no. I saw no need when—"

Shambley cut him off with a sneer. "You know what's wrong with you, Peake? You're lazy. Physically and intellectually. That's why you fouled up at the Friedinger." His eyes narrowed speculatively in his ugly face. "Or was it solely that?"

"What's that supposed to mean?" asked Peake, becoming cautious.

"I think it's time the board asked for a complete inventory. See if there's been any 'unauthorized deaccessioning' down here." He closed the file drawers he'd opened earlier and took the inventory folder from Peake's suddenly nerveless fingers.

"Listen," Benjamin Peake blustered, "if anything's missing, you can't blame me. Everyone knows Dr. Kimmelshue was senile the last three years before he died. Anything could have happened then."

Roger Shambley turned his huge head and haughtily waved Peake aside. "*Permésso*," he said languidly and left the office.

Mrs. Beardsley was becoming heartily sick of Dr. Roger Shambley's *permésso*. In a house this size, one would think a body that small could find a clear space in which to pass without shooing people aside as if they were witless flocks of chickens. And she wasn't taken in by his air of haughty politeness. Mrs. Beardsley knew all there was to know about using manners as a stick to beat those one considered inferior to oneself. Not that she ever did, she told herself.

Well, not without provocation, she amended.

She would admit that she was disappointed when Dr. Shambley received the trusteeship she had sought. She might not have his degrees or his growing reputation as an art scholar, but certainly she knew more about the soul of this house itself than any outsider could hope to. And her income was several times his. She'd checked. Considering the Breul House's financial difficulties, a trustee willing to give generous support should have counted for something, shouldn't it? Nevertheless, she had swallowed her disappointment and welcomed him as graciously as possible and what did she get for her graciousness?

Permésso.

Uptown, in the business office of Kohn and Munson Gallery, Hester Kohn listened in growing alarm as Benjamin Peake screamed in her ear about Roger Shambley.

"For God's sake, Ben, get hold of yourself," she interrupted crisply. "*Have* you taken anything from the house?"

"Of course, I haven't!" he howled.

"Then you've nothing to worry about."

"Yes, I have and you do, too, Hester. You didn't hear the way he said 'unauthorized deaccessions.' That bastard! He picks things out of the air. You know what art historians are like."

"Give them a flake of blue plaster and they'll prove a Giotto fresco once covered the wall," the woman sighed. She looked up as her secretary entered with a letter that required her signature. "Hold on a minute, Ben," she said and tucked the phone between her shoulder and ear while she signed, then told the secretary, "I want to see those consignment sheets before you call the shippers, and don't forget to remind Mr. Munson about tomorrow night."

She waited until the secretary had closed the door behind her, then spoke into the receiver. "There's no way Roger Shambley will start speculating about what really happened unless you give him that first flake of plaster."

But for several long minutes after she'd hung up, her hazel eyes were lost in thought as she wondered if she'd made a mistake in encouraging Jacob to sponsor Shambley on the Breul House's board of trustees. She'd considered it a minor quid pro quo when Shambley approached her about the vacancy in October. She didn't know how Shambley had heard about her tutorial sessions with young Rick Evans or how he knew she'd prefer Jacob not to learn of them, but smoothing his way onto the board seemed a small price to pay for his silence.

Not that he'd been crass enough to threaten her. Open confrontation was not Shambley's way. The man was oblique indirection: a lifted eyebrow, a knowing twitch of his lips, a murmured phrase of ironic Italian. His victim's guilty conscience would do the rest.

Only . . . had she drastically mistaken which situation Shambley meant her to feel guilty about?

In the office across the hall, Jacob Munson unwrapped a peppermint drop from the bowl on his desk. He had not intended to eavesdrop on the conversation between Benjamin and Hester and had almost announced his presence on their line when something in Benjamin's voice kept him silent. A lover's quarrel, he'd thought at first.

When he'd realized last year that Hester and Benjamin were occasional lovers, he'd hoped that it might lead to marriage. Thirty-four, Hester was, and time was running out if she wanted children.

That would have made an appropriate solution to the gallery's uncertain future—Horace's daughter and the best friend of Jacob's only son. To his disappointment though, their relationship had never gotten out of bed. When dressed, they didn't even seem to like each other most of the time. So what was all this about plaster flakes?

He sighed and absently tucked the cellophane candy wrapper into his pocket. Maybe it was a sign. Maybe blood was best after all. Surely it was not too late to train young Richard to carry on the Munson heritage at Kohn and Munson?

By closing time, Rick Evans had shot the last roll of film that he'd brought with him to the Breul House. He climbed down from Pascal's tall aluminum stepladder and unplugged the floodlights he'd used to light the plaster moldings on the ceiling of the third floor hallway.

"I guess we'll call it a day," he told Pascal Grant, and began packing up his cases.

Pascal bent to help, his smooth face so near Rick could have touched it with his own. His beautiful eyes met Rick's trustingly. "Will you need my ladder anymore, Rick?"

"Not for now."

They collapsed the light stands and carried everything through the frosted glass doors, down to the end of the hall and the mannequin maid, where they loaded it all on the dumbwaiter—easier than carting everything up and down by hand. Together they carried the ladder down the back service steps and unloaded the dumbwaiter down in the basement next to Pascal's room.

"Want to go get a pizza?" Pascal asked hopefully when they had stowed Rick's equipment in an empty cabinet. "We can eat it in my room and listen to some more jazz."

Rick hesitated; then, with a fatalistic *que sera sera* shrug of his shoulders, he nodded.

* * *

"Dr. Shambley?"

The patrician voice floated through the marble hall, startling him as he descended the main staircase, now dimly lit. For a moment, he almost thought he'd been addressed by the elegant female mannequin on the landing. Then he realized it was that Beardsley woman speaking to him from the doorway of the darkened gallery beyond the massive fireplace.

"Cretina!" Roger Shambley mumbled under his breath. He thought everyone had left for the day and that he was alone except for the simple-minded janitor somewhere in the bowels of the house.

Mrs. Beardsley turned off the lights in the cloakroom, leaving only the security lights in the hall, then buttoned her red wool coat and pulled on her gloves. "You won't forget to let Pascal know when you're leaving tonight, will you, Dr. Shambley? The burglar alarm wasn't switched on till almost midnight last night because he thought you were still here."

"I'll remember," he said brusquely. *"Buona notte."*

Dismissing her, he crossed the hall and entered the library, pettishly turning on the lights she had extinguished only moments before.

A slam of the front door restored the earlier silence. Already, the automatic thermostat had begun to lower the temperature here. For a moment, he contemplated finding the master control and turning it up again, then decided it was pointless.

He'd begun to despair of finding the letters he knew Erich Jr. must have written during his brief months in France. He had already leafed through all the personal papers still stored in Erich Breul's library. Except for that one tantalizing letter misfiled in the attic, there was nothing later than the spring of 1911 when young Breul wrote to say how pleased he was that both parents were coming to Harvard, that he'd reserved rooms for them at Cambridge's best hotel for graduation weekend, and that "although you will find her much altered since her father's death, Miss Norton trusts that her health will enable her to receive you at Shady-hill."

Charles Eliot Norton! Shambley had marveled when he read that. One of the patron saints of fine arts—an intimate of

Ruskin, Carlyle, Lowell and Longfellow—and the Breuls, *padre e figlio*, had been guests in his home!

Disconsolate, Shambley twirled Erich Breul's large globe in its teak stand. Those letters might as well be in Timbuktu for all the chance he had of finding them at this point.

Sophie Breul had saved her son's toys, his schoolwork, his best clothes. Surely she would have saved his letters as well. Yet he'd exhausted all the logical places and no more of Erich Jr.'s last letters were to be found.

He gave the globe a final twirl, switched off the lights, and crossed the hall to the cloakroom for his overcoat, the hollow sound of his footsteps on the marble floor echoing eerily from the walls all around him.

He started to leave, remembered Mrs. Beardsley's injunction, and descended the stairs to the basement, muttering to himself. As if he had nothing better to do than remind another cretin of his duties!

At the bottom of the steps, Roger Shambley paused, uncertain exactly where the janitor's room was. Lights were on along the passageway beyond the main kitchen and he followed them, noting the storerooms on either side. Late last week he had checked through the racks of pictures that Kimmelshue had consigned to the basement on the off chance that the old fart really had been as senile as Peake claimed. A waste of time. No silk purses hiding among those sows' ears.

No pictures stacked behind that pile of cast-off furniture, trunks, and rolled carpets, or—

He stopped, thunderstruck.

Trunks?

Slowly, almost holding his breath, he found the light switch, pulled a large brown steamer trunk into an open space, and opened it.

Inside were books, men's clothing, turn-of-the-century toilet articles, and a handful of—*Dio mio*, yes! Programs from Parisian theaters, a menu from a Montparnasse café, and catalogs from various art exhibits.

Excitedly, he pawed to the bottom. A few innocuous souvenirs, more clothing, nothing else. Erich Breul Jr.'s last effects didn't even fill one trunk.

Well, what did you really expect? he jeered at himself.

Retaining the catalogs, he shoved the large trunk back in

place and lifted the lid of the smaller one to see yellowed feminine apparel, an autograph album from Sophie Breul's childhood, and what looked like an embroidered glove case. He almost pushed it aside without opening it, but scholarly habit was too strong and as soon as he looked, he knew he'd found treasure: fourteen fat envelopes, thick with European postage stamps. The top one was postmarked August 1911 and had been mailed from Southampton, England; the last from Lyons in *Octobre* 1912. And *si! si! SI!*—near the bottom was an envelope postmarked *XXXI Août 1912*.

His hand was shaking so that he could hardly read the faded city.

Lyons?

If he remembered rightly from his one course in Post-Impressionism, Sorgues lay south from Lyons in the Rhône River valley.

In 1912, Pablo Picasso and Georges Braque, the co-founders of cubism, had spent the summer in Sorgues, where, in a burst of creativity, the two friends had invented the first collages.

For a moment, as he experienced a pure rush of excitement, Shambley's ugly face was almost attractive. Here was every scholar's dream: the discovery of primary documents, a chance to become a permanent footnote in history. He wanted to sit down and read them immediately; but innate, self-serving caution made him put the letters back in the glove case and slide it and the catalogs into his briefcase until he could be certain of no interruptions.

Leaving the storage room as he'd found it, he switched off the light and retraced his steps. Beyond the stairs, he noticed a door that was slightly ajar, and when he pushed it open, he realized he'd found the janitor's bedroom. No janitor, though.

In his state of excitement, the room's ornate sensuousness neither surprised nor interested him. All he cared about was scribbling the dummy a note—assuming the dummy could read—that he'd left the house for the evening.

He propped the note on the mantelpiece and, from force of habit, read the signature of the saccharine oil painting there. Idly, his eyes drifted over the posters with which the janitor had lined his walls and at the doorway, he paused, amused by the coincidence of seeing a reproduction of an early Braque collage when his head was so full of the possibility that Erich Breul had actually met Braque.

He hesitated, eyes on the poster. Braque or Picasso?

In later years even Picasso had trouble identifying which works were his and which were Braque's, so why should he be any more knowledgeable? The wood-grained paper overlapping a sketchy violin said Braque, but something about the lines of the head—a monkey's head?—said Picasso.

Curious, Shambley leaned closer, searching for a signature. There was none. Suddenly, a frisson of absolute incredulity shot through his very soul. This wasn't some poster issued by the Museum of Modern Art. That scrap of yellowed newsprint at the edge of the picture was real! He ran his hand ever so lightly across the surface of the picture and felt the irregularities where one piece of paper had been layered over another.

Very gently, he removed the bottom two thumbtacks by which the paper was held to the wall and lifted it up. With a minimum of contortion, he could read the words scrawled in charcoal on the back by two clearly different hands: "*A notre petit singe américain—Picasso et G. Braque.*"

Hardly daring to breathe, he carefully replaced the thumbtacks precisely as before and moved to the two pictures nearby. Even in this soft light, he could now see that they, too, were no mere reproductions but oil paintings unmistakably by Fernand Léger, another master of cubism. Indeed, the canvases still held faint crease marks from where they had been rolled and squashed.

The trunk, Shambley thought. The collage was small enough to lie flat on the bottom, but the pictures must have crossed the Atlantic rolled up in that trunk and there they'd stayed for the next seventy-five years because Kimmelshue had his ass stuck firmly in the nineteenth century and Peake was too damn lazy to get off his. A goddamned fortune thumbtacked to a janitor's bedroom wall.

"And little ol' *piccolo mio*'s the only one who knows," he gloated, wanting to kick up his heels and gambol around the room.

The distant sound of a closing door and young male voices raised in laughter alerted him. He quickly snatched up his note and stepped outside, pulling the door shut just as Rick Evans and Pascal Grant walked into the main kitchen carrying pizza and a bottle of Chianti.

Shambley was startled. Young Evans he'd met and had treated with courtesy because of his relationship to Jacob Munson, but he had never really looked at the janitor. The guy usually had his head down or his back turned when Shambley was around and he always wore rough green coveralls and mumbled when he spoke.

Tonight, Grant was dressed in tight Levi's and a beige suede jacket, his blond curls had been tossed by the icy December wind, his fair skin was flushed with cold, and his face, his beautiful face, was so animated with laughter that it was impossible to believe that he was the same slow-witted Quasimodo who had ducked in and out of his presence these last two weeks.

The two youths halted at the sight of him. Pascal Grant's laughter died and he lowered his head fearfully as they waited for the trustee to speak.

"A party?" Shambley asked. He'd meant to sound friendly, but it came out a sneer and for some reason, Munson's grandson flushed.

Instantly, Shambley knew why and was swept with a jealousy which he could hardly conceal. Deliberately, he walked over to Grant, put out his small hand, and lifted that soft round chin, but the handyman trembled and wouldn't meet his eyes.

"Take your nasty hand off him!" Rick Evans snarled, stepping toward him.

"Or you'll what?" asked Shambley. "Give me a proper thrashing?"

Without waiting for an answer, he released Grant and waved them both aside. "I'll let myself out this way. *Buona sera.* Enjoy your"—he let his voice turn lewd—"pizza. Or whatever."

As he passed through the shadowed passage to the front door, he almost forgot his first discoveries in the contemplation of this last: old Jacob Munson's grandson a *femminella.* Well, well, well.

* * *

Back in the warm security of his nest-like room, Pascal Grant rubbed his chin where Roger Shambley had touched him. "I don't like him, Rick."

"I don't either," Rick Evans said and his soft Louisiana voice was grim.

On any clear winter night, Søren Thorvaldsen could look upriver from his desk and see the distant George Washington Bridge strung across the Hudson like a Victorian dowager's diamond necklace, but it was not half so beautiful to him as the cruise ship docked almost directly below his office window. The *Sea Dancer* was lit from stem to stern by her own glittering lights and she would sail on Saturday with eighteen hundred winter-weary customers.

A soft trill drew him from the window back to his desk where a winking button on his telephone console signaled a call on his private line.

"Thorvaldsen here."

"*Velkommen hjem*, Thorvaldsen." A gurgle of Irish laughter warmed her golden voice as Lady Francesca Leeds stumbled over the word for home.

Her attempts at Danish amused him. "I tried to call you from the airport," he said.

"I know," she replied. "I'm sorry. I was tied up with a client tonight."

He looked at his watch. Nearly ten. "Is it too late for a nightcap?"

"I'm afraid so," she murmured regretfully. "But I have good news for you."

"Oscar Nauman's agreed?"

"Not exactly. But he hasn't said no, either, and this is the closest anyone's come yet. I've arranged a small cocktail party tomorrow evening at the Erich Breul House. Jacob Munson's going to bring Nauman to look at the space. You'll come?"

"*Helt sikkert!*" he assured her happily.

Her voice turned teasingly miffed. "I think you'd rather see Oscar Nauman than me."

He laughed as she said *godnat* and hung up, but her teasing held a shadow of truth. Francesca Leeds excited him more than any woman in years. It wasn't solely because she so outranked him in birth, although bedding a woman out of his class had always been an aphrodisiac. It was her special blend of sophistication and earthiness that was so irresistible to the self-made Dane, who had learned to hold his own in the drawing room without ever quite forgetting what went on out in the kitchen. She was capricious enough to keep him off balance, uncertain of victory.

Yet past successes, spiced with a tinge of cynicism, let him savor the chase. For the first time, he enjoyed prolonging the preliminaries. Inevitably, she must surely come to his bed.

In the meantime, Oscar Nauman was even less predictable and Thorvaldsen looked forward to meeting the artist whose pictures had given him so much pleasure, pictures that were as much a reward for his years of hard work as sex with a beautiful woman.

"A party?" Sigrid asked, dismayed. "I'm no good at parties, Nauman. You should know that by now."

"I want you to meet Munson. You don't have to dress up. Besides," he reminded her, "you're the one who thinks I ought to have this retrospective, so you might as well come along and see the place. Meet me there at seven and we'll have dinner afterwards."

Remembering that her housemate had mentioned something about a pickled boar's head in honor of the season, Sigrid decided that a party was probably the lesser of tomorrow's two evils.

". . . so there we were—my machine smashed at the bottom of the tree, Chou-Chew hurling simian curses from the top, while I lay trampled beneath the paws of a monstrous dog who determined that my battered body should provide a footstool to raise himself closer to my hysterical pet.

Fortunately, help was immediately at hand. The brute's master pulled him from me with apologies which owed as much to the Spanish language as to the French."

Letter from Erich Breul Jr., dated 8.30.1912
(From the Erich Breul House Collection)

V

Wednesday, December 16

The caterers arrived at the Erich Breul House shortly
after six, and Mrs. Beardsley, delegated by Lady Francesca
Leeds, was there to direct them through the door under the
main stairs and into the butler's pantry.

In the dining room, the formal table was relieved of its
extra leaves and draped in dark red linen with green plaid
runners. The caterers had brought their own silver-plated
canapé trays and their own chafing dish for the hot hors
d'oeuvres, but the dozen or so sterling candelabra that would
soon light the long room with tall white tapers belonged to
the house.

An arrangement of cedar, red-berried holly, and shiny
magnolia leaves had been delivered earlier, and as Mrs.
Beardsley centered it between the candles, Pascal Grant
paused with table leaves in his arms. "Do you want me to do
anything else, Mrs. Beardsley? Bring up some more chairs?"

She glanced about the room. Sophie Breul's Sheraton
dining table could be expanded to seat forty, but twenty
chairs were its normal complement and Lady Francesca had
said tonight's party was to be quite small.

"Just three or four of the trustees, Dr. Peake and his
secretary, the art people, Mr. Thorvaldsen, and of course
you, Mrs. Beardsley. When Oscar Nauman asks about the
history of the Breul House, we must have someone who can
tell him."

Mrs. Beardsley had known she was being buttered, but
that didn't diminish her pleasure. It was such smooth butter.
Now she smiled at Pascal Grant. "I think we have enough
chairs for anyone who might wish to sit. You go ahead to your

60

movie, Pascal, and you needn't worry about coming up later. We'll put everything back as it was first thing tomorrow. Just don't forget the alarm when you come back tonight."

"I won't, Mrs. Beardsley. Good night, Mrs. Beardsley."

"Good night, dear," she said absently, giving the room a final check.

Everything seemed quite under control. Gas logs blazed upon the open hearth next to the glittering Christmas tree and together, they lent the great marble hall an almost Dickensian warmth and cheer. Paneled pocket doors between the drawing room and gallery to the left of the hall had been pushed back to form one long open room and a hired pianist was familiarizing himself with the baby grand at the street end of the drawing room. The caterers had set up their bar in the pantry, appetizing odors were coming from the oven, and Miss Ruffton had returned from the cloakroom wearing a red skirt shot through with gold threads, a gold ribbon in her hair, and a party smile on her face. Even Dr. Peake had changed his tie before drifting in to lift the domed lid of the largest silver chafing dish and sample a hot savory.

"It's beginning to look a lot like Christmas," he said, licking his fingers like a mischievous boy.

Earlier in the afternoon, Mrs. Beardsley had slipped across the square and changed into her own holiday dress, a black wool sheath topped by a red Chanel jacket, her grandmother's three-strand pearl choker and earrings, and an emerald-and-ruby pin that seemed appropriate for the season. Now she decided it was time to complete her own costume, to exchange her sensible low pumps for the patent leather T-straps waiting for her in the cloakroom.

As she crossed the hall, the door swung open for Francesca Leeds, her windswept red hair swirling upon the collar of a dark mink coat, which she wore like a cloak over an evening suit of raw gold silk. "Show time!" she caroled.

Uptown, along the broad avenues, Salvation Army Santas were jostled for sidewalk space by three-card monte dealers and free-lance Santas who hawked "genuine Rolex watches, jus' twenny dollar—check it out" between nips from their hip flasks.

Skaters twirled and circled before the blazing tree at

Rockefeller Center; a string quartet sheltered in the street-level jog of a huge skyscraper to play German carols, while an artist chalked the sidewalk in front of St. Thomas's Church with an ambitious choir of angels. Further up Fifth Avenue, wide-eyed toddlers, blissfully indifferent to the monetary worth of diamonds and rubies, were lifted up by their parents to watch Muppets romp among the gems in Tiffany's windows.

As customers streamed through the doorways of lavishly decorated stores, seasonal Muzak occasionally floated out to mingle with the Salvation Army bells. The vaguely religious music fell equally upon the warmly dressed and upon the shabby bundles of rags who tried to hunker deeper into the few dark corners. For many, the street people added just the right tinge of guilt to the general thank-God-*I'm*-making-it aura of self-satisfaction, a sort of memento mori that made modern yuletide hedonism all the more pleasurable.

In the art gallery just off Fifth Avenue, Oscar Nauman refilled his empty cup from the fat china pot on Jacob Munson's desk, leaned back in the comfortable leather chair, and smiled at his friend. "I must be getting old, Jacob, when I prefer your hot chocolate to your cold whiskey."

"*Ja*, sure," the old man jeered, unwrapping another of his perpetual peppermints. They were imported from France especially for him and were made with particularly pungent oils that bit the tongue and almost compensated for his forbidden cigarettes. "Wait till you are my age. At least you don't have doctors telling you what you can drink. I look at you, Oscar, and I see still the boy who first came through this door with those charcoal drawings of Lila under his arm."

"The hair," said Oscar.

It was true. That thick mane of hair had turned completely white before he was thirty. His height helped, as did the probing intelligence in his intensely blue eyes, but it was the white hair that gave him such an aura of timelessness. Munson tried to look at him objectively, to catalog the fine wrinkles around his eyes, the lines beneath his firm chin, but it was hard to perceive the softening of age in that strong face. He did recognize that inward-turning melancholy however. Lila's name still had that power.

If only the woman would die, he thought. Die or be cured. God knows she'd tried to kill herself often enough in the past twenty-five years. Jacob sipped his cocoa and refrained from looking at Oscar's left ear. He knew that the scars Lila's knife had left there were almost invisible. And the scars on Oscar's psyche should have faded as well, but how could they while the woman remained alive in that prison for the criminally insane?

"I'm sorry," he murmured. "I'm a stupid old man to mention her."

"It isn't just Lila." Nauman cradled the cup with the fingertips of both hands and gazed at it bleakly. "That's the worst of this retrospective business, Jacob. I'll have to look again at so many things I thought I was finished with. I don't think I want to do that."

"For a *real* retrospective, perhaps not," Munson agreed, stroking his wispy beard. "But the Breul House—this we will treat like a preview, *ja?*" he said coaxingly. "The space is small. Friendly. This you will do for your old friend?"

"Preview?" Nauman growled.

"*Ja*, sure. How much longer can I keep working, Oscar? I tell you alone: I am eighty-two. Most men my age are dead but I cannot retire before we do your retrospective." He tried to sound frail and pathetic, but his small body was still too wiry and agile and there was a jaunty glint in his black eyes. "You are killing me."

"*Ja*, sure," Oscar said sardonically.

The office door was ajar and Hester Kohn, vivid in red and purple, stuck her head in. The lush scent of her gardenia perfume floated in ahead of her.

"Car's here," she said, holding out Jacob's coat and muffler.

Munson beamed. "Good, good! Now we meet your lady fireman."

"Lady policeman," Oscar grinned.

Sigrid had intended to leave work early enough to allow herself plenty of time for a long hot shower and a leisurely hour to dress, but in the late afternoon, she'd been called to an unexpected meeting that ran past six-thirty.

If she hoped to make Sussex Square before the party was over, Sigrid knew she could forget about that shower, much less changing into something more glamorous than the shapeless black wool suit and white turtleneck sweater she'd pulled from her closet this morning.

She rummaged in her shoulder bag and found a tube of lipstick and some mascara. She'd been running late the day before yesterday and had planned to duck into the locker room here at work, then completely forgot about makeup as soon as she saw the papers that had accumulated on her desk over the weekend.

Well, mascara and lipstick were better than nothing, she thought, and headed for the locker room where she washed her face and hands, pushed her hair into place and started on her eyes.

It looked so simple when other women did it. And really, what was so difficult? A steady hand, a bit of bravura and *voila!*

"Oh, damn!"

"Something wrong, Lieutenant?"

Sigrid whirled to see Detective Elaine Albee peering around the bank of lockers.

"No." She turned back to the mirror where she saw that the pretty blond officer was frankly staring at the smeared dark black rings around her eyes.

Sigrid was torn with frustration and embarrassment. "I'm supposed to be at a cocktail party in Sussex Square in exactly thirteen minutes and I look like a goddamned panda!"

"I was wondering if someone had given you a black eye," the younger woman ventured. This was the first time she'd ever known the lieutenant to worry about her looks and Elaine wasn't quite sure how to react. Lieutenant Harald could freeze a blast furnace with her tongue when annoyed.

"It's probably because the light's so bad in here," she said diplomatically.

"This is ridiculous," Sigrid said, grimly washing off the smeared mascara. "I'll just call and say I can't make it."

"Let me help," Albee offered. "I keep a few things in my locker for emergencies."

"You have emergencies like this?" Sigrid asked curiously. "You always look so put together."

"Come with me," Elaine grinned and Sigrid soon found herself seated on a bench in front of the other woman's locker.

Five minutes later, her eyes were expertly lined and shadowed, the planes of her cheeks subtly enhanced with blusher, her lips—

"My lip gloss is wrong for you," Elaine frowned. "I'm blond, you're brunette. You need something richer than anything I have here."

Sigrid brought out her own lipstick. "Will this do?"

Elaine uncapped it, examined it critically and handed it back with approval. "Perfect for you. How did you stumble—" She caught herself. "I mean—"

"I know what you meant," Sigrid said dryly as she leaned toward the mirror on the door of Albee's locker and applied the lipstick. "It was the woman who cut my hair last month. She picked it out. I've just tried to follow her directions."

She capped the lipstick and looked at the finished result as impersonally as if her face belonged to someone else.

"Uh, Lieutenant?"

"Yes?"

Elaine reached into her locker for a plastic bag with the name of a dress shop located in the next block. "I picked this up on my lunch hour today. It was on sale and looked like something that might come in handy during the holidays. You can borrow it, if you want."

It was a scoop-necked shell of gold sequins that glittered and sparkled like Christmas lights when Elaine lifted it from the bag.

Sigrid made one weak protest, then shucked off her jacket and sweater, remembering just in time not to smear her lipstick. The sequinned top fit fine. Albee was curvier, but she was taller, so it balanced. With her jacket left unbuttoned, she looked almost glamorous.

Elaine was getting into the sport of it now and pulled out some gold-colored costume jewelry: bracelets and a pair of earrings.

Sigrid accepted the bracelets but regretfully confessed, "My ears aren't pierced."

"You have to have earrings."

Another woman entered, greeted Albee by name, then gave Sigrid a formal nod and a curious glance.

"I'm late," Sigrid said, looking at the clock on the end

wall, but Albee was lost in thought. "Quaranto!" she exclaimed suddenly. "In Records. She keeps a wad of costume jewelry in her desk."

"I have to go," Sigrid objected.

"Not without earrings," Albee told her firmly and neither woman noticed that in this area it was now Albee who commanded. "I'll meet you by the elevators on the first floor in two minutes."

She sprinted for the door. Sigrid folded her turtleneck and left it in her own locker, put on her heavy coat, then took an elevator downstairs.

True to her word, it wasn't much more than two minutes later that Elaine Albee raced down the stairs with a glittery dangling earring in each determined hand. Without a shred of self-consciousness, she stood on tiptoe to clip them on Sigrid's ears, then fluffed her hair and stepped back to look at what she'd wrought.

"Your coat!" she cried. "I think I know someone—"

"No!" Sigrid protested, clutching her camel hair topcoat protectively.

"Well—" said Elaine. "But take it off the minute you get there, okay?"

"Okay." Sigrid hesitated and awkwardly held out her hand. "Thanks, Albee."

"Any time, Lieutenant." Feeling almost maternal, the younger woman watched as her boss hurried out into the winter night, earrings swinging with each long stride.

"There you are," said Jim Lowry when she returned to the squad room. "What's funny, Lainey?"

"Nothing," she grinned. "Except that now I know how the fairly godmother felt when she sent Cinderella off to the ball."

"Huh?"

"Skip it. Didn't you want to make the early movie?"

The cabbie had bent the speed limit, and Sigrid, who normally hated fast driving, gratefully added a little extra to her tip as he let her out in Sussex Square. It was only nineteen minutes past seven. Fashionably late, she told herself and hurried up the brick walk.

Remembering her promise to Elaine Albee, she slipped her coat off as soon as she entered the Erich Breul House. There she was greeted by a dignified gray-haired woman in a red jacket and beautiful pearls.

"Welcome to the Erich Breul House," said the woman, directing her to the cloakroom. "I'm Eloise Beardsley, senior docent."

"Sigrid Harald," she responded and handed her coat over to an attendant. "I think Oscar Nauman's expecting me?"

"Ah, yes." Mrs. Beardsley led her past an ornate Christmas tree and gestured toward the arched doorway near a wide marble staircase. "There he is now."

Suddenly all the silly panic over her clothes and makeup seemed worth it for the look in Nauman's eyes as he crossed the hall to her.

"Very nice," he said, handing her a bourbon-and-Coke. "I was afraid you might not come."

"Not come?" she asked. "Why would you think that?"

Seated at the desk in his makeshift office up on the fourth floor, Roger Shambley happily fingered the pack of letters. He had read them so many times since last night that he'd virtually memorized whole passages. For the most part they chronicled the usual unexceptional adventures of an earnest young man released from schoolbooks and given permission to play for a year or two before settling into adult responsibilities.

After graduation in the spring of 1911, young Erich Breul Jr. had spent the summer at the family's vacation "cottage" near Oswego on the eastern end of Lake Ontario. (Nowhere near as grand as the "cottages" at Newport, the Breuls roughed it each summer with a mere eighteen rooms and a live-in staff of only five.)

In August he sailed to England for a month in London, then entrained for Vienna by way of Antwerp, Cologne and Frankfurt. Christmas and most of January were passed with his mother's people in Zurich. Spring found him in Rome. In each great art center, he dutifully visited the appropriate museums and churches, attended the expected concerts and operas, and afterwards, with filial rectitude, recorded his impressions of each for his "dear Mama and Papa" back home.

As spring turned to summer in those letters, Shambley could read between the lines and sense young Breul's growing saturation with the old masters, lofty music, and approved lectures in fusty rooms. June made him restless for open air and manly exercise. Accordingly, he had sent his luggage ahead to Lyons and, in company with several similarly minded youths, had hiked along the Mediterranean coast from Genoa to Marseilles.

At Marseilles, he had somehow acquired a pet monkey, Chou-Chew. The details of that acquisition were glossed over; Shambley suspected a rowdy night in one of those waterfront taverns frequented by seamen from all over the world.

In any event, Breul had parted from his friends, who were going on to Barcelona, purchased a bicycle, and, with the monkey in an open wicker basket on the front, had pedaled northward up the Rhone valley. He meandered through small villages where he bought bread and cheese or a night's lodging; and as he entered the fertile plains north of Avignon, he enjoyed both the blazing sun overhead and the cool shaded avenues of plane trees that lined the irrigation canals.

It was mid-August and the young vagabond was dawdling along a back road near the nondescript village of Sorguessur-l'Ouvèze when his innocent reveries were suddenly interrupted by an enormous white dog that bounded over the hedgerows, barking with such deceptive ferociousness that the startled young American promptly crashed his machine into the nearest tree.

Enter Picasso and Braque, thought Shambley, who had spent most of the night reading everything he could put his hands on concerning their summer of 1912.

The dog was Picasso's, a Great Pyrenees, one of those shaggy white creatures as big as a Newfoundland or Great Dane. His whole life long, Picasso had adored animals, from exotic zoo specimens to the most common domestic cat. How could he resist a monkey?

Braque, himself a cyclist, was more concerned about the damage done to Breul's new bicycle.

While Picasso quieted his dog and charmed the frightened monkey from the tree with his dark expressive eyes and coaxing voice, Braque hoisted the crumpled machine over his broad shoulder. Together, they led the youth to the nearest blacksmith's, left the bicycle for repairs, and insisted that he go with them for a glass of wine.

As so often happens—even with strictly reared young Lutherans—one glass of wine led to two and before long, the first bottle was empty and Picasso ordered a second in which to toast *"le grand Vilbure,"* that great American whom he and Braque admired above all others and whose death that spring had so impoverished the world. The Spaniard spoke French with such a heavy accent that Erich Jr. had to ask him to repeat the name twice. Even then, Picasso had to spread his arms and make engine noises before Breul understood that they were toasting Wilbur Wright.

Eventually, the blacksmith's apprentice tracked them down and informed M'sieu Breul that it would be three days before his bicycle could be repaired. His master had sent to Orange for the necessary part. One must be patient.

"But I'm due in Lyons day after tomorrow!" said M'sieu Breul. "I'm to meet friends there. It's my birthday."

"Tant pis," shrugged the blacksmith's apprentice.

"Never mind," Braque and Picasso told him. "We will celebrate your natal day here."

Although this would be the last summer that Picasso had to worry about money, the two artists had deliberately chosen Sorgues for two reasons: it was cheap and no one knew them there. But perhaps they missed Apollinaire, Max Jacob, Derain, Manolo, Juan Gris, Havilland and all the other friends with whom they socialized back in Paris. Or perhaps their kindness to the young American sprang from a combination of great personal and professional happiness just then. Not only did their work intoxicate them, so did their women.

Braque and his Marcelle still considered themselves newlyweds and Picasso had only that spring taken a new mistress, the lovely and delicate Eva, *"ma jolie,"* who was to die so young.

In any event, Picasso volunteered to nursemaid Chou-Chew and Braque arranged for Breul to stay with him and his wife at Villa Bel Air, a rather dreary and commonplace house that was more beautiful in name than in fact.

Shambley wished Erich Jr. had written less about Braque's domestic arrangements and much more about Braque's studio, the pictures he saw there, or the conversations that must have passed between the two artists when Picasso arrived the next morning with the monkey on his shoulder.

Instead, after a brief reference to Braque's *trompe-l'oeil* technique and how he used combs and varnishes to duplicate the appearance of marble or grained wood on his canvases, Erich Jr. wrote that he did not think dear Papa would find the work of his new friends very meaningful. "I fear that you, with your deep love and knowledge of pure art, would scorn their *papier collé* and the strange analytical shapes of their designs, but their experiments interest me very much and when they explain what they are doing, their excitement infuses me as well."

Having seen the results, Shambley could use his imagination to fill in the details Erich Jr. so lightly touched upon. They made him sit in a chair all afternoon, gave him Braque's violin to play and, while the monkey clambered at will over sitter and artists alike, began to devise a birthday portrait, using their new techniques. In the evening Marcelle and Eva produced a special dinner and Breul gave them most of his pocket money for wine. By midnight, the portrait was declared finished (even though it had taken on certain simian details as more bottles were emptied) and both artists had signed it on the back before making a formal presentation to the birthday boy.

In return, Erich Jr. had risen to the occasion with a speech about Spanish-French-American friendship, in token of which he now gave his bicycle to Braque and his monkey to Picasso. Early the next day, with his portrait tied up in brown paper, a slightly queasy young American—"I think it must have been the sausages," he wrote his parents—caught the morning train to Lyons, where his *wander jahr* returned to its prescribed paths.

Except that it hadn't quite, thought Shambley, turning to the letters written after Breul settled in Paris for what was to be his final six months before sailing home. He was discreet about his sorties into bohemia, and his assurances of studious application to conventional art and culture were probably written in response to pointed questions from home.

But the catalogs and Montparnasse menus, not to mention the two Légers hanging four floors down in that zoo of a janitor's room, gave ample evidence that the junior Breul had spent as much time among the avant-garde of Paris as in the venerable Louvre.

Shambley returned the last letter to its envelope and blocked them between his small hands like a deck of cards. At that moment, Dr. Roger Shambley was a deeply happy man. All his life he'd chased those capricious goddesses, Fame and Fortune.

Native intelligence and dogged hard work had made him a well-regarded expert in nineteenth-century American art. His first two books had gained him tenure; his third confirmed his reputation for good solid scholarship, which translated into speaking engagements, magazine articles, even an occasional spot on the *Today Show* when a feature story required an art historian's authoritative comment. If that art historian came across the tube as acerbic and witty, all the better.

Yet everyone dreams of immortality. No matter how competently and wittily written, few books survive their time if they only rehash previously known data; but the discoverer of new material will always be read simply because he was *first*. That's why every scholar dreams of new finds—that Greek statue only a shovelful of dirt away, that major missing piece of the puzzle. Discoveries automatically turn on the grant machines and roll out appointments and promotions.

With these letters and a description of how he found an unknown seminal work, Shambley knew he could write a monograph that would become a permanent appendage to the Picasso-Braque legend. Not only that, he would become a hero to everyone connected to the Breul House. Once it was made public that this dead-in-the-water museum contained the only documented example in the entire world of a Picasso-Braque collaboration, they'd have to put in a conveyor belt to keep the crowds moving.

Which took care of fame.

As for fortune . . .

Those two Léger canvasses presented interesting possibilities, none of which involved the Breul House. Today, he had gone to the Museum of Modern Art and bought two

Léger posters as nearly like the two on Pascal Grant's wall in size and composition as he could manage. He had already stashed them in one of the basement storage rooms. In the next day or so, as soon as he could substitute them for the real pictures, he would announce his discovery of the Picasso-Braque collage.

There would be such an instant uproar of excitement that even if the janitor noticed the difference between the posters and the authentic paintings, who would pay him any mind?

No one. He'd be home free with two Légers of his very own. Too bad he couldn't openly offer them for sale at, say, Sotheby's. Auctions always brought the highest prices. But Sotheby's required a legal history of the artwork it put on the block: documents, canceled checks, and bills of sale; and the only provenance he could offer would be the 1912 catalog he'd found in Erich Jr.'s effects.

No, he'd have to find someone with a love of modern art, a streak of larceny, and the resources to indulge expensive tastes.

He looked at his watch. Time to put in an appearance downstairs. He started to put the letters back in his briefcase, then hesitated. Maybe it would be safer to leave the letters here for now. There were a million hiding places in this cluttered attic but, as most scholars knew, a misfiled letter is a lost letter.

Shambley opened a drawer marked "Miscellaneous Business Correspondence: 1916/1917" and craftily filed the packet under "August 1916."

At that moment he felt positively gleeful, as if the ghost of Christmas Present had upended an enormous bag of toys at his feet. If the attic stairs had possessed a free-standing banister, he would have slid right down it, and it was all he could do to keep from chortling aloud. He stepped into the servants' lavatory on the third floor, smoothed his unruly hair, and put his pugnacious face into a semblance of professorial dignity.

But as he walked downstairs to join the party, it occurred to Roger Shambley that perhaps he wouldn't have to look very far for the buyer he needed.

The Breul dining room was the scene of many elaborate and festive dinners. Sophie Fürst Breul's mother was famous in Zurich for her brilliant dinner parties and her daughter brought the Fürst touch with her to New York. Although extravagant, perhaps, by our 1950's standards, Mrs. Breul's dinners were considered small and select in their day and the guest list never exceeded forty, the number which could be comfortably seated at her table. Like Scrooge after his conversion, it could be said that the Breuls "knew how to keep Christmas well, if any [couple] alive possessed the knowledge"; and it was their custom to invite a few friends for "supper" on Christmas night. The following is from Mrs. Breul's menu files and was dated "Christmas 1906."

Crème d'asperge

Hûtres   *Sardines*   *Dinde fumée*

Rôti de boeuf

Haricots verts   *Pommes*

Sacher Torte   *Noix glacée*   *Topfenstrudel*

Vermouth   *Bordeaux*   *Champagne*

---

from *Welcome to the Breul House!—An Informal Tour*, by Mrs. Hamilton Johnstone III, Senior Docent. (© 1956)

VI

"Sigrid Harald?" asked Søren Thorvaldsen. *"Er De dansk, frøken Harald?"*

"My father's father was from Denmark," Sigrid acknowledged, "but I'm afraid I know very few words of Danish."

And not much more than a few words of party talk either, she thought as she listened to a small white-haired woman quiz Thorvaldsen about the frivolous names he'd given his cruise ships.

"I think ships deserve more stately names," said the woman, whose own name Sigrid couldn't remember. "Something like *Empress of the Sea* or *Queen Margrethe.*"

"But those are for serious ships," Thorvaldsen answered her playfully. "My ships *are* frivolous, Mrs. Hyman."

Hyman, Sigrid told herself. Hyman. Wife of David Hyman, trustee. And next to Mrs. Hyman was Mr. Herzog. Albert. Husband of Lydia Herzog, another trustee, whom she hadn't yet met but of whom Mrs. Hyman had whispered, "Lydia was a Babcock, you know."

Sigrid did not know, but had dutifully placed a mental star next to Mrs. Herzog's name and attached a Babcock in parentheses since Mrs. Hyman seemed to think it was important. It was the sort of remark that reminded Sigrid of going through reception lines with her Southern grandmother. If Mrs. Lattimore's hierarchal memory of bloodlines and obscure degrees of kinship had ever failed her, Sigrid was unaware of it.

"I shouldn't have thought you'd find much profit in running Caribbean cruises out of New York," Mr. Herzog observed.

"Oh, you might be surprised how many people like the extra time in our casino," Thorvaldsen said with pleasant candor.

With a vague smile as Thorvaldsen elaborated on Caribbean fun ships, Sigrid detached herself from the group standing near the piano in the drawing room and wandered back to the gallery. So many pictures stacked on the walls like cordwood both fascinated and repelled her. As did everything else she'd seen of this house so far.

It was too full of *things*. How could anyone relax in a place so visually distracting? Even tonight, with the lights lowered and candles to soften the impact, the busyness of the decor made her edgy. She tried to imagine the walls stripped of the pictures Erich Breul had collected, the furniture surfaces cleared of vases, ornaments and other bibelots. Even so, would these ornate rooms really make an appropriate exhibition space for Nauman's abstract pictures?

Evidently she wasn't the only one who wondered that, for immediately after her arrival, while still talking to Jacob Munson, whose old-world courtliness had charmed her, a tall storklike man in formal evening clothes strode into the Breul House, spotted Nauman, and immediately cried, "Oscar! What's all this crap about a retrospective *here*?"

"Behave yourself, Elliott," laughed Francesca Leeds, swooping down upon them, "or we shan't let you play, shall we, Jacob?"

The newcomer murmured appropriately as Sigrid was introduced to him, but his eyes were for Lady Francesca and Oscar Nauman. Arguably the hottest curator in town, Elliott Buntrock did not recall having met Sigrid at a Piers Leyden opening back in October. Nor did he seem to consider her someone with whom he need bother tonight.

Which suited Sigrid. As the other four began to discuss the possibilities of an exhibit here at the Breul House, she had followed the sound of a piano into the drawing room where Mrs. Beardsley had introduced her to Thorvaldsen and some of the trustees of the Breul House.

And now she had examined all the pictures hung one above the other on the gallery walls and, except for the Winslow Homer drawings, the only work that really captured her interest was a still life of bread and cheese. It reminded her empty stomach she'd eaten nothing since a pushcart hot dog around noon. Back at the far end of the drawing room, Thorvaldsen and the Hymans had been joined by Francesca Leeds and Jacob Munson; a young black woman entered the gallery in animated conversation with a vivacious middle-aged blond who exhibited a slight limp; and, as Sigrid crossed the great hall at the upper end, she saw Nauman and Elliott Buntrock walking slowly in her direction.

Both men were tall and lean, but while Nauman looked fit and moved easily, the curator seemed all joints. In his formal black-and-white evening clothes, he looked like some sort of long-legged water bird, a stilt or a crane, picking his way across a shallow lake, on the alert for any passing minnows. He had neglected to check his long white evening scarf and it hung down over his jacket. Occasionally he would forget and gather both ends in a large bony hand and pull his head forward while making sweeping uncoordinated gestures with his free arm. Nauman had an expression on his face which did not bode well for whatever Elliott Buntrock was propounding.

Sigrid prudently continued into the dining room.

"You're too important for this place," said Buntrock. "A Nauman retrospective's big business. Where's your head on this, Oscar?"

"*If* I do it—" Nauman began mildly.

"You're doing it!" the curator interrupted. "And high time, too."

"—it'll be for Jacob."

"Loyalty. How touching. But why here? With your reputation and my connections, we could easily have the Whitney. Or what about a triple header? Any three galleries you name, any part of the city. Uptown, downtown, Soho, the Village—you say it, you've got it. But for the love of God, Montresor, not here."

"Nobody's threatening to wall you up with a cask of Amontillado," Nauman grinned. "You don't have to get involved. It was Francesca's idea; I told her you wouldn't be interested."

"Francesca Leeds is the only one with any sense on this whole damn project. Of course I'm interested."

The art world was always a little crazy but Elliott Buntrock was beginning to feel as if he were caught in a comic opera version of "This Is the House that Jack Built." Francesca Leeds' wealthy shipowner wanted to sponsor a Nauman retrospective. Everyone knew Nauman refused to have one. Somehow Francesca had known that Munson was Nauman's

Achilles' heel, so she'd gone looking for Munson's, and, of all the absurd people in the world, wouldn't you know it'd turn out to be that goof-up Benjamin Peake?

Buntrock wasn't quite sure *why* Peake's well-being was important to old Jacob Munson. Francesca thought it had something to do with Munson's only son who'd been killed years ago.

Anyhow, there they were: Peake's career was wobbling again, so once Jacob Munson was persuaded that a Nauman show would shore it up, he'd put the screws to Nauman, who was evidently unwilling to refuse his old friend.

Exasperated, Buntrock pulled harder on his silk scarf, which only hunched his angled head forward and increased his resemblance to a reluctant stork being pulled along to his doom. Only a fool would turn down the chance to curate a major Nauman exhibition, but *here*?

They had entered the gallery. It was the first time Buntrock had ever been here and he just stood shaking his head from side to side. "The most important abstract painter of our time in a shrine to nineteenth-century kitsch? You're crazy, Oscar."

Until their conversation, Nauman had not made up his mind but now the trendy curator's patent dismay roused the imp of perversion that lurked in his soul.

"The Breul House or no house, Buntrock. Take it or leave it."

"Done!" Elliott Buntrock groaned, already hearing the disbelieving jeers that would rise from his compatriots in the art world when they learned what he'd agreed to. He looked down the long space beyond the archway, to the drawing room, where the others were gathered around the piano. "Shall we tell them the wedding's on?"

"Be my guest," said Oscar. "I want another drink."

In the dining room, a waiter had taken Sigrid's empty glass and promptly returned with a full one.

At the buffet table were a gray-haired man and woman who both smiled as she approached. "The pâté's good," said the man, gesturing to the platter with a hearty friendliness.

"So are the crab puffs," said the woman, who was so

painfully gaunt beneath her diamonds and pearls that Sigrid couldn't believe anything more caloric than lettuce and water ever passed her lips.

Another couple at the end of the table broke apart from what seemed like an intense conversation. The dark-haired woman wore a vivid red-and-purple dress with panache and she turned with an equally vivid smile on her attractive face. "Miss Harald? I'm Hester Kohn, Jacob's partner. Have you met Benjamin Peake? He's director of the Breul House."

"So pleased," the director murmured and took her hand and looked into her eyes as if he'd waited all his life to meet her.

Unfortunately for the effect, he immediately turned that same look upon the thin woman beside them, "Mrs. Herzog! Have you met Miss Harald, Oscar Nauman's friend? Miss Harald, Mrs. Herzog. And this is Mr. Reinicke. They're two of our most dedicated trustees, Miss Harald."

"Winston Reinicke," said the man. "Great admirer of Nauman's work. Fine painter. Fine."

"Thank you," Sigrid replied inanely as the man pumped her hand.

Mrs. Herzog continued to smile graciously, but Sigrid suddenly felt herself inventoried, cataloged and ready to be shelved. Mrs. Herzog ("She was a Babcock, you know") was not deceived by gold sequins and costume jewelry. "We at the Breul House would feel so honored if an artist of Oscar Nauman's standing should come to us."

"Is it quite settled then?" asked a languid voice behind them.

A man approached from the stairs beyond the arched doorway. Sigrid noted that he was several inches shorter than she with a slender, almost childlike body, and the head of someone much bigger. His thatched brown hair grew low on his forehead, almost meeting his thick shaggy eyebrows, and as he crossed to join them by the table, he carried his chin thrust upward at such an angle that Sigrid was reminded of a haughty ape.

"He hasn't definitely committed himself," said Benjamin Peake, "but Hester thinks Jacob may persuade him tonight. Perhaps Miss Harald knows?"

The newcomer looked at her curiously as Sigrid disavowed any insider knowledge of Oscar Nauman's ultimate decision.

"We haven't met," he said, offering her his hand. Its smallness and delicacy was surprising after the visual impact of his massive head, but the lack of physical vigor made the limpness of his clasp almost an insult. "I'm Roger Shambley."

"Dr. Shambley's our newest trustee, Miss Harald," boomed Mr. Reinicke. "A fine scholar. He's going to put the Breul collection on the map, eh, Dr. Shambley?"

For a moment, Shambley's ugly face was lit by sly glee. "You could say that," he drawled. "Yes, you could definitely say that."

Winston Reinicke beamed at him. "Spoken with the enthusiasm of a real scholar! A *catalogue raisonné* of the whole collection, eh?" His vigorous arm gesture took in all the pictures that lined this room as thickly as in the gallery across the hall.

"Not exactly," Shambley corrected him disdainfully. "My new book will merely cite some of these works as examples of general currents in the late nineteenth century. And it will probably sell fewer than five thousand copies nationwide, Reinicke, hardly enough to start a stampede for the Erich Breul House."

"Of course, of course," Winston Reinicke said heartily. "Still, one never knows what will further the cause, eh? Something for everyone."

"Speaking of which," said Shambley, "I'm told that Rockwells and Sharpes are rising in value. Have you considered them for your empty spaces?"

Sigrid sensed a sudden intake of silence around the buffet, almost as if everyone had stopped breathing.

Then Reinicke said, "Lydia, my dear, shall we take Albert and Marie some of these crab puffs? They must think we've gotten lost, eh?"

Murmuring polite phrases, the older couple arranged several hors d'oeuvres upon a plate and departed.

"Still pulling wings off flies, Roger?" Hester Kohn's tone was light but there was a wary look in her hazel eyes.

Shambley ignored the other woman's gibe. "Are you in the art world, too, Miss Harald?"

"No."

"Miss Harald's a police officer," Hester Kohn told him.

Shambley looked at Sigrid with the most animation he'd shown yet. "How appropriate. Robbery, may one hope?"

"No," Sigrid replied, wondering why Shambley had glanced so pointedly at Benjamin Peake. "If you don't expect your book to sell many copies, Dr. Shambley, what *are* you planning for the Breul House?"

"Publicity comes in many forms, Miss Harald," he said. And with a languid wave of his small hand, he parted a space between Sigrid and Hester Kohn. "*Permésso,*" he said and drifted toward the door.

Hester Kohn exchanged a glance with Benjamin Peake, then flashed her professional smile at Sigrid. "Would you excuse us, please, Miss Harald?"

Sigrid barely had time to nod before the two followed Shambley from the room.

At the end of the table, a waiter lifted the lid on the silver chafing dish.

"Swedish meatballs?" he asked.

Sigrid nodded hungrily.

Jacob Munson hesitated in the doorway of the drawing room. Only a moment before he'd seen Hester out here in the hall, a flash of purple and red followed by Benjamin, and he had thought it would be pleasant to tell them of Buntrock's announcement. But when he reached the hall, there was no sign of them. He crossed the hall, peering into the cloak-rooms, and finally heard voices from the library—Benjamin's voice raw with anger, Hester's intense and cold, and another voice that held a lazy sneer. He listened a moment and realized the third voice belonged to Dr. Roger Shambley.

"*Was ist los?*" he asked, peering around a bookcase at the three who stood there glaring at each other. In his agitation, he realized he'd spoken in German. "What's going on?" he repeated in English. "Hester? Ben?"

"A hypothetical question," Shambley said smoothly. "To which they gave a hypothetical answer. *Scusatemi, per favore.*" He smiled and walked past Munson into the great marble hall.

Before the inner woman was completely satisfied, Sigrid was joined by Nauman.

"Worked through lunch again, hmm?" he asked, eyeing her plate of appetizers.

"Have a stuffed mushroom," she advised. "I think they just came out of the oven."

"You'll spoil your appetite."

"Never."

He laughed. "You must be the only woman in the western world who doesn't worry about her figure."

A lot he knew, she thought, watching Francesca Leeds across the room on Søren Thorvaldsen's arm. Now there was a figure worth worrying about. There was no envy as she noted the way Lady Francesca's copper hair fell in artful tangles around her lovely face, the way the silky gold fabric enhanced her perfect figure. Yet, Sigrid did find herself wondering again why Francesca Leeds seemed so familiar, almost as if they'd met in another life or something.

There was a pleased expression on Thorvaldsen's rugged face and Francesca was smiling.

"Elliott said you've agreed, Oscar. That's grand of you." With a graceful gesture, she laid her cool fingers on his neck and pulled him down so she could kiss his cheek.

"How pretty!" said Roger Shambley, who had approached unnoticed. "Portrait of the artist with harem?"

Thorvaldsen frowned. "That's a tasteless remark, sir."

"Unlike your taste?" drawled Shambley. "But then you and Oscar Nauman have identical tastes, don't you?"

His eyes glittered beneath his heavy brows as they swept Francesca's body with an insulting deliberation that was like a physical pawing. Thorvaldsen's brawny hand shot out and grasped Shambley by the lapels and for a moment they could see the brawling stevedore he'd once been as his right hand drew back in a fist. Sigrid started forward, but Nauman had already caught his arm before it could throw the punch.

Immediately, Thorvaldsen released Shambley with a muttered apology.

Shambley straightened and drew himself up arrogantly. "I think you will pay for that," he told Thorvaldsen, then turned from the room and walked up the wide marble staircase.

The restaurant was intimate and candlelit, but dinner had become strained.

"Will you stop projecting your guilt feelings onto me?" Sigrid said tightly. "For the third time, I'm not angry and I am *not* jealous."

Her fork clattered sharply against her plate as she put it down and reached for her wine glass.

Nauman pushed a broiled scallop around his plate moodily, wishing all the hurtful words to come were already said so that he could touch her hand or make her gray eyes dance with laughter again.

"If you'd just let me explain—"

"Damn it, Nauman, there's nothing to explain." Her gold-colored earrings swung back and forth with each word. "There can't be many sixty-year-old virgins walking the land and what you did before we met is none of my business. Aren't you going to eat your scallops?"

He handed them over. He didn't know which annoyed him more: that she'd thrown his age in his face or that she could still be hungry after realizing he and Francesca had been lovers.

"You really *don't* give a damn, do you?" he asked disconsolately.

"It's illogical to be jealous about things that were over and done with before I knew you," she said, transferring his scallops to her plate. "I just mind that I was so stupid."

"Stupid?" he asked hopefully.

"Stupid. I knew she seemed familiar, but I thought it was my imagination. And all the time, there was that portrait of her in your apartment."

He paused in the act of signaling their waiter. "Portrait? I've never done a portrait of Francesca."

"Of course you have. It's hanging over that Spanish chest next to your door. I know it's not a literal representation, but still—"

Nauman shook his head and his white hair gleamed in the candlelight. "That painting is a purely abstract construction generated from sets of inverse Cassinian ovals. That's all there is to it."

"It's also—" She fell silent as their waiter approached.

"Everything all right?" he asked.

Nauman handed him their empty wine bottle. "Another one of these, please."

"It's also a portrait of Francesca Leeds," Sigrid said as the waiter left them. "The way her hair falls away from her face when she tilts her head back and laughs. All that orange and gold and brown. And those big canvasses in your studio up in Connecticut—the ones you said you painted year before last—most of those use the same colors, too. Francesca's colors."

He started to deny it, then looked at Sigrid with perplexed admiration. "I'll be damned, Siga. You're right."

Nauman never tried to analyze why he painted as he did. Let others theorize after the fact; when things were working, he only knew that they felt right. Nevertheless, it was interesting to catch his subconscious off guard. He had enjoyed Francesca, her beauty, her sophistication, her body. But she was more uptown than he, more interested in the right social circles. It had exasperated her that he wouldn't capitalize on his fame, so they had parted as amicably as they'd begun and he hadn't realized that she'd affected his palette.

Now he remembered that violent purple-and-black study Francesca had pulled from the back of his storage racks up in Connecticut last weekend. He fingered his left ear unconsciously. Blacks and purples that sloped into somber browns.

Lila.

His mind shied at the thought of Lila, locked away all these years; and he willed himself to consider instead the vivid, almost garish colors he'd used during those exuberant postwar years with Susan; or those serene pastels that had echoed Cassandra's quiet blond loveliness. Odd that he hadn't seen—hadn't let himself see?

Four women. All different.

And what would Sigrid bring?

"Don't!" she said sharply, and gold sequins shimmered like moonbeams on water as she flinched from his gaze.

"What?" he asked, bewildered.

"You look at me sometimes as if I'm a—I don't know. As if I were a thing, not a person."

The waiter arrived with more wine, filled their glasses, and departed.

Nauman lifted his glass in tribute. "Oh no, my dear. Never that," he said, and was glad to realize that their fight seemed to have ended before it ever began.

A clock was chiming nine-thirty when Roger Shambley came downstairs to use the telephone on Hope Ruffton's desk. The caterers had long since gone and the rooms were dark and silent. He called information for the number he wanted, dialed and, when an answering machine beeped at the other end of the wire, spoke the cryptic words he'd rehearsed, then hung up.

He crossed the echoing hall to unlock the front door and as he returned, a figure appeared in the doorway of the darkened library.

"*Gesù e Maria!*" he exclaimed. "You startled me. I thought you left hours ago."

In the warm snug Hobbit-hole room, the last tape had come to an end and Rick Evans was enjoying the comfortable silence when he suddenly stiffened like a burrowing animal that hears the dogs above him.

"What's wrong, Rick?" Pascal Grant asked sleepily.

"Sh! I thought I heard a noise out there."

Pascal raised himself to a kneeling position beside Rick. The only light in the room was a small amber lamp shaped like an owl near the door and both held their breath, listening. Rick looked around for a weapon of some sort. "You have a stick or something, Pasc?"

"Like my softball bat? Sure."

Rick slipped off the mattress and pulled on his trousers. "Where is it?"

"Behind that chair." Then realizing what Evans meant to do, Pascal Grant clutched at his leg. "No, Rick. Don't go out there. Please!" His voice grew louder as he became more agitated. "I don't like Dr. Shambley. He scares me."

Of course, Rick thought, Shambley. That dirty little coward. What gives him the right to sneak around down here? Was he hoping to find Pasc alone? He thinks he knows what Pasc and I are, but we *know* what he is and he's not going to wreck things.

With angry, confused thoughts running through his head,

Rick grasped the bat, unlocked the door, and stepped out into the kitchenette.

"Who's there?" he called, suddenly caught by conflicting emotions.

In the dim warmth behind the half-closed door, Pascal Grant huddled uneasily on the bed, wishing Rick would come back and lock the door and they could talk some more and listen to the old Louis Armstrong tape Rick had brought and forget about Dr. Shambley. Before yesterday was bad enough, Pascal thought unhappily, but ever since last night when he put his hand on my face— And today, he keeps looking at me and he makes me feel dirty, like Mr. Gere at the training center—

Pascal shivered and tried not to think of Mr. Gere and what Mr. Gere had wanted him to do.

There was a thump and clatter out in the main kitchen and Pascal sprang from the bed and ran to the door. "Rick?"

An icy draft of air met him at the kitchenette and he glanced across the dim stretches of the main kitchen to the passageway that wound out to his spiderweb door.

A forty-watt security light burned over the stairs off to his left and something dark lay crumpled at the bottom. Half whimpering with terror, Pascal edged closer. "Rick?"

A moment later, with the bat clutched in his hand, Rick emerged from the dark hallway into the main kitchen and found Pascal shivering over a twisted bundle at the foot of the stairs.

"Dr. Shambley," Pascal whispered.

Rick drew near. The ugly little man lay face up on the tiles, his eyes stared unblinkingly at the light, his lips were drawn back almost in a snarl.

"Is he dead?" asked Pascal.

It reminded Rick of finding a dead snake in the road. Neither wanted to touch him. Rick nudged Shambley's head with the bat. It flopped to one side and they saw that his shaggy brown hair was matted with blood. Rick knelt down then. There was no pulse in the man's lifeless wrist.

"Did you hit him?" asked Pascal. "I heard the bat."

"No," Rick said sharply. "Someone else was here, too—in the hallway. I ran after them but the bat banged into the wall and I dropped it. Whoever it was must have pushed him down the stairs and then run away."

"Why?"

"I don't know," Rick said grimly, "but we can't leave him here."

"Why, Rick?"

"Because they might think *you* pushed him. Or me."

"But we'll just tell them we didn't. I'll call Mrs. Beardsley. Or Dr. Peake. They'll know what to do."

"No!" Rick looked at Pascal's beautiful innocent face despairingly. "Look, if you call them, you'll have to tell them I was spending the night with you and they wouldn't understand."

"You're my friend."

"I know, but most people would think that was wrong."

"Wrong to have a friend?"

"Wrong to let him sleep over with you. They'd make something dirty out of it. They think everything is sex."

"Oh," said Pascal. He caught his lower lip between his teeth and nodded.

"We'll take him up to the third floor and leave him at the bottom of the attic stairs. Those steps are steeper. They'll think he tripped and fell up there."

Still shivering, Pascal reluctantly agreed to Rick's plan. Even though Shambley's body was small, neither youth was strong enough to carry him very far. Instead, they rolled him onto one of the blue rag scatter rugs, loaded him inside the dumbwaiter, and hoisted him aloft.

Up on the third floor, they carried him across the wide hall to the foot of the uncarpeted steps and Rick tried to arrange those limbs into a natural-looking sprawl.

When they were finished, they lowered the dumbwaiter and, as a precaution, Rick stopped it at the butler's pantry beside the dining room.

Back in the basement, they were left with a patch of sticky blood on the tiles where Shambley's head had lain. They swabbed up the worst with the blue rag rug since it already had blood smears on it. While Pascal got a mop and scrubbed away the rest of the blood, Rick bundled up the rug, stashed it in one of the storage rooms, then returned to Pascal's room to finish dressing.

"Aren't you going to stay?" asked Pascal. His large blue eyes were frightened.

"Listen, Pasc," Rick said seriously. "If you want to let's stay friends, you have to do exactly what I tell you, okay?"

"Okay."

It took almost a half-hour before Rick was certain the janitor had their story straight: they had gone to a movie, come back and listened to jazz for a while, then Rick had gone home at nine and Pascal had fallen asleep without remembering to set the burglar alarm.

"I could set it now," Pascal said.

"Better not," Rick said. "Otherwise they'll ask you if you checked to make sure Dr. Shambley was gone."

"Oh. Okay."

"You didn't see Dr. Shambley."

"I didn't," Pascal agreed. "Not till—"

"Not at all," Rick reminded him. "You didn't see him since before the party, okay?"

"Okay." Pascal looked up at his friend trustingly. "I wish you could sleep over, Rick."

"Another time," he said and clasped Pascal's shoulder as he stood. "I promise."

At the spiderweb door beneath the main stoop, he drew on his gloves, pulled his collar snugly around his neck, and stepped out into the freezing night as Pascal locked the door behind him.

Shortly after eleven, Rick let himself into the apartment on the upper West Side. His grandfather usually went to bed early, but he was a light sleeper. Tonight, a muffled snore was all Rick heard as he crept past Jacob Munson's closed door and gained the sanctuary of his own room. He expected to lie awake reliving the horror of the evening; yet no sooner did his head touch the pillow than he was instantly and deeply asleep.

* * *

Mrs. Beardsley awoke near midnight with a painful leg cramp. Groaning, she pushed aside the covers and made herself stand up and walk around the room until the spasms passed. Her bedroom faced Sussex Square and, though she told herself it was childish, she lingered at the window to watch the tall spruce tree turn off its lights. The automatic timer was set for midnight, and there was something magical about catching the precise moment.

There! The tree's blaze of colored lights vanished, leaving only the old-fashioned gaslights to illumine the square. Pleased, she started to turn from the window when a movement diagonally across the park caught her eye. Someone was coming down the front steps of the Breul House. She strained to see.

Dr. Shambley?

No, Dr. Shambley was shorter than she and this man—if it were a man—was taller.

The figure came down the steps, head hunched into the turned-up collar of the topcoat, and hurried along the brick walk. At the corner, the figure became recognizable as he passed beneath the electric streetlight there, turned west at the corner, and disappeared from her view.

Now why, wondered Mrs. Beardsley, had Mr. Thorvaldsen come back to the Breul House so late at night?

Sigrid turned in the night and found her bed empty. "Nauman?"

The room was quite dark but there was a movement by the door. "I didn't mean to wake you."

"What time is it?"

"Not quite five. Go back to sleep," he whispered.

She raised herself on one elbow and looked at the luminous clock dial in disbelief. "Five! Why are you up so early?"

"I couldn't sleep and there're things I need to do."

He came and sat on the edge of the bed and gathered her into his arms. She smoothed back his hair and felt the rough stubble along his chin line. "Come back to bed."

He kissed her then, a yearning, tender kiss that transcended carnal desire, and tucked the blanket around her body. "I'll call you tonight."

Too sleepy to argue, she snuggled deeper into the covers.

Zurich

My dearest husband,

Mama's health is so much improved this week that I begin to think I may soon be released from sickroom duty and may truly begin to plan our return. You will be surprised at how our son has grown since you last saw him in April. He all but tops my shoulder now.

In these three short months, his German has become quite fluent. He has made great friends with Papa's friend, Herrn Witt, one of the directors of the new art museum, and a visit to that magnificent institution is his dearest treat. Herr Witt asked him how he came by such a fine eye for art at so early an age and young Erich replied, *"Es kommt von meinem Papa!"*

I will always regret, *mein Lieber*, that God in His infinite wisdom did not see fit to bless us with a dozen children, yet I can never give thanks enough for the angel-child He *did* lend us . . .

Letter from Sophie Fürst Breul to
Erich Breul Sr., dated 6.20.1899.
(From the Erich Breul House Collection)

VII

Sigrid had dropped Albee's sequin top at a dry cleaners near headquarters and waited to have the claim ticket stamped paid, so she was a few minutes late for work. Jim Lowry, Matt Eberstadt, and Elaine Albee were already in the staff room with coffee and doughnuts and the morning papers. Sigrid had tucked the costume jewelry into a small plastic bag and she handed it and the ticket to the young blonde with a quiet, "Thanks again, Albee. And thank Quaranto for me, too."

Any other woman in the department and Elaine Albee would have asked how the evening went. With the lieutenant, discretion was always the better part of valor, so she smiled and said, "Any time, Lieutenant," and went back to reading aloud the *Daily News* follow-up story on the "Babies in the Attic Case," as it called the discovery of the infant remains found in that East Village row house.

They had reprinted earlier pictures, including one of Detectives Harald and Lowry as police officers who appealed to the public for any information about former occupants from forty years earlier.

"'Baby-killer still stalking East Village?'" read Albee. "'Area residents mum.'"

"*Are* area residents mum?" Sigrid asked, taking the last glazed doughnut in the box.

Matt Eberstadt regarded the empty box with mild sorrow. Now in his late forties with a wiry, iron gray hairline that had receded to the top of his head, he'd been put on a strict diet by his wife Frances—"You'll lose six more pounds before Christmas or no strudel for you this year," she'd threatened—but his heart wasn't in it.

"The problem may be finding any longtime residents, talky *or* mum," Lowry said pessimistically. "So far, the canvass hasn't turned up anybody earlier than 1954. I think Bernie's over checking records this morning."

Eberstadt shifted his girth in the chair and slipped his thumb into his waistband. Not as snug as last month, but not nearly loose enough to satisfy Frances. He met Lieutenant Harald's gaze and hastily reported, "Those fingerprints we found on the newspaper have been on the wire almost a week. Nothing so far."

"And I don't suppose Cohen has anything more for us yet?" Sigrid asked. "No? Okay, on to other matters."

The next twenty minutes were devoted to cases still pending, then Albee and Lowry settled into paperwork while Eberstadt went off to review his testimony for a court hearing.

Bernie Peters returned with some names he'd dug out of public records. Now that his infant son was finally sleeping through the nights, he seemed to have more energy for work again.

"That block was mostly Polish and Ukrainian in the thirties," he said. "Still is, to some extent."

By cross-referencing real estate and tax records, he'd learned that the house was sold in 1934 to a Gregor Jurczyk, who'd converted it to an eight-unit tenement. Old telephone directories turned up a single telephone listed in Jurczyk's name, at that address, until he died in 1963 and left the house to his sisters, Angelika Jurczyk and Barbara Jurczyk Zajdowicz. Even after his death, the telephone continued to be listed in his name until 1971, which would lead one to believe at least one of his sisters was still in residence there until the property was sold to a developer who went bankrupt in 1972, at which time the house was taken over by a bank.

"And after that I didn't bother," said Peters. "I called a friend of mine in Vital Records. Angelika Jurczyk died in 1970, age sixty-seven. No death record for Barbara Zajdowicz."

Sigrid jotted the figures down on her pad. "That would have made her forty-four in 1947 when the last infant was put in that trunk. Any idea of the age of her sister?"

Before Peters could answer, they were abruptly interrupted. A patrol officer in Sussex Square had requested the assistance of investigators at the Erich Breul House where a dead male had been discovered.

"*Where?*" Sigrid asked, startled.

"Sussex Square," Elaine Albee repeated. "Wasn't that where you were last night?"

Patrol cars had driven up onto the bricked walk around Sussex Square and eight or ten uniformed officers clogged the doorway when Sigrid arrived with her team.

"Too many unnecessary personnel," Sigrid said crisply, as they entered the vaulted marble hall. "Clear them out, Cluett."

Detective Third Grade Michael Cluett was an old-timer from Brooklyn who'd been wished on her by Captain McKinnon. He didn't seem to resent taking orders from a woman, but he was too close to retirement to worry about impressing anyone. His only ambition seemed to be finishing out his forty years on the force without screwing up. He hitched his belt up around a belly that sagged worse than Eberstadt's and moved off to carry out the lieutenant's instructions.

Dr. Benjamin Peake was speaking to a uniformed officer at the rear of the hall and his handsome face grew bewildered at the sight of Sigrid.

"Miss Harald!" he exclaimed. "I'm afraid we're closed—"

"Lieutenant Harald," she said, pointing to her badge. She was almost as surprised to see him. They'd been told only that a man had been found dead under suspicious circumstances at the Breul House, not who the man was, and for no good reason she'd halfway expected it to be Peake. "Who—?" she asked him.

"Dr. Shambley. A dreadful accident. Dreadful. Fell down the attic stairs. I'll show you," Peake said.

"That won't be necessary," Sigrid told him.

Elaine Albee was beside her as she started up the wide marble staircase. "This is one of the places I keep meaning to come see," said the younger woman. She noticed the rich details of the dress worn by the female dummy on the landing. "How did Breul make his money? Railroads? Oil?"

"Canal barges, I think," Sigrid said, threading her way past the uniformed officers who loitered in the second-floor hallway frankly sight-seeing at the moment. She could only hope they'd had the sense to keep their feet out the actual crime scene.

"That's nice stained glass," Albee said, pausing beneath the oval Tiffany window where spring flowers blossomed on this December day.

Tiffany glass seldom appealed to Sigrid and she didn't break her stride as she continued up the last flight of steps to the third floor.

"Through there, Lieutenant," said a patrol officer, who was posted to limit access to the rear half of the third floor.

They passed through the frosted glass doors which were blocked open and at the end of the hall found Officer Paula Guidry already photographing the body, which lay sprawled on the bare floor at the base of some steep wooden steps. A frosted glass window high in the rear wall flooded the area with cold north light.

Across the wide landing, a mannequin dressed in the long bib apron and starched white cap of an old-fashioned maid smiled at them serenely.

Sigrid was glad to see that the end of the hall was roped off and that everyone seemed to be respecting the integrity of the crime scene. "Who was responding officer?" she asked.

A uniformed patrolman in his late twenties stepped forward. "Officer Dan Monte, ma'am."

Without being asked, he flipped open his notebook and described how he'd been dispatched to number 7 Sussex Square in response to a call placed by a Miss Hope Ruffton, the secretary here.

"This place opens at ten A.M. and a Mrs. Eloise Beardsley—I think she's a volunteer—came upstairs at approximately ten forty-five and discovered the body lying face down just as you see it. She said she tried to find a pulse, then realized the individual was dead."

Officer Monte had arrived at 10:57, observed certain inconsistencies, and immediately requested investigators.

"What inconsistencies?" asked Jim Lowry.

"Not enough blood," the patrol officer replied succinctly. "You can see from here—the back of his head's pretty messed up and blood's clotted in his hair, but it didn't run down his face and there's none on the floor beside his head. The stairs

are bare wood and I guess he could have hit his head on one
of the sharp edges coming down, but again, no blood."

Sigrid watched as Guidry indicated she'd taken enough
pictures of the body and its immediate surroundings. While
the photographer waited for someone from the medical examiner's office to turn it over, the crime scene unit began
processing the area around the body.

"Who was in the house when you arrived?" Sigrid asked.

"Just the secretary, the Beardsley woman, the live-in
janitor, and the director," answered Monte. "They're all downstairs. The ambulance crew got here at eleven oh-two and
confirmed death."

For a moment, Sigrid almost forgot and looked around
for Tillie, the officer on whom she most relied, the one who
usually acted as her recorder and could be trusted to note
every minute detail.

Unfortunately, Detective Tildon was still recovering from
the bomb blast that had nearly killed him in October. He was
home from the hospital now and healing nicely, but was not
expected back at work till next month. Mick Cluett was
certainly no substitute and Albee was already catching her
share on other cases. Sigrid told Lowry he'd won recorder's
job and the younger man gave a mock groan as he continued
to measure distances for sketching the scene.

Bernie Peters, directing the application of fingerprint
powder on the stair rail, grinned in sympathy.

Cohen arrived from the medical examiner's office and
greeted her sardonically. "We gotta quit meeting like this,
Lieutenant."

A few minutes later, he'd agreed with Officer Monte's
suspicions. "Lividity's not much help if he was moved within
a half-hour of death, but that wound bled like hell and there
ought to be a puddle under his head. He didn't die face
down though. And see this?"

Cohen pulled back the collar of Shambley's shirt and
Sigrid saw that a thin trickle of blood had run down inside to
his back.

She nodded thoughtfully. "So he was upright when he
received the wound?"

Cohen shrugged. "He did most of his bleeding while

95

lying supine; but yeah, I'd guess the blow came while he was sitting or standing."

"He didn't hurt himself in a fall?"

"Maybe. But I can't see him standing up again after getting this wound, so how'd blood run straight down his neck?"

They would keep it in mind, Sigrid told him as Guidry photographed the stain.

The dumbwaiter shaft had been discovered and a good set of prints were found on the enamelled wood molding that framed the hinged doors. Officer Monte had managed to keep everyone off the back stairs, so Albee started down to determine the dumbwaiter's current location, being careful to keep to the center of the treads and on the lookout for anything out of the ordinary.

Cohen finished his preliminary examination and stripped off thin latex gloves as he stood. "Funny-looking guy, isn't he? Little Ed with the big head. Something odd about that head."

"Besides its size?" asked Lowry, who had chalked an outline of the body's position before Cohen began.

"Not our old friend the blunt instrument?" queried Bernie Peters.

"I'll let you know after I've taken a look at that wound in the lab," Cohen told them.

Guidry stepped back in for more pictures now that Cohen had turned the body face up.

"Want to estimate a time of death?" Sigrid asked.

Cohen shrugged. "Rigor's complete, but there's still a little body warmth, so we're talking maybe twelve to fifteen hours, no more than sixteen hours max."

They looked at their watches. Between 7:15 and 11:15, always taking into account that the temperature in this hallway may have been measurably higher or lower than it was now, or that the dead man had some physical quirk that would quicken or retard rigor mortis.

"I saw him alive between eight and eight-thirty last night," Sigrid said.

Bernie Peters shot Lowry a telling glance. The lieutenant had a reputation for coldness, but she hadn't turned a hair upon seeing the body. Even Cohen looked at her curiously. "Friend of yours?"

"No," she answered distantly. "There was a party here last night and he came, too. We met briefly and he left early. Or rather he went upstairs early. I believe he was doing research on some papers in the attic."

Elaine Albee reappeared on the back stairs. "The dumb-waiter's on the first floor," she reported, slightly out of breath. "And there looks like a smear of blood inside."

"Probably turn out to be roast beef," Cohen grinned. "You guys ready for me to take him?"

Sigrid queried her people. Guidry was satisfied with the number of photographs she'd taken and Lowry and Peters had just finished with their inventory of Roger Shambley's pockets, so everyone stood back as Cohen's assistants lifted the body onto a collapsible gurney, covered it, and strapped it down. Rigor mortis made for a bulky shape and Sigrid was not the only one reminded of a grotesque and badly wrapped Christmas package.

"By the way, Lieutenant—" Cohen paused before fol-lowing the body downstairs. "You'll get my official report late this afternoon, but I can put it in an eyedropper right now: On the bones last week, you can forget about actual age, sex, race—hell! I couldn't even swear they aren't monkey bones. All I can say is that they're consistent with what you'd find if a newborn baby was wrapped in newspapers and stuck in a trunk for thirty years, give or take a week."

"What about the mummified one?" Sigrid asked.

"Caucasian girl," he replied promptly. "And before you ask, yeah, she was born alive. I found lint in her breathing passages. Looks like she no sooner got herself born than she got herself smothered."

With a laconic "Ciao for now, *amici*," he trailed after the gurney, never realizing that he'd allowed Roger Shambley one final exit in Italian.

With the body removed from the landing, Sigrid went up the steep attic stairs to examine the makeshift office Roger Shambley had created amid file cabinets and storage boxes. Later, someone would go through the papers and folders so neatly stacked upon his work tables, but for now she simply wished to sit in the art historian's chair and try to get a better feel for the man she'd met so briefly last night, some sense of why he'd died.

The tabletop directly in front of his chair was bare, so she assumed he'd probably finished work for the night and cleared away his papers. Into one of those folders, perhaps. Or into his briefcase, which still sat beside the chair. A methodical man?

She rather thought there had been method in Shambley's calculated insults last night—to that trustee, Mr. Reinicke, to Søren Thorvaldsen and, by extension, to Nauman and Francesca Leeds—but she'd observed him too briefly to understand the motive for his rudeness. There had been a certain electricity in his manner, though; as if he were so wired about something that he hardly knew or cared what he was saying.

Or to whom.

Power, Sigrid thought. Shambley had acted like someone who'd just won a lottery or inherited a throne and suddenly felt free to ride roughshod over everyone else.

"Lieutenant?" Jim Lowry's voice at the attic door drew her back to the present. "We think we've found where he died."

They went down the narrow back stairs, past the butler's pantry on the first floor where Officer Guidry had photographed the dumbwaiter before the crime scene technicians took a sample of its stains for the lab, and from the butler's pantry, on down the broader, more commodious stairway to the basement.

As they descended, Sigrid noted and carefully sidestepped three chalk-circled spots.

At the foot of the steps, a portable floodlamp lit up the area and made it quite apparent that the floor there had been recently—and inexpertly—mopped. They could clearly see a circular spot where dried streaks of water left dull swirls upon the shiny dark tiles.

"Bonded commercial cleaners come in every Monday," said Elaine Albee as they watched a technician fill small glass vials with samples of a brown sticky substance he'd scraped from the joints between the tiles. "According to the woman who found the body, the cleaners bring their own equipment

98

and part of their routine is to wax and buff the floors down here."

A mop, still damp, had been found in the scullery, she told Sigrid. It, too, would be taken to the lab for analysis.

"And the blood on the stairs themselves?" Sigrid asked, referring to those chalk circles.

"Couple of small splashes up on the tenth and eleventh treads; a bigger one down here on the third," said Bernie Peters. "Nothing on the upper landing and, from the shape of the drops, he was moving down at the time."

It was consistent with what Cohen had told them. Until they uncovered data to disprove it, their working theory would be that Shambley had started down the basement steps when he was struck a tremendous blow on the head from behind. He had fallen here, bled copiously, then his body had been hauled up to the third floor soon afterwards.

"Why not leave him here in the basement where he fell?" Sigrid wondered aloud.

"The perpetrator wanted him found quickly?" speculated Lowry.

"Maybe he *didn't* want him found quickly," Albee countered. "There's a live-in janitor who has a room down here. Maybe the perp wanted time to get away and set up an alibi before the janitor stumbled over him."

"Or maybe it was an individual that just didn't want us taking too close a look at the basement," suggested Peters.

"In which case," said Sigrid.

The others tried not to groan as they looked across the crowded Victorian kitchen to the warren of storage rooms beyond.

"There's still a bunch of uniforms wandering around upstairs," Mick Cluett reminded her.

"Might as well put them to use," Sigrid agreed. "And start a canvass of the square, anyone seen entering or leaving these premises last night. In the meantime, Lowry, you and I will begin with the staff."

They commandeered the stately, book-lined library for questioning their witnesses and lunchtime came and went before the two police detectives had heard all that the Breul House staff were prepared to tell them.

With commendable initiative, the secretary, Hope Ruffton, had typed up a guest list from the previous evening, complete with addresses, which helped them track departures. Sigrid knew that the three trustees and their respective spouses had left shortly after eight, and that she and Nauman left at 8:20. After that, as best the others could reconstruct, the curator, Elliott Buntrock, said good-night at 8:30, followed soon by Søren Thorvaldsen and Lady Francesca Leeds, Hope Ruffton, Hester Kohn and Jacob Munson, in that order.

Hope Ruffton had been collected by three friends for a musical comedy playing up in Harlem and she supplied the detectives with a separate list of her friends' names and addresses.

Benjamin Peake declared that he'd planned to wait until the caterer's men had gone, but Mrs. Beardsley, the senior docent, had volunteered to stay in the director's place since she had only to walk across the square after she'd locked up.

"Mr. Peake left about eight-forty," Mrs. Beardsley told them. "The caterers were finished shortly before nine; then I double-checked to make sure no candles were still burning, turned out the lights, and went home shortly after nine."

"All the lights?" Sigrid asked. "What about Dr. Shambley?"

"I refer, of course, to the main lights," Mrs. Beardsley replied, sitting so erectly in the maroon leather wing chair that Sigrid was reminded of one of Grandmother Lattimore's favorite dicta: a lady's spine never touches the back of her chair. "The security lights are on an automatic timer and they provide enough illumination for finding one's way through the house."

"And you didn't see Dr. Shambley after the party last night?"

"No. Dr. Shambley often worked late," said the docent with a slight air of disapproval.

"What about the janitor?"

"Pascal Grant had permission to attend a movie. I assume he hadn't yet returned by the time I left."

"Permission?"

"When you speak to Pascal, Lieutenant Harald, I think it will be evident why we give him more guidance and direction than an ordinary worker. This is his first job since he left the shelter and I do hope you'll be patient with him. He's really quite *capable* within clearly defined limits. You'll see."

"So as far as you know, Dr. Shambley was alone in the house when you left?"

"Y-es," she said, but something unspoken lingered indecisively on her face.

Pressed, Mrs. Beardsley described how she'd awakened at midnight and seen Mr. Thorvaldsen descending the front steps of the Breul House.

Sigrid went to the library window and asked Mrs. Beardsley to point out her house across the square. It was a windy gray day and the reporters who crowded around below to question the police guard outside had bright pink cheeks and blown hair. "You're positive it was Thorvaldsen?"

"Absolutely," the lady said firmly. "He's quite tall and when he passed under a streetlight at the corner, I saw his fair hair."

On his identity, Mrs. Beardsley could not be budged, although she was quick to admit that she hadn't actually seen the Dane exit from the house. "I thought perhaps he might have returned for something he lost or else forgot and left behind."

"Who has keys to this place?" asked Lowry from his place at the end of a polished wooden library table.

"All the trustees have keys." Mrs. Beardsley patted her purse with a proprietary air. "I, too, of course, as senior docent."

Seated across the table from her, Sigrid looked at the growing list of names on her notepad. "Thorvaldsen, as well?"

"Oh, no, he's not a trustee. But Lady Francesca might since she's going to be in and out a lot if Mr. Nauman's retrospective takes place." She gave Sigrid a friendly social smile and began to describe how surprised everyone was to discover that last night's Miss Harald was today's Lieutenant Harald.

Jim Lowry was diverted by these clues to the lieutenant's off-duty life. Odd to be taking down her testimony as background for a case. Oscar Nauman's name rang a vague bell, but he couldn't quite recall why. Besides, wasn't she supposed to be living with an oddball writer named Roman Tramegra? Maybe Lainey would know.

The lieutenant's cold gaze fell on him and he started guiltily. "Um—*keys*," he croaked. "Who else has them? The janitor?"

"Oh yes. Not to the main door, but to an outside door in the basement." The gray-haired woman hesitated. "And Miss Ruffton and Dr. Peake, of course."

"Of course."

Miss Ruffton shared with them her impression that Dr. Shambley had been up to something besides pure disinterested research, but did not suggest what that something might be.

Dr. Peake grew defensive, mistook their questions for innuendoes, and wound up revealing more animosity toward Dr. Shambley than he'd intended.

"A busybody and a snoop," declared Peake. "With delusions of mental superiority and the reverse snobbism of the proletariat."

"Really?" Sigrid asked, not having heard that epithet since her college days.

"Proletarian roots compounded by his shortness," Peake theorized. "He always insulted his superiors."

Sigrid thought of last night. "At the party, he was rude to Mr. Reinicke, Mr. Thorvaldsen, and Professor Nauman."

"Well, there you are." Peake nodded. "They're all much taller."

When it was his turn to be questioned, Pascal Grant sat in one of the heavy library chairs with his ankles crossed like a schoolboy and kept his head down when spoken to. The janitor was so uncommunicative that Sigrid at first wondered if the young man fully understood what had happened to Dr. Shambley, and she and Lowry found themselves phrasing their questions in words of one syllable.

"I didn't see Dr. Shambley at all last night," he said, looking up through thick golden lashes as he answered. "Rick and me, we went to the movie."

"Rick?"

"Rick's my friend," Grant said softly.

"What time did you get back here?" asked Lowry.

"I don't know. We listened to tapes, Rick and me. Then Rick went home and I went to bed. I didn't hear anything."

Sigrid looked up from her notes. "Your friend Rick was here?"

"He went home," said Grant, darting quick glances at both of them. "He didn't hear anything either."

"Does your friend Rick have a last name?"

Pascal Grant concentrated a moment and then his face lit up with a beautiful smile. "Evans. His name is Rick Evans. He's Mr. Munson's grandson."

They could extract no further information. The young handyman continued to insist he and Evans had neither seen, heard, nor spoken to Roger Shambley the previous evening.

Unfortunately for him, Bernie Peters came up just then to announce that their search had turned up a bloody scatter rug hidden behind some boxes in one of the storerooms, and that a softball bat found beside Pascal Grant's bed seemed to have a suspicious stain at the business end.

"Is that how you killed him?" Sigrid asked gently.

Young Grant shook his head and tears pooled in his blue eyes. "No, I didn't. We didn't see him. We didn't do it."

Feeling rather like the schoolyard bully, Sigrid sighed. "Take him back to headquarters for further questioning," she told Peters. "And have Rick Evans picked up, too."

Mrs. Beardsley was so outraged by Pascal Grant's removal to headquarters that Sigrid was not overly surprised to reach her office and find the woman had gotten there before her. Nor to see that she had brought along her own lawyer, a thin dry man with tonsured hair and an ascetic manner. Harvey Pruitt might be more at home dealing with wills and deeds and other civil matters, but for Mrs. Gawthrop Wallace Beardsley's sake, he seemed prepared to represent Pascal Grant should the young janitor be detained on criminal charges.

Rick Evans had been located at the Kohn and Munson Gallery, and an equally protective Hester Kohn had accompanied him downtown. Three minutes after their arrival, they were joined by the gallery's attorney, a tall, brown-haired woman in what looked like Eskimo mukluks, a deerskin parka lined with fur, and gold-rimmed granny glasses. Ms. Caryn DiFranco.

The two lawyers immediately went into a huddle, then requested and were given a private room in which to confer with their respective clients.

It was long past lunchtime, so Sigrid and her team took advantage of the lull to send down for sandwiches. Mick Cluett had been sent off to check Shambley's apartment and to notify his next of kin; but Eberstadt, back from court, joined them with an enormous corned beef on rye.

"If Frances could see that," said Bernie Peters, shaking his head.

"Salads are for summertime," Eberstadt said defensively. "In December, a man needs something that'll stick to his ribs."

"Just what you need." Elaine Albee grinned. "More meat on those puny ribs."

Eberstadt laughed and as they ate, the others filled him in on Roger Shambley's death amid such Victorian surroundings.

They had taken a set of elimination prints from staff members at the house. "Just eyeballing it, I'd say the Grant kid's the one who left prints on the dumbwaiter," said Peters.

"You should see his bedroom down there in that basement," Jim Lowry told Eberstadt. "Looks like a Chinese whorehouse—red velvet and gold satin, snaky lights, and art posters or calendar pictures on every square inch of wall space."

"Calendar pictures?" Eberstadt leered. "Art posters?"

"Get your mind out of the gutter," Albee told him. She reached across the table to commandeer his kosher dill pickle. "He's talking abstract art, not *Playboy* art."

"Yeah, it's funny," said Peters. "You'd think a guy like him—not too swift on the uptake—would have pictures that looked like real things."

"Probably sees enough of those upstairs," said Albee. Between crunches of Eberstadt's pickle, she described for him the tiers of gilt-framed pictures that lined the walls of the main galleries at the Erich Breul House.

Matt Eberstadt savored the last morsel of corned beef and licked his fingertips. "Frances keeps saying we ought to go tour the place. She likes old things," he said, wiping his hands on a less than clean handkerchief.

"Like you?" gibed Peters.

Sigrid ate her own tuna sandwich swiftly and quietly, with one eye on some paperwork and only half an ear for their give and take. Casual camaraderie had never been easy for her, although now that Nauman had entered her life, she found these unofficial sessions a little easier than before.

She skimmed through one report a second time, then passed it down the table to Bernie Peters. "The neighborhood canvass turned up someone who remembers the Jurczyks."

The others looked at her blankly, trying to place the name.

"Oh, yeah," said Peters. "Those baby bones."

He read the highlights of the report aloud. "Mrs. Pauline Jaworski remembers the Jurczyk sisters from her childhood in the fifties. Thinks her mother may still be in touch with Barbara Zajdowicz. Mother's name, Mrs. Dorota Palka. Currently resides at Lantana Walk Nursing Home up in Queens."

Elaine Albee's head came up. She had briefly worked undercover there back in the spring. "Lantana Walk? Queens? I thought they put that place out of business last spring."

"The director testified against his partners and got off with a suspended sentence and a hefty fine," said Sigrid, who had followed the situation and been disappointed by its outcome.

As they wadded up foam cups and paper napkins from their impromptu lunch, word came that Pascal Grant and Richard Evans were ready to make their statements. Sigrid checked her watch. "Lowry, I want you and Albee to sit in on this, too. Peters, see if you can get a statement from that Palka woman."

"Just how I wanted to spend the afternoon," Bernie Peters grumbled to Eberstadt when the other three had gone. "Freezing my ass off on the F train to Queens."

"Better than surveillance," replied his partner, who had done his share of sitting in cold cars on icy winter streets.

Flanked by their lawyers, Pascal Grant and Rick Evans each appeared very young and very intimidated when they entered the interrogation room; but once all the legal formalities and stipulations were out of the way, their statements were quite straightforward.

They were questioned separately and then together. The second time around, Rick Evans did all the talking at first, in a soft voice full of southern inflections. Sigrid listened without questions as he described again the noises they had heard the night before, his impression that someone had left through the basement door, Pascal Grant's discovery of the body, and his own decision to move it to the third floor using the dumbwaiter.

When he finished, Sigrid said, "Do you have anything to add to that, Mr. Grant?"

Looking like a frightened Raphael angel, Pascal Grant darted a quick glance at her through thick sandy-blond lashes, then bit his lip and shook his head.

"You didn't set the burglar alarm, therefore anyone who had a key could have walked in without your knowing. Is that right?"

He nodded without lifting his eyes.

"What if that person *didn't* have a key?"

Puzzled, Pascal Grant looked at her. "He couldn't come in?" he guessed.

"No," Sigrid said patiently. "I meant what would happen if someone rang the bell? Would you hear?"

"Oh. Yes," he nodded vigorously. "It's right over the door in my room. Makes a real loud noise even if my tapes are on." He hesitated. "Or did you mean the bell board in the kitchen? It's nice. The bells jingle and a little flag comes up to show which one it is. Mrs. Sophie had a bell and Mr. Erich and—"

"No, I meant the doorbells," Sigrid said, interrupting his enthusiastic description of how Victorian employers had once summoned their servants to particular rooms of the house.

"The doorbells ring in the office and they buzz in my room," said Pascal Grant. "A big buzz means it's the upstairs door and a sort of littler one means it's the spiderweb door."

"And did you hear either buzzer last night?"

Pascal shook his head.

"You're sure of that?"

He nodded solemnly.

The two youths described how they had returned to the Breul House from an early showing of *Round Midnight*, entered through the basement door, and headed straight to Pascal Grant's room without going upstairs and without seeing anyone.

"So you were in your bedroom listening to jazz tapes," Sigrid said, "and you heard someone outside. What time was this?"

Pascal's smooth brow furrowed in concentration. "Around ten-fifteen, I think. Maybe ten-thirty."

"Yet you didn't go out to investigate?"

"I thought it was Dr. Shambley," Pascal said slowly.

"Did Dr. Shambley often come down to the basement that late?"

"He was everywhere."

"Did you like Dr. Shambley?"

"No," said the golden-haired janitor before his lawyer could stop him.

"My client's personal feelings toward the deceased had nothing to do with his death," said Harvey Pruitt.

"Then you won't mind if he tells us why he disliked Dr. Shambley?" Sigrid asked.

"I'm afraid I can't allow that at this time," Mr. Pruitt said austerely.

"Very well. What about others at the house, Mr. Grant? Who else didn't like Dr. Shambley?"

"Mrs. Beardsley didn't like him."

"Why not?"

Mr. Pruitt started to object, then sat back.

"I don't know," said Grant. "She said he got her place or something."

Sigrid looked at the lawyer, but Pruitt shook his head. "This is sheer hearsay, you realize?"

"Of course."

She turned to Rick Evans. "You said you had an impression that someone else was there in the passageway when you came out of the bedroom. Who did you think it was?"

Rick shook his head. "I didn't think. I just heard—like footsteps or something. And then I felt a draft from the open door and heard it close."

"Did you go down and look through the door window?" asked Lowry.

"I didn't see anyone," Evans said.

They asked Pascal Grant to explain once more why there was blood on his softball bat if he hadn't hit Shambley with it.

"I didn't!" Pascal said.

"He's telling the pure truth," said Rick in his soft Southern voice. "I was the one carrying that bat. The whole time. I didn't want to touch Dr. Shambley at first. I thought he was dead. He *looked* dead and I just sort of poked him to make sure he really was."

The weakest part of their story was the reason they gave for moving the body and not calling the police. No matter how many times the police detectives returned to that point, the story remained that they were afraid to have Shambley's body found so close to Pascal Grant's door. Period.

While Jim Lowry and Elaine Albee pressed the two youths for stronger reasons, Sigrid leaned back in her chair trying to decide whether or not to charge one or the other or both with the murder. They'd had a weapon, an opportunity, and probably a motive if that lawyer's reluctance to let Grant discuss his distaste for Shambley meant anything.

On the other hand, Grant said he hadn't heard a doorbell, yet that Beardsley woman claimed she'd seen Thorvaldsen there at midnight.

And what was Rick Evans holding back? That he and Grant were sleeping together. Was that all?

She was almost grateful when a uniformed officer opened the door, peered in, and signaled that she had an important phone call.

"Sorry to interrupt, Lieutenant," he said when she came out into the hall and closed the door to the interrogation room, "but Dr. Cohen said you'd probably want to know right away."

The assistant medical examiner was as laid-back over the telephone as in person. "You know that softball bat you people just sent over? Forget it. Too big. You're looking for a rod, not a club."

"A rod?" Sigrid was surprised. "With a wound that messy?"

"I told you there was something odd about that head,"

Cohen reminded her. "He had a big skull, but it was paper thin. Want the Latin for it?"

"Put it in your report," she said. "What do you mean by a rod? Like a curtain rod?"

"One of those solid brass ones, maybe. Or a broom handle."

"What about that mop handle?"

"Not thin enough. We're talking something no thicker than my thumb. A cane, maybe, or a poker or the handle of an umbrella even. Anyhow, as thin as his skull was, it wouldn't have taken much force whatever they used."

Back in the interrogation room, Sigrid told the two lawyers that as soon as a statement could be typed up and signed, their clients would be free to leave.

Rick Evans gave an involuntary sigh of relief and smiled at Pascal Grant. His smile faded though when she added, "Of course, there will probably be further questions in the next few days, so we expect you not to leave town."

"I won't," Pascal Grant said earnestly.

"No easy solutions," Sigrid told Elaine Albee and Jim Lowry when Grant and Evans had signed their statements and departed. The younger officers were disappointed to learn that the blow which killed Shambley could have been delivered by either a man or a woman, or possibly even a determined child.

"Did any of those people last night carry a walking stick?" asked Albee.

"Not that I noticed," said Sigrid. "The wife of one of the trustees, Mrs. Reinicke, walked with a slight limp, but I didn't see her with a cane." She described the animosity she'd witnessed between Shambley and Reinicke, then checked the time. "I'll take Thorvaldsen and Lady Francesca Leeds; you two can split the trustees—the Reinickes, the David Hymans and Mr. and Mrs. Herzog."

Sigrid's voice was cool and her face perfectly serious as she told Lowry, "Mrs. Herzog was a Babcock, you know."

"Huh?" said Lowry.

Later, he and Albee stood on a chilly IRT platform, surrounded by Christmas shoppers with brightly wrapped packages, and debated whether or not the lieutenant's last remark was meant to be humorous.

As the Lexington Avenue train squealed to a stop, they decided it probably wasn't.

In a cab headed uptown, Hester Kohn and Caryn DiFranco discussed the pros and cons of contact lenses while Rick Evans sat sandwiched between them on the rear seat with his feet drawn up on the transmission hump.

The furry hood of Ms. DiFranco's parka brushed Rick's nose as the lawyer leaned over for a closer look at the lenses in Hester Kohn's eyes.

"I just can't wear mine," she sighed. "I looked absolutely gorgeous in them, but I can't see a damn thing. Besides, I've decided glasses are who I am. People expect me to look like this. *I* expect me to look like this."

The round gold frames of her granny glasses had slipped down on her little button nose and she pushed them up in a delicate gesture.

"I know what you mean," said Hester Kohn. "I wore glasses for almost twenty-five years. They were such a part of me I felt naked the first few times I went out without them."

Caryn DiFranco peered into Rick's brown eyes. "Do you wear contacts, Rick?"

"No, ma'am."

"*Ma'am?* Omigod! That makes me sound like I'm eighty years old."

Rick flushed. "Sorry. I keep forgetting people don't say that up here."

"It's okay, kid. You'll be as rude as the rest of us soon enough." She caught a glimpse of passing street signs and tapped the driver on the shoulder. "Let me out at Macy's, okay?"

The driver grunted.

"I've got to buy and mail presents to half of Michigan," she complained to Hester Kohn. "Be grateful you're Jewish."

"I frequently am," Hester said dryly.

As the taxi double-parked in a no-parking zone and Caryn DiFranco opened her door, Hester added, "Thanks for coming down, Caryn."

"Don't thank me. You'll get the bill. Speaking of which, do we bill that MCP partner of yours or the gallery?"

"The gallery."

"Right. Stay out of mischief, Rick, and don't talk to any strange cops."

"Thanks, Miss DiFranco," he said.

She rolled her eyes, slammed the door and disappeared among the crowds of Christmas shoppers.

The cold air that rushed in when Caryn DiFranco got out had briefly dispersed Hester Kohn's gardenia perfume, but as the cab swerved back into the flow of traffic, the sweet scent again filled the space between them even though Rick had moved to the far side of the seat. For him, it was a disorienting smell, one connected with hot drowsy summer days, swinging on the porch of his mother's house, a porch surrounded by those glossy bushes heavy with waxy white blossoms. Somehow it seemed all wrong to be smelling his mother's gardenias here in this New York City taxicab on a cold December afternoon. Especially with the new associations the heavy scent of gardenias now held.

Dusk was falling and rush hour had begun in earnest. All lanes were clogged at Forty-second Street.

Forty-sixth, Forty-seventh, another snarl in front of Radio City Music Hall.

Hester Kohn smoothed her dark hair and loosened the top button of her red wool coat. "Want to tell me what's really bothering you?"

"Nothing." Without a camera to shield himself from her quizzical face, he unconsciously sank deeper into his corner and kept his eyes on the neon-lit stores and buildings they were now creeping past.

A complex blend of affection and irritation and a few stray tendrils of pity as well swept over Hester as she remembered Rick's first few weeks at the gallery.

Her own virginity had been lost so long ago that she had forgotten what terrors true sexual innocence could hold. Despite their age difference, she had dazzled him, made him want her, made him helpless to resist; yet, until they were well into the act, she hadn't even considered the possibility that it might be his first time. In that moment she had become tender and sentimental and had almost broken it off because she suddenly found herself panged by a conscience she didn't know she still possessed.

If I'd known, I would have made it more beautiful, she thought.

Too late. Already the sweet liquids of youth were spilling from his touchingly inept body.

With those first hot rushes of manhood, another boy might have become immediately cocky and boastful, a royal nuisance. Instead, Rick came to each subsequent session reluctantly and seemed miserable and guilty afterwards.

As he was now, in this overheated cab. It wasn't only his involvement in Roger Shambley's death that made him shrink into that corner, yet Hester knew that if she removed her glove and touched his bare, chapped hand with hers, he would be unable to resist. She considered testing her power, but they were now too close to the gallery.

Instead, she sank back into her own corner and wondered if young Rick had, after all, seen or done more last night than he was willing to admit.

Over in Queens, an artificial Christmas tree decorated the main lobby of the Lantana Walk Nursing Home and an electric menorah stood on the reception desk with two bulbs lit for this second day of Hanukkah. As Detective Bernie Peters soon discovered, he had arrived at the most restless hour of the day for ambulatory residents, and Mrs. Palka was not in her room.

"The dinner shift is promptly at five," explained the new resident director, "but they begin gathering outside the door by four o'clock. No doubt that's where we'll find Mrs. Palka."

They walked through halls wide enough for two wheelchairs to pass each other, into a lounge decorated with more symbols of Hanukkah and Christmas. There they found a querulous elderly woman with thick glasses and a hearing aid struggling to understand what she could expect for dinner as her incurably cheerful friend read the menu aloud.

"Roast ham?" she sniffed. "We had ham for supper last night and dry, stringy fodder it was, too, with a smidgen of honey glaze or pineapple."

"Lamb!" her friend enunciated loudly. "Roast *lamb*, Maureen. And you know perfectly well the doctor said you can't have sweet things."

"Wheat beans? What're wheat beans? Do speak up, Dora."

"There she is," said the director, gesturing toward the cheerful little dumpling of a woman, who leaned heavily upon her aluminum walker and watched their approach with lively curiosity.

The director introduced Detective Peters to Mrs. Palka, pointed them to a quiet corner of the lounge, and expertly vectored Mrs. Palka's hard-of-hearing friend toward another group of residents waiting for their dinner.

"My daughter told me someone from the police might be up," beamed Mrs. Palka. She lowered herself painfully into a chair, refusing Peters's help. "I had a hip replacement two years ago," she explained. "Eighty per cent who get it can go dancing in six months. I'm part of the twenty per cent who have to hang up their dancing shoes."

"I'm sorry," Bernie Peters said awkwardly. The infirmities of age made him uncomfortable. Even though he knew intellectually that everyone grows old, he was still young enough to believe he would somehow be exempted.

Mrs. Palka patted his hand. "Don't be sorry. I danced plenty in my lifetime, believe me." She sat erectly in her chair and cocked her small white head. "So! Dead babies in Gregor Jurczyk's attic. Whose babies were they?"

"Well, that's what we were hoping you could tell me, Mrs. Palka. Your daughter thought you were friendly with the Jurczyk family and might remember some of the people who lived in that house."

"Pauline says between 1935 and 1947. That right?"

"Those were the dates on the newspapers we found them wrapped in," Peters nodded.

"Now let me think. The Depression was going strong then and then came the war. They couldn't have been Barbara's. She was very good, very religious and would never. Besides, she and Karol—that was her husband, lovely man— they couldn't have babies. And Angelika was a business-woman, worked as a secretary in one of those big-shot investment places on Wall Street. She never married, so it couldn't have been her. There was a Mr. and Mrs. Rospochowski, but they had a new baby almost every year. When did she have time to slip in four more? Now there *was* a pretty little red-headed thing. What was her name? Anna? Anya?

"Ah, but what am I talking?" Mrs. Palka shook her head ruefully at what she considered a failing memory. "That one didn't come till after the war started."

"What about Mr. Jurczyk? Was he married?"

"Not that one. Too interested in the almighty dollar to spend a penny on a wife."

The dining room opened and residents began a modest surge through the doors. The smell of roast meat and steamed broccoli spread through the lounge and stirred those still seated to action. Even Mrs. Palka began to move her walker into a ready position.

"But really, Barbara's the one who could tell you better about the people who lived there," she said. She took a slip of paper with a Staten Island address from the pocket of her pink cardigan and gave it to Peters. "*If* she'll talk to you. We used to call each other up on the phone at least once a month, but she's gone downhill so much this year. Last time I talked to her—back in August that must have been—I don't believe she knew who I was. But then she *is* eighty-seven, four years older than me."

Getting up from a chair seemed almost as painful to Mrs. Palka as sitting down, but as she regained her feet and had her walker pointed toward the dining room, her querulous friend impatiently called to her, "Hurry up, Dora! Loretta says we're having colicky moose for dessert."

A ridiculous mental image filled Peters's head, and plump little Mrs. Palka, her wrinkled face aglow with laughter, winked at him with such insouciant charm that he found himself laughing, too.

"That Maureen! She knows perfectly well that Loretta said chocolate mousse."

The Hymans lived on Central Park South, but the Herzogs and the Reinickes lived within three blocks of each other in the East Sixties, so Elaine Albee and Jim Lowry decided to interview them first.

Lydia Babcock Herzog was tall and gaunt in a high-necked tunic and slacks of ivory wool. The young police-woman admired her dramatic gold necklace, her diamond earrings, her beautifully furnished drawing room with its miniature gold Christmas tree set upon an intricately carved ebony stand, even her tall and dignified husband; but as far as Elaine was concerned, that old adage, "You can never be too rich or too thin," was only half right. Mrs. Herzog would have to gain ten pounds just to qualify for anorectic, never mind too thin.

Mr. Herzog was quietly handsome, like a fair-haired English film star of the forties, refined and reserved. He offered Jim and Elaine drinks and, when they refused, continued with the one he'd begun before they arrived.

Mrs. Herzog's drink remained untouched on the low table before her. She sat on a sofa of pale blue brocade, inclined her head graciously, and repeated how shocked they had been to learn of Dr. Shambley's untimely death. How utterly shocked, in fact.

Jim Lowry rather doubted that. Mrs. Herzog seemed too detached to have ever been shocked by anything, but he nodded. "We understand that he hadn't been there very long?"

"He was appointed at our semiannual meeting in September," said Mrs. Herzog. "Jacob Munson put his name forward. I wasn't quite sure he was right for the Breul House—he was on sabbatical from the New York Center for the Fine Arts, you see—but Jacob assured us his academic credentials were impeccable and we did lack a scholar on the board." She watched her husband refill his martini glass from a silver shaker on the antique Chinese sideboard. "I suppose we shall have to find ourselves another scholar."

"This time from the *Institute* of Fine Arts," her husband murmured as he sat down again in a pale blue chair by the sideboard.

"Yes." She lifted her own drink from the gleaming teak table and held the long-stemmed crystal cocktail glass with skeletal fingers while she stared at the small white object awash in clear liquid.

A Gibson, Elaine decided. Martinis had olives, Gibsons had pearl onions.

Of course.

Onions also had fewer calories than olives. Not that it actually mattered.

Without touching the glass to her lips, Mrs. Herzog returned it to the table.

"Were you aware of any animosity between Dr. Shambley and anyone else at the Breul House?" asked Jim Lowry.

"We hardly knew him, Detective Lowry. Marie Reinicke arranged a luncheon at the house for everyone to meet him, early last month. He was quite witty that day. A bit *too* witty for my taste, but then perhaps I—"

She hesitated as her husband stood and casually poured himself another drink, then looked at her inquiringly. "Another for you, my dear?"

"No, thank you," she replied. "I still seem to have some."

"We were told that he was witty at Mr. Reinicke's expensive last night," said Elaine Albee.

"Precisely my point. Winston was devastated when he had to part with his Van Gogh drawing, and for that odious little man to make light of it—!"

Her voice lost its detachment and Mr. Herzog completed the thought for her in a dignified tone. "He was no gentleman."

"Was Mr. Reinicke angry last night?" asked Lowry.

"Winston Reinicke *is* a gentleman," said Mrs. Herzog. "If you're really asking if he remained behind last night and exacted revenge for Dr. Shambley's insults, he did not. The four of us left Erich Breul House together shortly after eight and shared a car uptown. We dropped the Reinickes at their own door well before eight-thirty."

"Are you quite sure I can't fix someone a drink?" Mr. Herzog asked courteously.

When they regained the street some twenty-seven floors below, Elaine Albee and Jim Lowry unconsciously paused to draw in several deep breaths of frigid night air.

Lowry laughed when he realized what they were doing. "That's how it must feel in a submarine or a spaceship," he said. "Every crack hermetically sealed and all the air recycled over and over until there's no oxygen left in it."

Rush hour traffic was still building and streams of headlights could be seen all the way down Park Avenue. The Reinickes lived in a building that fronted the park and as she and Jim walked over to Fifth, Elaine said, "Before we do the Hymans, let's stop in at F.A.O. Schwartz if we finish up with the Reinickes in time. I need to see some kids talking to Santa soon or I'm going to lose all my Christmas spirit."

The Reinicke apartment rose high above Central Park. The living room was furnished with an eclectic mix of beautiful antiques, modern couches, small collectibles and a large, bushy Scotch pine squashed into a corner window; its colored lights overlay the lights of the park and were reflected back into the room. Despite the clutter, the place seemed warm and cozy after the airless precision of the Herzogs' home.

Mrs. Reinicke was a vivacious blonde of late middle-age and seemed totally unselfconscious about her limp.

"Polio," she said cheerfully when she noticed Jim Lowry's surreptitious glance at her rolling gait. "Jonas Salk was eight years too late with his vaccine for me. Even so, I was lucky. My baby sister died."

She tilted her blond head to them. "So much anxiety now with AIDS but we've forgotten the sheer terror of the polio epidemics, haven't we? I do hope there's a heaven. Dr. Salk and his colleagues so deserve one."

Winston Reinicke, bluff and hearty, patted her hand tenderly. "So they do, my love, so they do."

"Forgive my asking," said Elaine, "but do you ever use a cane?"

"Oh, no. Not for me. I tried once but such a nuisance you wouldn't believe! Getting in and out of cabs, and they always slide off your chair and trip up the waiters. I have an Irish shepherd's crook for tramping around our country place, but here in the city I simply can't be bothered. Winston, do fix these two young people something to drink."

She waved aside their demurrals. "It doesn't have to be alcoholic. We have juice, Perrier, or—I know! In honor of the season, what about some eggnog without the nog or mulled apple cider?"

The detectives had not wanted to accept drinks from the Herzogs, but somehow it seemed all right from the Reinickes and soon they were sipping hot cider, warmed inside and out by the spicy bouquet of cloves and cinnamon.

"I grew up on an apple farm in Pennsylvania," Lowry said contentedly, "and this smells like Christmas at home."

Both Reinickes looked as if they'd much rather discuss apple farms or Christmas customs or even Lowry's mother's recipe for mulled cider than Roger Shambley; but it was clear that someone had already given them all the news about the art historian's death. Once the initial awkwardness wore off, they freely answered questions about the previous evening as if the detectives were there solely to gather background material. Neither seemed to realize that Mr. Reinicke might be a suspect.

"It was an informal sort of get-together," explained Marie Reinicke. "Four or five of the trustees and their spouses, some art people, people from the Breul House. Organized by Lady Francesca Leeds with, I suppose, Mr. Thorvaldsen picking up the tab?" She looked doubtfully at her husband.

"Quite right, quite right," agreed Mr. Reinicke. "All their idea, and a tax write-off to boot, so it's only right, eh? Our funds are too low for impromptu parties, I'm afraid. And don't forget Oscar Nauman."

"Of course," Mrs. Reinicke nodded briskly. "He was the whole point of the party. You've been told that though?"

"He's a painter—going to exhibit some of his pictures there, isn't he?" Lowry asked hesitantly. "And that's supposed to help bring in more money?"

"And publicity." Mrs. Reinicke cocked her blond head at Lowry's uncertainty and charitably elucidated, "Yes, you might say Oscar Nauman's a painter. Like Donald Trump's a carpenter or Pavarotti sings a little. Nauman's never had a summary exhibition and to have his first at the Erich Breul House—! There'll be lines all around Sussex Square."

Jim and Elaine exchanged glances. Neither had realized that Lieutenant Harald was involved with someone of that stature.

"And the Kohn woman, Jacob Munson's colleague at the gallery," said Mr. Reinicke, who was still reconstructing last night's party, "and that quiet young woman with those extraordinary gray eyes. She came with Nauman. Did you meet her, Marie? A Miss Harald. Tall woman. Didn't say much, but had a nice smile."

"He never listens to a thing I tell him," Mrs. Reinicke

confided to Elaine and Jim. "Now, Winston, don't you remember when Hope Ruffton called to tell us about Dr. Shambley? She said that the police officer in charge of the investigation turned out to be the same woman who was there last night with Oscar Nauman."

"Eh?" Mr. Reinicke drew himself up and looked at Lowry and Albee with the first signs of suspicion. "Well, then. You must already know everything that happened, eh?"

"Not really," Elaine Albee said smoothly. "Lieutenant Harald was there as a guest, like everyone else, and she was only one person. She couldn't have seen everything Dr. Shambley did."

"But she *did* hear his exchange with me, eh?" He glowered down at her.

"Now, Winston—"

"She said he seemed like a very rude man," Elaine answered diplomatically.

Mr. Reinicke flexed the tension from his shoulders and smoothed the lapels of his tweed jacket. It was like watching a farm dog lower its hackles and become good ol' Shep again, thought Lowry.

"Dr. Shambley was rude to you last night?" asked Mrs. Reinicke. "You didn't tell me, Winston."

"No need, my dear, no need at all," he said gruffly. "He'd heard about our Van Gogh and it amused him."

"*Amused* him?" Mrs. Reinicke began to grow indignant.

"And then he had the unmitigated gall to suggest I could upgrade my collection with a Norman Rockwell or a Pierson Sharpe."

"My dear!"

"Sharpe?" asked Jim Lowry, who rather liked Norman Rockwell's down-to-earth pictures and didn't see where the insult lay in Shambley's remarks.

"He's the man who draws those kids with the big sad eyes," Elaine told him. "The one my sister-in-law likes so much."

Lowry knew what Lainey thought of her sister-in-law's taste and began to understand the Reinickes' annoyance.

"No wonder you and Cheevy were gone so long last night," said Mrs. Reinicke sympathetically.

"You went out again last night?" asked Elaine.

"Needed a good long tramp," Winston Reinicke nodded. "Walked around the edge of the park to Columbus Circle, then up to Lincoln Center and back down Broadway to Times Square. Don't mind admitting the fellow got to me. Nobody likes to admit he's failed."

"Oh, for heaven's sake, Winston!" Mrs. Reinicke stood, plucked her husband's empty glass from his hand and stumped over to their liquor cabinet to pour him a fresh drink. "You had a temporary setback. And you were hardly alone. I never liked that Van Gogh anyhow."

"Well, *I* did!" he said testily, waving away the drink she offered him.

Mrs. Reinicke evidently knew her husband's moods quite well, for she continued to hold out the glass until he sighed and took it.

"Suppose that lieutenant woman wants to know what it was all about," he told Lowry and Albee. "Black Monday. Took a real bath on the Street. Overextended. More than I could raise to cover all my margin calls. Elliott Buntrock'd had his eye on my Van Gogh for years and he offered to help liquidate some of my collection in a hurry if I'd give him first shot at that drawing. Didn't try to fudge the prices either. Damned decent of him. Might've gotten a bit more if I'd put them up for a proper auction; but if I could've waited for an auction, wouldn't have had to sell out in the first place, eh?"

"And now you can have the fun of building a new collection," Marie Reinicke observed indulgently.

"Not the same," said her husband, taking another swallow of his drink. "Not as much fun having people to dinner any more either."

"It was a very gloomy drawing," Mrs. Reinicke told the young officers. "But some people were impressed to learn they were dining in the same room with a Van Gogh and Winston loved to show it off. Personally, I miss the Cassatt pastel more and no one ever paid it a shred of attention."

"After Dr. Shambley's remarks, though, it's certainly understandable that you'd want to walk off some steam," said Elaine Albee.

It all sounded very much like a tempest in a teapot to Jim Lowry, but he knew that murders were committed every day for even sillier reasons. It was lucky that Mr. Reinicke had an alibi.

"Did your friend come home with you?" he asked.

Mr. Reinicke looked blank. "Friend?"

Elaine realized that Jim was trying to avoid raising Mr. Reinicke's ire again. "You said that you and a Mr.—Cheever, was it?—took a long walk together," she said helpfully. "If you could give us his full name and address—"

"Cheevy?"

Mrs. Reinicke lay back in her chair and whooped with laughter. "*Mr.* Cheevy!"

"Cheevy's our dog," chuckled Mr. Reinicke, his good spirits partially restored. "A King Charles spaniel out of Scorned Lady of Winterset, so we had to name him Cheevy. First name,"—he chuckled some more—"Miniver, of course."

Mrs. Reinicke took pity on the detectives' puzzled looks. "From the Edwin Arlington Robinson poem," she smiled. "You know: 'Miniver Cheevy, child of scorn'?"

Elaine looked at Jim, then sighed and took a deep breath. "I'm sorry, Mr. Reinicke, but we have to ask you exactly what time you left this apartment, when you returned and if you met anyone you recognized during that time?"

Traffic was beginning to thin out, and as they walked down Fifth Avenue to see if the famous toy store were keeping late Christmas hours, a sharp arctic wind swept across the park. With mittened hands, Elaine pulled her woolly blue knitted hat further down over her face and turned up her collar till only her eyes and her pink-tipped nose could be seen.

Jim Lowry had not worn a hat or cap since he was twelve and still under parental control, but he turned up his own collar and wrapped his wool scarf tighter so that his ears were somewhat protected. His breath blew out in white clouds before him as he said gloomily, "I don't think Lieutenant Harald's going to accept the testimony of a King Charles spaniel."

Elaine pulled him to a stop. "Look down there," she said, gesturing with her head. "Cohen said a rod or a stick, right? Do you suppose Mr. Reinicke has one?"

On the sidewalk a few yards ahead of them, a man was

cleaning up after his poodle with a device that looked something like a long-handled dustpan.

Jim began to laugh. "You gotta promise I can be there when you ask the lieutenant if Shambley could have bought it with a pooper-scooper."

With a fuzzy hat pulled down over her ears and a long fur coat that swathed her tiny body like a djellaba, Søren Thorvaldsen's middle-aged secretary tripped up the gangplank and across the wide deck as if the frigid gusts whipping off the Hudson River were nothing more than spring zephyrs.

Probably one of those dauntless Nordic types that went from steaming saunas to splashing among ice floes, thought Sigrid as she shivered along behind in a utilitarian coat and hood of heavy black wool that had weathered nine winters. The usual river traffic seemed to be out on the choppy water tonight, but the wind made her eyes so teary that she could only distinguish blurred lights in the darkness.

When she called earlier to set up this meeting, Sigrid hadn't expected it would take a half-mile hike to find Thorvaldsen. But she'd arrived at his office overlooking the river to find a Danish pixie who, after a quick telephone conversation conducted in Danish, had immediately encased herself in an envelope of fur and led Sigrid through a maze of hallways and elevators and eventually across a bone-numbing expanse of windswept pier and up onto the deck of his cruise ship, the *Sea Dancer*.

"She's supposed to sail Saturday at noon," explained the pixie, a Miss Kristensen. Even in high-heeled leather boots, the woman barely came up to Sigrid's shoulder and her words were almost blown away as she trotted along ahead of the tall police officer. "—partial loss of power in one of the main generators."

She tugged open a heavy steel door and they were suddenly and mercifully out of the biting wind and into the silence of a glass-enclosed promenade. Through another door and this time they entered true warmth. Sigrid pushed back the hood of her coat and felt her face begin to thaw.

They were inside a spacious lobby decorated in tones of peach, melon and sunshine yellow, but Sigrid was given no time to play tourist. Already, Miss Kristensen was halfway across the wide expanse of floral carpeting, heading for a bank of elevators. Sigrid almost expected to see her pull out a large turnip watch and murmur something about being late. She lengthened her own stride and caught up with the other woman just as the elevator arrived.

Instead of descending to the depths of the ship, or wherever they kept generators—Sigrid was weak on engineering details—the elevator rose. Soon she was once more following Miss Kristensen through a maze of confusing twists and turns, then down a wide, paneled hall carpeted in rich patterns of luscious tropical colors.

Abruptly, Miss Kristensen opened the door of a luxurious room with a sweeping view of the river. "Mr. Thorvaldsen's suite," she murmured. "If you'll wait here, Lieutenant Harald, he'll join you shortly." She flicked on a soft light over a fully equipped bar that gleamed and sparkled with chrome and crystal and cut-glass decanters like a tiny, perfect jewel box. "May I get you something to drink while you wait?"

"No, thank you," said Sigrid.

"Then I'll say *godnat*." Wrapping her furs tighter around her small form, the secretary hurried away.

Sigrid was drawn to the bank of windows at the end of the room where a wide couch had been built into the curve of the window. Upholstered in buttery soft leather of a tawny topaz color, it invited one to curl up and enjoy the view. She slipped off her coat and rested her strong chin on the back of the couch to stare through the glass.

The 180-degree night view was breathtaking. Across the water, a huge neon coffee cup dripped its good-to-the-last-drop in front of New Jersey's lights; on the near shore, the skyscrapers of midtown Manhattan became towering tiers of cubed light; while upriver, the George Washington Bridge spanned the two shores with graceful, glittering loops.

The city's stately nighttime beauty, coupled with the ship's warmth and quiet, made Sigrid relax. It had been a long day and as the moments passed, relaxation turned to increasing lethargy. Just as she was beginning to think she ought to take a turn about the deck to wake herself up, the door opened and Søren Thorvaldsen entered.

He was casually dressed in dark wool slacks and a white hand-knit fisherman's sweater that had a fresh smear of grease on the left cuff, and he was followed by a waiter whose tray held a silver thermos jug of steaming hot drink and plates of cheese and crackers and smoked fish.

"Can't offer you much," Thorvaldsen said as the waiter spread the food on the blond oak table before her, then left. "The kitchen staff's off duty until tomorrow morning."

"This wasn't necessary," Sigrid told him, but she was suddenly conscious of hunger and took the plate he offered with no further protest.

The hot drinks were Tom and Jerries, not a concoction Sigrid cared for, although she could appreciate how fitting it was for the cold night and for the yuletide season.

"*Glaedelig jul,*" said Thorvaldsen, lifting his glass toward her.

"*Skål,*" she replied.

The spicy hot rum slid down easily and began to create its own inner warmth.

"I didn't realize you were such a hands-on shipowner," Sigrid said, watching Thorvaldsen dab with a linen napkin at the grease on his sweater. There was an unpretentious, raw vitality about the man that kept one subliminally reminded of the working-class roots even when he wasn't boasting of them.

"That generator could wind up costing me an extra eighteen hundred unnecessary meals if we're a half day late leaving port," the Dane said with a shrug. He finished his drink and poured another from the thermos. "Plus the extra time and labor to serve and clean up afterwards."

Sigrid cut herself a wedge of soft Havarti and spread it on a slice of dark bread. "All because it leaves in the evening instead of noon?"

"Everything that happens aboard ship, every detail, has a price tag. Leaving a half day late could mean getting into Bermuda long after lunch instead of well before. This is a very competitive business. Something goes over cost, it comes out of profits. When that happens, I want to know why."

The serious lines in his open rugged face crinkled as he grinned and added, "Eighteen hundred lunches would just about buy one Oscar Nauman painting."

Sigrid followed his eyes to a picture on the far wall, in a place of honor beyond the bar. Its colors and rhythms were arresting: very manly, very—now that she looked at it—Nauman. She was surprised to realize that she could recognize the painting as indisputably his. It was a large abstract in those topaz and rust tones that she now identified with Francesca Leeds.

In fact this whole room with its blond oak, its amber and russet-colored couches and chairs, its gold chrome and its touches of burnt orange might have been designed as a setting for Francesca Leeds.

"Which came first?" she asked, curious. "The picture or the decor?"

"The picture, of course," he answered, apparently surprised that she would need to ask.

Sigrid gave an inward sigh. It was awkward to be the only person in Nauman's world who wasn't particularly enthusiastic about his work. She didn't wonder that this self-made millionaire could respond so directly to the strength of Nauman's art. Intellectually, she, too, could appreciate the games Nauman played with color and mathematics, with subtle rhythms and thematic variations; and she wished she liked it more. But it was just too abstract to move her emotionally, unlike the old German painters whom she loved for their spare asceticism and because they *were* rooted in the particular.

"—and perhaps it appeals to me precisely because I have spent so many years in hard serious work, but there's always Nauman's playful quality," Thorvaldsen was saying.

Wasn't there just, Sigrid thought wryly, momentarily diverted from Thorvaldsen's enthusiasm by certain memories of Nauman's playfulness.

"—an artist of his own time and one who isn't afraid to leave the loose ends. The high purpose of art is to remind us that something is always left undone—to remind us that it's not human to expect too much from method and plan. Only third-rate artists paint perfect pictures. Real life isn't tidy," said Thorvaldsen. "Look at this ship—all a fantasy!"

Thorvaldsen tilted the nearly empty thermos jug inquiringly. "More?"

Sigrid shook her head and covered the top of her glass with her hand. "No."

She pulled a notepad from the outer pocket of her coat

and placed it on the table. "You *do* realize this isn't a social visit?"

"Too bad." His voice was slightly slurred, but his eyes were wary.

He seemed to be drinking quite a lot, Sigrid noted. That was the trouble with mixing alcohol with eggs and spices. Those hot Tom and Jerries were like eggnog: if one hadn't eaten, it was too easy to treat them like food instead of drink.

Sigrid patted her other coat pockets and finally the pockets of her dark blue jacket and gray slacks without finding a pen.

Smiling, Thorvaldsen handed her his, a slim gold-filled object. His fingers brushed hers and lingered a moment before he released the pen.

Deliberately?

"Thank you," she said stiffly. "I gather you'd already heard about Dr. Roger Shambley when I called before."

"Yes. Someone told Francesca and she telephoned me." Thorvaldsen buttered a cracker, added a morsel of smoked fish, and popped the whole thing in his mouth.

"How long had you known Dr. Shambley?"

The shipowner swallowed. "I didn't. Heard his name, of course, and knew he was an art historian writing a book, but that's all."

"What did you think of him?"

Thorvaldsen gave a short explosive laugh and spoke a couple of one-syllable words in Danish that need no translation. "You were there, *frøken* Harald. You heard him threaten *me*."

"Yes. What did he mean?"

The big Dane shrugged. "Who knows what small men dream?"

"You weren't afraid of his threat?"

"Of course not."

"Would you describe, please, what happened at the Breul house after Nauman and I left?" asked Sigrid.

"After you and Nauman left, it became boring." Thorvaldsen leaned back in a creamy leather chair with his left ankle resting on his right knee and his brawny hands clasping his left shin. "I spoke with that curator chap, Buntrock, for a few minutes. Very knowledgeable about Nauman's work. Then I left with Lady Francesca Leeds. About eight-thirty, I think."

"Shambley didn't reappear?"

"He did not."

"And then?"

"And then?" he mimicked. "You wish to know what happened *after* we left the Breul House?"

"You had words with Dr. Shambley, laid hands on him, almost hit him," Sigrid said calmly. "A few hours later, he was dead. You may not want to answer without a lawyer—"

"*Lawyers!*" Thorvaldsen snorted scornfully.

"—but I have to ask you to account for those hours up until, say, one A.M."

"Eight-thirty till one A.M.," he repeated slowly.

"Yes."

"We had dinner reservations at Le Petit Coq," he said, naming an expensive French restaurant a few blocks west of Sussex Square. "After that I put Francesca into a taxi for the Maintenon and came back to my office to work."

His blue eyes were sardonic. "You have a most unprofessional look on your face, *frøken* Harald. You are surprised to hear that she went back to her hotel alone?"

"Not at all," Sigrid lied. "You and Lady Francesca parted at what time?"

"Ten-fifteen, ten-thirty. I didn't look at my watch."

"And then?"

"I worked until midnight, went to my apartment on the top floor, had a drink, and went to bed. Alone."

"Is there anyone who can confirm that? Miss Kristensen, perhaps?"

"Not even Miss Kristensen is that dedicated."

"What about a night watchman or a cleaning person?"

He shook his head and his fair hair was like old mellow gold in the lamplight of this golden stateroom. "Sorry. There's only my word."

"Your word?" Her eyes were skeptical chips of gray slate as she lifted them to his.

"You're an odd woman," he said, standing abruptly. He stretched out his hand to her. "Come, please."

Puzzled, Sigrid stood up.

He pointed toward the glass.

Out in the channel, a tugboat moved slowly past the *Sea Dancer*. Car lights passed in an intermittent stream along the expressway, and high above the Palisades could be seen the red and green flashes of airplane lights.

"In the glass," Thorvaldsen murmured and Sigrid saw themselves reflected as in a dark mirror.

"It did not surprise me that Oscar had taken Francesca," he said thickly. "But you—!"

He tried to pull her to him.

"Mr. Thorvaldsen—"

"Oscar Nauman is a man of fire. You can't be as cold as you look."

He put his arms around her as if to kiss her.

"Are you crazy? Stop it!" she cried and, when he didn't release her, kicked him in the shins. Hard.

As Thorvaldsen tightened his hold, Sigrid's police training shifted into automatic. She abruptly relaxed, leaned into him, and a moment later, sent the Dane crashing to the floor.

Instinctively, her hand went to the handle of the .38 holstered in a shoulder harness beneath her jacket as she waited to see how Thorvaldsen would react.

At that moment a voice behind her said, "Is this a private game or can anybody play?"

Sigrid released the gun handle, took a deep breath, and slowly turned. "Hello, Lady Francesca."

Francesca Leeds closed the door behind her and looked from Sigrid, breathing hard in the middle of the room, to Søren Thorvaldsen, now sitting on the floor and rubbing his left eye where it had banged against the low table. Her smile was tentative as she said, "I'm sure there's some perfectly rational explanation for what's happened here."

"Not really," said Sigrid. "Mr. Thorvaldsen was a bit uncertain about a woman's ability to defend herself and I'm afraid he goaded me into a demonstration. Quite unprofessional of me. I apologize, Mr. Thorvaldsen."

She had expected him to be sullen. Instead, he came to his feet with an easy smile and a shrug.

"No apologies, *frøken* Harald. You showed me what I wished to know." He greeted the elegant redhead with a kiss on her cool cheek. "You see, *Lsøde ven?* I'm still an Ålborg roughneck."

Not fully convinced, but willing to let it pass, Francesca threw her mink coat over a nearby chair, added her gloves to the heap, and headed for the bar. "I feel as if I'm two drinks behind. Fix anyone else something?"

"Not for me," Sigrid murmured.

"Just an ice cube," Thorvaldsen said ruefully, as his fingers examined the lump swelling beneath his eye. "You come in time to rescue me, Francesca. I'm being grilled about Dr. Shambley."

Francesca paused with a decanter of Irish whiskey in her graceful hands. "Should I be leaving then, Sigrid?"

"Why?" asked Thorvaldsen.

Sigrid stood. "Perhaps it would be better if you both came to my office tomorrow and made formal statements."

"Me?" Francesca seemed surprised. "Why on earth would you need a statement from me? I barely knew the man."

"But you have a key to the Breul House, don't you?" asked Sigrid.

"Well, yes, but— Oh, don't be daft, Sigrid! He was a grotty little man but you can't think I went back there last night and sneaked in and killed him?"

"Can you tell me where you were between eight-thirty and one A.M.?" Sigrid asked bluntly.

"To be sure, I can," she said in her Celtic lilt. She brought Thorvaldsen an ice cube wrapped in a napkin and sat down with her drink at the other end of the couch from Sigrid. "Søren and I finished dinner shortly before ten, then I took a cab to the Maintenon. Some friends of mine were just going into the lounge when I got in around ten-thirty—George and Bitsy Laufermann—and they insisted that I join them. We stayed for the midnight show. I'll give you their phone number, if you wish, and you can also ask the maître d'. He'll tell you I was there."

Sigrid jotted down the names and numbers, then asked, "What about your key to the Breul House? Do you carry it with you?"

"On my key ring, yes," said Francesca. "I suppose you'll be wanting to see it."

She moved so beautifully, Sigrid thought, watching as the other woman crossed to her fur coat. Tonight she wore a dark brown taffeta dress edged with a stiff, narrow self-ruffle at the neck and wrists, shot with gold threads that gleamed with every swing of the skirt. Her lustrous hair fell in copper tangles about the perfect oval of her face.

Even as Sigrid went through the formalities of this interview with one level of her mind, another level catalogued Francesca's almost flawless beauty. Thorvaldsen's advances had been clumsy and insulting and she should have decked him harder, but she could almost sympathize with his basic confusion. How could Oscar Nauman possibly be attracted to her when he'd had one of the most beautiful women in New York?

Last night she had meant it when she told Nauman she wasn't jealous of the women he'd known before her. Tonight, on this ship, she found herself wondering who had initiated their split—Francesca or Nauman?

Francesca Leeds dug into one of the deep pockets and came out with a handful of keys. She detached one and handed it to Sigrid. It was tagged *EBH*.

"I'd like to keep this for now," Sigrid said, wrapping it in a clean sheet of notepaper. She quickly wrote out a receipt for it. "One more question: do you know why Roger Shambley was killed?"

The copper-haired woman resumed her place on the couch and her brown eyes regarded Sigrid humorously. "Because he couldn't keep his mouth shut?"

Sigrid looked up inquiringly.

Francesca shrugged. "I only know what I've heard."

"Which is—?"

"Word around art circles is that Roger Shambley liked to know things. He listened and he heard and he was a bloody genius with insinuations. People often thought he knew more than he did, but by the time they realized he didn't, it was too late because they'd already let too much slip." She looked into her glass and laughed. "Does that make any sense?"

"He was a *røven af fjerde division*," Thorvaldsen growled, the ice cube still held to his eye.

"That, too, if it means what I think it does," Francesca nodded. "He liked to know unpleasant things about you and then rub your nose in it." She tilted her glass to her lips and drank the rest of her undiluted whiskey. "Or so I've been told."

More specific, she would not be; so Sigrid turned her gaze back to the man, who had taken Francesca's glass over to the bar for a refill. "Would you prefer to finish your statement down at headquarters tomorrow, Mr. Thorvaldsen?"

"I thought I had finished already," he said, pouring Irish whiskey into two glasses.

Sigrid flipped back several pages in her notebook. "You told me you worked until midnight and then went to bed."

"*Ja.*"

"Yet we have a witness who saw you at the Breul House at midnight."

That finally got under the shell of amused condescension which he'd adopted since Francesca's arrival.

His blue eyes narrowed. "He must be mistaken."

"No," she answered flatly.

Francesca looked up at him as he returned with her new drink.

"Søren?"

He ignored her. "And if I say he lies, it is my word against his. Then what happens?"

"Then your people here will be questioned. No matter what you think, if you returned after midnight, someone will have seen you. Lady Francesca's key to the Breul House will be analyzed. If the lab finds any waxy or soapy residue, that might indicate that it'd been duplicated without her knowledge. We would probably look more closely into your activities, see if Roger Shambley had learned something interesting about you—how you acquired all the pieces in your art collection, for instance. And then—"

"Enough, enough." He turned to Francesca. "I did *not* use your key."

"But you did go back to the Breul House," Sigrid prodded.

"*Ja,*" he sighed and walked over to the windows to stare out at the dark river.

Francesca's eyes met Sigrid's and both women waited silently.

With his back to them, Thorvaldsen said, "When I returned to my office last night, there was a message on my machine from Dr. Shambley. He apologized for what he'd said about Francesca and Nauman and said he wanted to make it up to me."

"Is the message still there?" Sigrid asked.

"No, I erased it." Thorvaldsen sank heavily into the tawny leather chair opposite the low oak-and-glass table, his full glass cradled in those strong hands. The red lump under his eye had begun to turn blue.

"Did he say what he planned to do?"

"Not in so many words. Francesca told you before: he could say one thing, but you knew he meant something else." He looked at his glass, then set it on the table without drinking.

"This you must understand, *frøken* Harald—I did not get here by following every rule."

He made a sweeping gesture of his hands that encompassed their luxurious surroundings here on the high deck of this ship and, by extension, all that it symbolized. "If I'd done that, I'd still be breaking my back under bales of smoked herring on a dock in Ålborg. Back then, *ja*, maybe I did sail too close to the wind. But that was then and this is now. Now, my money makes more money. All by itself, and all legal. Now, I want things I never dreamed of when I was a kid in Denmark. Now, I have time to learn what these things mean, and money to pay for them."

He gestured toward the painting across the room. "Twenty-three years ago, I was walking along a street in København and I saw a picture in the window of a gallery. A little thing, so—" He sketched a small rectangle with his hands, approximately twelve by eighteen inches. "—and it stopped me cold. I didn't know why, I just knew I had to own it. It took me two years to pay for it. My first Nauman picture. Now I own eleven Naumans and they form the heart of my collection. I've collected other artists, of course—two Picassos, a Léger, a wonderful Brancusi sculpture, and a number of works by lesser-known practitioners of what I call 'cerebral abstraction.'"

Francesca slipped off her brown high-heeled boots and tucked her legs up under her skirt with a rustle of taffeta, but Sigrid remained motionless as Thorvaldsen abruptly reached for his glass.

"And for all these works," he said, "I have documents, bills of sale, certificates." He drank deeply. "But every now and then, people come to me with very beautiful, very rare things and they don't always have documents and I don't always ask for receipts. Shambley knew this."

Thorvaldsen gave Francesca a crooked smile. "Or, as you said, *min dame*, he made me think he knew this."

"He offered to sell you a stolen painting?" Sigrid asked.

"Not in those words, but yes," Thorvaldsen admitted. "At the same time, he made me think that if I didn't come, questions would be raised by others. Just now—"

He broke off and gave a sardonic shrug of his broad shoulders. "Let's say that at this particular moment, I don't want controversy. *Any* controversy. Next month, okay. Now, no."

"So you went to the Breul House?"

"Not immediately. But the more I thought of this other matter, the more I decided I had to go, at least hear what he wanted to say. I walked over to Eleventh Avenue and caught a cab going downtown. Got out near Sussex Square. He said to come in without ringing; the front door would be unlocked."

"Was it?"

His affirmative grunt was halfway between a *ja* and a yeah.

"And the time?"

"A few minutes past eleven, I think. The great hall was dim inside. I called his name. No answer. A light was on in the library, so I went in there and sat until I almost fell asleep. Finally, I began to think it was some kind of stupid joke, so I left."

"What time was that?"

"Midnight." A more genuine smile flitted across his rugged features. "As I came down the steps, the lights on the Christmas tree in the middle of the park went off."

Sigrid found it hard to believe that a man like Søren Thorvaldsen would sit meekly in a library and wait almost an hour for someone like Shambley to jerk him around and she said as much.

Thorvaldsen finished off his drink and set the glass on the table between them with a decisive clink. "Think what you like. You wanted my statement. That's it."

The lump beneath his eye was nearly purple now and Sigrid saw that he winced when he touched it absentmindedly. It was probably pointless to continue with Thorvaldsen tonight, she thought. Better to wait and get him down to her office when he was less belligerent. Time enough then to ask if he'd had a look around for whatever shady art object Shambley may have planned to sell him.

She slipped on her coat, stowed the pad in one of its pockets, and pulled out her gloves.

"Did you leave a trail of bread crumbs coming in?" Francesca asked.

"No," Sigrid smiled, "but I think I can find my way out."

As she said good night and opened the door, Francesca suddenly slid on her boots and said, "Better let me point you toward the nearest gangplank. Back in a minute, Søren."

They walked down the wide passageway to the elevator. Sigrid said, "Do you suppose the ship's doctor is on board tonight? Someone ought to take a look at that eye."

Francesca was amused. "I'm sure Søren's had worse knocks than that. He made a pass at you, didn't he?"

"Not exactly."

They rang for an elevator and Sigrid felt the other woman's appraising eyes as they waited.

"He's really not like that," said Francesca. "You probably won't believe me, but I've been seeing him for two months now and underneath all that diamond-in-the-rough facade, he's been a perfect gentleman. *Too* perfect, in some respects."

The elevator arrived and they stepped inside. "In fact," she added, "I was beginning to wonder if he marched to a different drummer or if I was losing it."

"You?" Sigrid murmured, feeling like a drab country mouse next to Francesca's rich shimmer of brown-and-gold taffeta.

As the elevator doors opened for them, Francesca laid her hand on Sigrid's arm. "Does it make a difference to you, Sigrid? About Oscar and me, I mean? I saw your face last night when you realized what Roger Shambley meant."

Sigrid was silent. She rather doubted if Francesca Leeds had seen any more in her face than the redhead expected—or wanted?—to see; and she had never felt comfortable exchanging girlish confidences.

Evidently Francesca felt differently. "What Oscar and I

had was wonderful while it lasted, but it's been over for more than a year."

And what, Sigrid wondered mutely, was the proper response to that? I'm sorry? I'm glad? Were you glad when it ended? Was Nauman?

"Ah! There's the door I came in," she said, pulling on her gloves and raising the hood of her coat. "I think I can find my way out from here."

And beat a coward's quick exit.

It was after nine when Sigrid got home. She'd stopped off at a bookstore along the way to begin her Christmas shopping. This was a young cousin's first Christmas and she couldn't decide whether to get him a traditional *Mother Goose* or a lavish pop-up book, so she bought both. Baby Lars had been named for her favorite great-uncle, but she couldn't neglect the other five in Hilda's brood, especially when one stop could take care of the whole Carmichael family so simply.

She had spent a happy hour browsing through *Wind in the Willows, The Secret Garden, Watership Down, Treasure Island* and *Charlotte's Web*, leafing through dozens more before adding a newly published and beautifully illustrated book of fairy tales for Hilda, who collected them.

A book for Hilda's husband wasn't quite as simple. What does one give a CPA who has everything? Impulsively she chose a book on building Chinese kites. A man with six children might find that diverting.

Laden with bundles, she arrived at number 42½, a sturdy green wooden gate set into a high nondescript wall on an equally nondescript street full of rundown buildings at the western edge of Greenwich Village. She unlocked the gate and found Roman Tramegra stringing lights on the dogwood tree that stood in the center of their small garden. He was bundled against the icy December night in a bizarre white ski mask, multicolored scarves, and three layers of sweaters and he greeted her gaily in his deep booming voice as she piled her packages on a stone bench.

"Ah, *there* you are, dear Sigrid! Had I realized you'd be home so soon, I would have waited. No matter. I shall be the president and *you* can be the little child that leads us."

It had been almost a year since this late-blooming flower

child, to use Nauman's phrase, had wandered into her life and, by an odd set of circumstances, wound up sharing with her an apartment he'd acquired through arcane family connections.

Although only a few years older than she, he had adopted an avuncular manner and by now felt free to comment on her clothes, her hair, her makeup, and whether or not she was eating properly and getting enough sleep. He was so easily deflected, however, that Sigrid, by nature a solitary person, found him less of an intrusion than she'd feared. She discovered that she enjoyed coming home to a well-lit apartment full of occasionally entrancing dinner aromas—Roman was an adventurous cook; not all his adventures had a happy ending—and his magpie curiosity and verbal flights of fancy kept her amused more often than not.

He was tall and portly and there was just enough light in their tiny courtyard to make him look like a cross between a Halloween ghost and Frosty the Snowman. The eye and mouth holes of his white ski mask were outlined in black and the dark toggles of his bulky white cardigan marched down his rounded torso like buttons of coal on a tubby snowman as he positioned the last light and held out to Sigrid the plug end of the tree lights and the receptacle end of an extension cord that he'd snaked from the house.

"Everything's ready," he caroled. "Come along, my dear. No speeches, though I really should hum something appropriate. What did the Marine Band play the other night when they lit the White House tree?"

In his deep basso profundo, he began to hum the national anthem.

Laughing, Sigrid stepped up to the tree and, in a Monty Python imitation of ribbon-cutting royalty, plugged the two electric cords together and said, "I now declare this Christmas season officially opened."

A blaze of colorful lights twinkled through the bare twigs of the dogwood.

"God bless us, every one!" said Roman.

Although Mr. Breul never summarily disregarded expert opinion, he had no use for pedantry. Being well-educated and well-informed, he preferred to trust his own eye to pick out the one good thing from a gallery full of old pictures and to leave the bad behind and he had no need to lean upon the advice of others in so doing. So secure was he in his own taste, that he was never disturbed when, as it occasionally happened, an attribution of his purchase was afterward discredited.

"It matters not who actually painted it. The picture still retains the lofty qualities for which I chose it," he would say as he continued to give it high place within the collection.

Erich Breul—The Man and His Dream, privately published 1924 by The Friends and Trustees of the Erich Breul House

VIII

Sigrid moved the morning session briskly through the usual update on current cases. Matt Eberstadt brushed powdered sugar from his dark green shirt and maroon tie and reported a conviction in the drug-related homicide trial that finally went to the jury yesterday. "They were only out twenty minutes."

The neighborhood canvass around the house that held those infant remains had turned up no one else who could remember the Jurczyks or their tenants from the thirties, but Bernie Peters had already been on the phone to the nursing home in Staten Island, where a staff doctor confirmed Mrs. Palka's fears about her former East Village friend.

"Mrs. Barbara Jurczyk Zajdowicz has had a series of small strokes this past year," Peters said as he tore open a packet of dry creamer and added it to his coffee. "She's in a wheelchair now and the doctor says some days she's cogent, most days she's not. He suggests that we try her immediately after Saturday morning confession."

"Who's her next of kin?" asked Sigrid.

"None listed."

"Who pays the bills then?"

"I talked to an individual in their business office, and the way it works is that she paid into something like an annuity when she first went there back in 1971. Probably what she got for the house. On top of that, she signed over her husband's pension and social security and they're supposed to take care of her as long as she lives."

Elaine Albee shivered and pushed aside her jelly doughnut. She hated the whole idea of growing old, especially here in New York City, and tried not to think about it any more than she could help. It kept getting shoved in her face, though: bag ladies homeless on every street corner; women who once ran but now hobbled down subway platforms, fearfully clutching their lumpy shopping bags as they moved arthritically through doors that closed too fast; women like Barbara Zajdowicz, who'd outlived brothers and sisters and husbands and were now warehoused in nursing homes with no one to watchdog their interests or—

Lieutenant Harald's cool voice cut across her private nightmare. "Are you with us, Albee?"

"Ma'am?"

"Your interview with the Reinickes," the lieutenant prodded.

Feeling like a third-grade schoolkid caught goofing off by a strict teacher, a likeness subliminally underlined by the lieutenant's no-nonsense gray pantsuit and severe white blouse, Albee sat up straight and summarized what she and Lowry had learned from Winston and Marie Reinicke.

"So there's no alibi for Reinicke but his wife doesn't use a cane either," she finished, wadding up the scrap of paper Jim Lowry had slipped her under the table with *P—S???!!* scrawled on it in bold block letters.

"We did pick up something from the Hymans, though," said Lowry.

After looking at kids who were looking at toys in F.A.O. Schwarz, he and Lainy'd swung west to the Hymans' terraced apartment on Central Park South. David and Linda Hyman appeared to be in their midsixties. Mr. Hyman still looked like the rabbinical student he'd once been before he became an economist. His thick and curly beard was more pepper than salt and his dark eyes flashed with intensity as he spoke. A faint rusty glow through her soft white hair hinted that Mrs. Hyman had been a strawberry blonde in her youth. She was small and quiet, but her face had held an amused intelligence as her husband described the things they'd noticed last night.

"They said they saw Shambley come out of the library with a cat-that-ate-the-canary look on his face last night," Lowry reported. "He'd been in there with the director, what's his name? Peake? And the Kohn woman. The Hymans didn't hear what was said between them, but evidently old Jacob Munson came in on the tail end of the conversation and didn't much care for what he heard because he told Hyman that maybe he'd made a mistake when he recommended Shambley as a trustee last fall."

"After the Hymans left the Breul House, they went on to a dinner party in Brooklyn Heights so it looks like they're out of it," said Elaine Albee. "And Mrs. Herzog didn't like the way Shambley was riding Reinicke Wednesday night, but she and her husband alibi each other and their maid confirms it."

Sigrid reported the salient points of her interview with Søren Thorvaldsen and Lady Francesca Leeds and there was a brief discussion of how Thorvaldsen's movements fit into the timetable they were beginning to assemble.

Gray-haired Mick Cluett shifted his bulk in a squeaky swivel chair and phlegmatically reported that the Sussex Square canvass had drawn a blank. No convenient nosy neighbor with an insatiable curiosity about the comings and goings of the Breul House.

He had, however, found an address book in Roger Shambley's upper West Side apartment, which had helped him locate a brother in Michigan who would be flying in tonight. A cursory examination of the apartment revealed nothing unusual to Cluett's experienced eyes.

"Looked like standard stuff to me," he said. "Small one-bedroom apartment, nothing too fancy, but all good stuff, you know? Lots of books and papers, nice pictures on the walls. The brother said he'd let us know if he finds anything odd when he goes through the stuff."

They batted it around some more, then Sigrid laid out the day's assignments: in addition to ongoing cases, there were alibis that needed checking, interviews still to come, a murder weapon yet to be discovered, and that interesting possibility that Shambley might have brokered art works of questionable provenance.

Someone with a knowledge of art had been specialed in from another division to go through the papers Shambley had left behind in the Breul House attic, and Eberstadt and Peters were given the task of backtracking on Shambley's last few days as well as taking a quick poll of how his colleagues at the New York Center for the Fine Arts had felt about him.

Leaving Mick Cluett with a stack of paperwork, Sigrid left with Albee and Lowry to do another sweep through the Erich Breul House.

Elliott Buntrock leaned on a chair beside the desk like a great blue heron with a potential mullet in view and cocked his head at Miss Ruffton, who was a peppermint cane this morning in red wool suit and white sweater.

"Looking for something?" he asked. "Looking for what, for God's sake? And how would he know if he'd found it, as much *stuff* as this house has crammed into it?"

Miss Ruffton shrugged imperturbably as the electronic typewriter continued to hum beneath her capable brown fingers. "You asked me why he was acting so smug Wednesday night. I've told you what I thought. Now do you want me to finish with these dimensions or don't you?"

"I do, I do!" he assured her. With a stilt-legged gait, he picked his way across the marbled hall and through the gallery arch to glare at a picture of dead swans and market vegetables which had caught his eye high on the far wall. A passionate proponent of the latest in art, he considered "pre-art" anything exhibited in America before the Armory Show of 1913.

Kitsch, kitsch, and more kitsch, he thought, contemptuously dismissing the Babbages and Vedders. And all this recent fuss over Sargent. One of the few silver linings to the gloom of curating a show in this place would be the sheer pleasure of dismantling these stiff rows of gilt-framed horrors and seeing them stacked somewhere else for the duration. And he wouldn't limit himself to stripping the walls either. Much of the furniture and all of the tacky gewgaws would have to go as well.

Dressed today in black jeans and a fuzzy black turtleneck, he stood in the exact center of the long gallery with his arms akimbo, the tip of his right boot *en pointe* while the heel lay flat against his inner left ankle, and his bony chin angled forward and up as he considered the size and shape of the long room. This was his favorite contemplative pose and one that a clever photographer had once captured in black and white for a whimsical *New York Today* article entitled

"City Birds." To Buntrock's secret gratification, she'd captioned his portrait *Curatoris Hotissimus (Genus Arbiter Artem)*.

As he mentally cleared the gallery and the long drawing room beyond of their resident pictures and superfluous adornments, Elliott Buntrock had to admit that it was actually a rather lovely space, nicely proportioned, architecturally interesting. Maybe wrong for Nauman's work—the restrained sensuality of his middle period, in particular, would be killed by these ornate moldings and marble pilasters. But a Blinky Palermo or a Joseph Beuys, one of those early late-postmoderns—what a curatorial coup it would be to show *them* here!

It was hard, though, to keep his mind firmly fixed on an exhibition some twelve to fourteen months in the future when murder had occurred less than forty-eight hours in the past. He had barely known Shambley. Rumor tagged him a ravenous careerist, all the more dangerous for the depth of his expertise and the thoroughness of his scholarship.

Zig-zags of fashion being what they were these days, Dr. Roger Shambley would probably have had his fifteen minutes of fame, would have found a way to titillate the gliterati's gadfly interest in turn-of-the-century American art, perhaps even, Buntrock thought with a twist of the self-deprecation that made him so attractive to his friends, have been featured in a whimsical *New York Today* photograph of his own.

The telephone out on the secretary's desk trilled softly. He was too far away to hear her words, but Buntrock saw her answer, listen briefly, then hang up.

Hope Ruffton thought Shambley had spent the last couple of weeks looking for something specific and that his cocky arrogance Wednesday night meant that he'd found it. "He wanted the inventory sheets and he was rude about Dr. Peake's ability to recognize authentic work," Miss Ruffton had said.

Buntrock had cocked his bony head at that statement, wondering how much Peake's present secretary knew about the Friedinger brouhaha when Peake wrongly deaccessioned some pieces that later turned out to be authentic after all. And not only authentic, but valuable. No malfeasance had been charged, merely simple stupidity, which, in the art world, could be almost as damaging as a suspended jail sentence.

Innocent though Miss Ruffton's interpretation of Shambley's insinuations might be, Peake and several volunteer docents were even now up in the attic with the same set of inventory sheets that Shambley had used, trying to duplicate the dead man's discovery, if discovery it had been. They were aided by the strong back of that simple-minded janitor as they shifted trunks and furniture around the big attic.

"Taking that list and checking it twice," Buntrock whistled half under his breath as he ambled from the gallery into the drawing room, and from the drawing room back out into the great hall with its opulent Christmas tree. "Gonna find out if naughty Shambley took something nice."

Fully indulging his momentary mood of postmodern grand funk, he ignored the disapproving glance of an elderly docent who guarded the entrance against casual visitors. The Breul House was unofficially closed today except for a group of art students, who had booked a tour for this date several weeks ago and were due in this afternoon from a woman's college in Raleigh. Buntrock looked around for Hope Ruffton and found her desk unexpectedly vacant.

"Miss Ruffton went up to tell Dr. Peake that the police are coming back this morning," said the guardian of the gate.

"Very good," said Buntrock. "I'll just carry on."

Continuing his casual whistling, he circled the mannequin that stood below the curve of the marble balustrade. That masculine figure was still dressed in heavy winter garments suitable for a brisk morning constitutional and his blank face still tilted up toward the female figure on the landing as if he were being instructed to pick up a quart of milk and a pound of lard on his way home. Smiling at his own drollery, Buntrock ducked through the doorway under the main stairs.

Let Peake explore the high pikes, he thought; surely there was a reason Shambley had died down in the basement. He remembered that when he and Francesca Leeds discussed logistics Wednesday night, she'd murmured something about storage racks in the basement and Peake had said more would have to be built because old Kimmelshue, the previous director, had filled most of them with earlier culls from the collection.

The mind boggled. If Kimmelshue had kept in William Carver Ewing and Everett Winstanley, what in God's name had he weeded out?

At the foot of the stairs, Buntrock paused to get his bearings. Abruptly remembering that this was also presumably where Roger Shambley had got his, he moved away from the landing.

To his left stretched caverns measureless to man in the form of a large Victorian kitchen; to his right, beyond a sort of minikitchen adjunct, was a closed door. Buntrock automatically tried the closed door first.

The lights were on inside and as soon as he stuck his bony head around the door frame, all the colors and patterns of Victorian excessiveness beat upon his optic nerves and clamored for simultaneous attention. The rooms upstairs were models of harmonic taste and order compared to the chaotic anarchy of texture and design down here, with its clash of different cultures. Clinging to the door for support, Buntrock's disbelieving eyes traveled from the syrupy farmyard scene over the fireplace, to the modern art posters thumbtacked to turkey red walls, down to the layered scraps of patterned carpet on the floor.

When he spotted the twentieth-century tape deck and portable television beside the nineteenth-century pasha's mattress heaped high with silken cushions, the bizarre incongruities were explained. The janitor's room, he realized.

Of course. Lo, the wonder of innocence!

With a shudder that lent his fuzzy sweater a fleeting resemblance to ruffled egret feathers, he pulled the door closed again and moved stilt-leggedly through the kitchen in search of old Kimmelshue's storage racks.

Upon entering the Breul House, Elaine Albee immediately headed for the attic to see if that art expert on loan from another police division had learned anything pertinent from Shambley's papers, while Sigrid and Jim Lowry invited Benjamin Peake into his own office for yet a further discussion of his relationship to Dr. Shambley.

"Relations were quite minimal," said Peake. The dark

suit he wore was impeccably tailored and a turquoise tie made his blue eyes seem even bluer as he leaned back in his chair with careless grace. "Jacob Munson put him up for trustee back in the fall. I think it was his first trusteeship and, just between us, it went to his head. Got it in mind that he was actually supposed to *do* something."

He laughed deprecatingly. "Well, of course, he was supposed to be using some of Erich Breul's papers to document the price of original art works in the 1880's, here and abroad, for his new book."

"Yesterday, Miss Ruffton implied that Dr. Shambley's research had taken a different course," Sigrid said, "and, if you recall,"—she paused to consult her notes—"you referred to him as a 'busybody and a snoop with delusions of mental superiority.' Would you explain that, please?"

Peake smiled. "I thought I just did. Roger Shambley seemed to think he ought to be a new broom, clean sweep, stir up the old cobwebs."

"And did he?" asked Sigrid. "Stir up old cobwebs?"

"He tried," but he was going about it all wrong. Now I don't know how much you've heard about the Breul House's financial difficulties but I assume Nauman's told you—"

"I prefer to hear your version," Sigrid interrupted coldly.

"Certainly." Peake glanced at Detective Lowry, but that young man had his eyes firmly fixed on the notebook on his knee and his face was a careful blank.

"Well, then, perhaps we should start with the terms of Erich Breul's will," Peake said and pedantically described shrinking endowments, capital outlays, and dwindling grants. "It's simply a matter of attracting more money, but Shambley had begun to act as if the fault lay with the staff. As if we weren't already doing everything humanly possible."

"Why did he ask for a set of your inventory sheets?" Sigrid asked.

Peake shrugged petulantly.

"We've heard that he made certain insinuations."

"Look," said Peake defensively. "I don't give a damn what you've heard. That was an honest mistake. There was nothing unethical or illegal about what happened when I was at the Friedinger. I was caught in the middle up there. And you can go through our inventory sheets with a fine-tooth comb. There hasn't been a straight pin deaccessioned from the Breul House since I took over. If anything's missing, it didn't happen on my watch."

Cautiously, because this was the first mention she'd heard of the skeleton in Peake's closet, Sigrid said, "It would help us clarify things if we had your side of what actually did happen at the Friedinger."

Giving his side took Benjamin Peake almost fifteen minutes, an intense quarter hour in which he used nearly every technical and aesthetic art term Sigrid had ever heard in order to rationalize his actions. When he ran out of breath, she mentally translated his account into layman's terms for her own benefit.

According to Peake, the Friedinger had been presented with an opportunity to acquire an important Ingres. In order to finance the purchase, it was decided to sell (in museum talk "deaccession") some of the lesser pictures, including two cataloged "School of Zurbarán." Consequently, the pictures were sent to auction and sold, and a month or so later, the new owner jubilantly announced that his hunch had paid off: exhaustive scientific and aesthetic analysis conclusively proved that the pictures were not merely "School of Zurbarán" but authentic works by Zurbarán himself.

In view of the soaring values for that artist's work after the Met's splashy Zurbarán show, the two pictures were now worth more than the Ingres they were sold to help purchase.

Peake's immediate superior was technically responsible for approving the deaccessioning of any of the Friedinger's holdings, so public ridicule fell heaviest on him; but since the action had been based on Dr. Benjamin Peake's supposedly expert recommendation, Peake's resignation was also accepted. Very unfair, Peake claimed, since he was pressured from above to find things to sell and had relied on the advice of subordinates who claimed to know more about the Spanish master than he had.

From the way Peake glossed over certain details, Sigrid gathered that there had also been allegations of impropriety concerning other, lesser pictures which had been deaccessioned and sold through private galleries, but nothing quite as spectacular as the Zurbaráns.

Once more Sigrid remembered Shambley's cock-of-the-walk attitude Wednesday night, the electricity in his big homely face, the pointed look he had given Peake when he learned that she was a police officer.

"Robbery, may one hope?" he'd asked. "How appropriate." He had also informed her that publicity came in many forms.

Publicity, Sigrid wondered, or notoriety?

Her flint gray eyes rested on Benjamin Peake as she considered what he'd just told them about the Friedinger in the light of Shambley's insinuations.

Peake stirred uneasily behind his gleaming desk, unable to meet her gaze, and Lowry, who'd endured that unblinking basilisk stare more than once himself, felt a small twinge of sympathy for the man.

At last Sigrid dropped her eyes and turned through her notebook for yesterday's interviews. "We've been told that you and Miss Kohn had a later confrontation with Dr. Shambley in the library, a confrontation overheard by Mr. Munson."

"Our conversation was hardly a confrontation," Peake protested with a nervous laugh. "It was only artsy hypothetical cocktail-party nonsense."

"What was his hypothesis?" asked Sigrid.

"I'm afraid I really don't remember."

Sigrid let it pass for the moment. "You stated that you left here Wednesday night around eight-forty?"

"That's correct," Peake said, relaxing a little. "Mrs. B— that is, Mrs. Beardsley—volunteered to stay and lock up after the caterers had gone. There was no need for both of us to stay."

"Where was Dr. Shambley when you left?"

The director shrugged. "So far as I knew, in the attic."

"Alive and unharmed?"

Peake looked at her sharply. "Certainly! That's right, isn't it? I mean, he died much later in the evening, didn't he?" He appealed to Jim Lowry for confirmation.

"The medical examiner's office says sometime between eight and eleven-fifteen," Lowry told him.

"Well, there you are," Peake told Sigrid. "You saw him go upstairs around eight, didn't you?"

"He could have come down again before you left," she said mildly.

"Ask Mrs. Beardsley. She'll tell you."

Sigrid nodded. "What did you do after you left here?"

"Went home," he said promptly. "It'd been a long day."

"Can anyone verify that?"

Peake hesitated. "No." He started to amplify and then stopped himself. "No," he repeated.

Before Sigrid or Jim Lowry could push him further on that point, there was a brisk knock on the office door and Mrs. Beardsley opened it without waiting for a reply.

"Dr. Peake!" she exclaimed, her long face full of self-important concern. "Lieutenant Harald! Someone's stolen Mr. Breul's gold-handled walking stick!"

Oblivious to the stares and speculations of curious docents, the tall mannequin stood as serenely as ever in the well of the curving marble balustrade, his face turned toward the female figure on the landing above his head. He still wore a gray pearl stickpin in his tie, but there was no longer a cane in his gloved hand.

"Who saw it last?" Sigrid asked.

Four other docents had gathered and they murmured together uncertainly, but Mrs. Beardsley said firmly, "I definitely remember that I brushed a piece of lint from the collar of his overcoat on Wednesday night and straightened his stick at the same time."

"When Wednesday night?"

"Shortly before the party began. You know how one will look around one's house to make certain everything's in proper order before one's guests arrive?"

Her unconscious choice of words revealed her deep involvement in the place, thought Sigrid. She recalled glancing at the two mannequins during the party and again yesterday, but she couldn't have sworn to the presence of a walking stick. She glanced at Jim Lowry, who shook his head.

"Call Guidry and see if the mannequin's in any of the pictures she took of the hall yesterday," Sigrid directed. Then, turning back to Mrs. Beardsley and Dr. Peake, she said, "Describe the cane, please."

Peake looked blank. "It was black, I believe, and had a solid gold knob."

"And was about so long," said Mrs. Beardsley, stretching out her plump hand a few feet from the floor.

"Would you like to read how it's listed on the inventory?" asked Miss Ruffton, efficient as ever.

She handed Sigrid a stapled sheaf of papers labeled *Second Floor*. A subdivision under *Bedroom & Dressing Room—Erich Breul, Sr.* was *Wardrobe—Accessories*, and Miss Ruffton pointed to a numbered entry: "2.3.126. Man's ebony stick. 95 cm., two threaded knobs: (a) gold plate over solid brass, acanthus design; (b) carved ivory ball."

As Sigrid read the description aloud, Mrs. Beardsley said, "So *that's* what that ivory thing is! I didn't realize one could change the knobs. How clever."

"Gold *plated?*" Peake sounded personally affronted.

Sigrid was silent, thinking of ebony's strength and hardness. And when weighted with a solid brass knob at one end? Until they learned otherwise, Erich Breul's missing walking stick sounded like a perfect candidate for the rod that had smashed Roger Shambley's thin skull.

Lowry hung up the telephone on Hope Ruffton's desk and reported, "Guidry says she'll have to make a blowup to be sure, but she doesn't think the cane's in any of the pictures and she's got a long shot of this hall and doorway."

After telling the staff members that they were free to continue with their normal routine for the moment, Sigrid walked with Lowry over to the Christmas tree where they could confer unheard. The gas logs wouldn't be lit until just before the students from Raleigh were due to arrive, so the hearth was dark and cheerless. Someone had already plugged in the tree, however, and a hundred or more tiny electric candles sparkled in the vaulted marble hall.

"I suppose it would be too much to hope that the search team found a blood-smeared walking stick yesterday?" Sigrid asked, bending for a closer look at one of Sophie Breul's glass angels.

" 'Fraid so," Lowry said glumly. "They noticed smears on that softball bat in Grant's room, but I didn't hear anything about a cane."

Sigrid turned to cast a speculative glance at the mannequin. It stood so near the concealed door beneath the stairs. Say Shambley had gone through the door on his way to the basement, she thought. And say further that he was accompanied by someone suddenly so moved to violence that he (or she?) had grabbed for the first implement that came to hand: the mannequin's walking stick.

The scene was so vivid in her mind that she could almost see it.

The only thing she couldn't see was who had actually wielded the stick.

"Albee helped search," Sigrid remembered. She glanced at her watch. "What's keeping her upstairs? Go check, Lowry. I'm going to take another look at that basement."

As Sigrid crossed the large basement kitchen, she heard noises floating down the passageway beyond. She had thought that Pascal Grant was still up in the attic, so who—? She paused to listen and the odd sound defined itself as a whistle that rose and soared above muffled thumps even as she listened, a bouncy and rather familiar tune. As she turned a corner and saw light spilling from a doorway, she recognized Gilbert and Sullivan's "I Am the Very Model of a Modern Major-General."

With catlike tread, she stole to the door and there was Elliott Buntrock, his lips pursed in music as he slid one picture after another from a large wooden storage rack, removed its brown paper covering for a quick examination, then carelessly recovered it.

Sigrid leaned against the doorjamb, one hand in the pocket of her loose gray slacks. "Found anything interesting?"

Buntrock jumped like a startled bird, but made a quick recovery. "Nothing worth keeping," he said cheerfully. "Biggest pile of junk you ever saw."

"I thought nineteenth-century art was outside your area of expertise."

"Good art is timeless. You don't have to be an expert to recognize it. All you have to do is trust your eye."

"As Peake trusted his at the Friedinger?" she asked sardonically.

"Ben Peake couldn't tell his armpit from his—" He broke off with a laugh and undid another picture.

"What about Roger Shambley? Could he tell undoubted Raphaels from Gerard Dows and Zoffanies?"

Buntrock leaned the picture against the others, put his hands on his hips, and straightened up to give her his full attention.

"Well, well, well!" he said, cocking his head to look down at her from his full six foot two. "And here I thought Oscar was merely becoming eccentric in his old age. A policewoman who actually knows her Gilbert and Sullivan."

Sigrid shrugged. "Tarantara, tarantara," she said modestly.

"Now don't show off," he admonished.

She laughed and came over to look at the last picture he'd uncovered. It was a bathetic sickroom scene: an expiring young matron, a doctor who held her limp wrist with a hopeless air, the grief-stricken young husband being comforted by his innocent curly-haired toddler and a couple of weeping older women. There was a bronze title plate at the bottom of the picture frame but it was written in old-fashioned German script and Sigrid didn't recognize any of the words. Nor the artist's name.

"Probably part of Mrs. Breul's dowry," Buntrock hazarded. "Godawful, isn't it? Picasso painted scenes like this when he was about fifteen."

"Are all the pictures like that?"

"This is one of the better ones. Most of them are ladies, either at their spinets or spinning, or landscapes oozing with moral uplift, like the one hanging over the hearth in the janitor's room. Have you been in there?" A mock shudder shook his bony frame.

"Not yet. I keep hearing that it's an interesting experience."

"Don't bother," he advised her. "You'd find it a visual nightmare."

Buntrock watched as Sigrid pulled another picture from the rack.

"So how long've you known Oscar?" he asked.

"Since April. Do you think Shambley examined these pictures?"

He ignored her question and pounced on her answer. "April? That's when Riley Quinn was poisoned, wasn't it?"

"Yes."

"And in the process of catching his killer, you also caught one of the greats of American art?"

"Is he?"

"He must be. After all, I once called him the master of effortless complexity in an article I wrote for *The Loaded Brush*."

Sigrid pulled a picture of a snow-covered mountain from the rack. It depicted a late afternoon when the snow was cream and rose. Long purplish shadows stretched across the slopes, and the needles on a scrub pine in the foreground looked almost real. "Why? What makes a Nauman abstract a better picture than, say, this snow scene? It looks effortless enough."

Buntrock started to laugh, but something in her steady gaze stopped him. Instead, he found himself answering seriously. "Effortlessness is one thing, a breezy want of substance is quite another. True art's always been made for an elite, Lieutenant. The elite of the eye. It places visual *demands* on the viewer and it rewards with visual delights. That snow scene demands nothing. It's only meant to soothe and please or, at worst, *edify*, for God's sake.

"Nauman goes to the core of experience and makes visible the invisible. His pictures are more than the merely fungible formulations of generic abstraction, and they're never *ever* tricked-up literary sentimentality like *that* thing!"

Caught up in the heat of his rhetoric, Buntrock flung out a hand and thumped the offending canvas scornfully. "Nauman's pictures deal with critical masses and elemental tensions. His best are like the moment before the big bang!"

Buntrock's arms fluttered erratically as he searched for the precise phrases, as if he expected to pluck them from the walls of this cramped storage room. "It's as simple as that, Lieutenant: Oscar Nauman makes the invisible visible. Either you see it or you don't."

He flexed his bony shoulders and assumed his contemplative pose. "Nauman was the quintessential risk-taker in his time," he said with a valedictory air. "He may no longer be on the cutting edge. The parade does move on. Modernism gives way to postmodernism as day yields to night. But his place within the matrix of aesthetic discourse is secure. And do you know what triggers his genius?"

A bit dazed, Sigrid shook her head.

"He knows what to leave out!" Buntrock said triumphantly. "He is the master of elision."

She had listened without comment and when he finished, she formally inclined her head—rather an interesting head now that he looked at it closely—and said, "Thank you."

Buntrock was intrigued. She was almost like a Nauman painting herself: a seemingly simple surface that concealed unexpected complexities. "Don't you like his work?" he asked.

"It's not that. There are things that I can like that I don't understand. That's not the point. It's the things I don't like that I *want* to like that give me trouble."

"Ah," he smiled. "I think we're not talking about art anymore."

There were hurried footsteps out in the kitchen and Lowry's voice called, "Lieutenant?"

"Down here," she answered.

"Could you come up? They've found something interesting in Shambley's briefcase."

Sigrid turned to go. "If *you* find something interesting among these pictures, you will share it, won't you?"

In a series of jerky movements, Buntrock threw up his hand and touched his thumb to his little finger. "Scout's honor."

A faint expression of surprise flitted across his bony face. "Oddly enough, I mean it," he said and rearranged his long fingers to form a Vulcan peace sign.

Oddly enough, thought Sigrid as she joined Lowry and started up to the attic, she believed him.

In the attic, Elaine Albee introduced Sigrid to Dr. Ridgway of Special Services, who immediately described how she'd found Roger Shambley's briefcase under the desk. "Inside were the usual papers, and this."

"This" was a heavily-embroidered pink satin envelope lined in white satin and tied with red cords. It measured approximately twelve inches long by seven inches wide and although it was now empty, they could clearly see that it had once held something that had left an imprint upon the lining, a rectangular object that measured ten by four and a half inches.

"Any guesses?" asked Sigrid.

"Could be anything," said Dr. Ridgway. "A diary, letters, maybe even a jeweler's box. I haven't come across anything here that fits though."

In fact, she reported, she'd been through everything on Shambley's makeshift desk and had found nothing untoward among the murdered man's papers. "It seems to be the usual scholarly hodgepodge of raw data right now," she said, running her fingers through her extravagantly curly hair. "He had cross-referenced Erich Breul's bills of sale for various pictures with what similar pictures were fetching in the U.S. at the time. He wanted to check what a middleman like Bernard Berenson got for some of the pictures he represented as compared with dealing directly with the owners as Breul did, for instance."

"You've matched those bills with the actual pictures?" asked Sigrid.

"Only on the inventory sheets," said Dr. Ridgway. "Shambley seems to have already checked them off himself, but I'll redo it, if you like."

"I would."

"Okey-doke," she said.

As Dr. Ridgway returned to her work, Sigrid drew Albee and Lowry aside and asked Albee about yesterday's search of the basement. Lowry had already told her about the missing cane and the policewoman shook her blond head. "We were specifically looking for anything that could have been used as a weapon so I'm sure it would have been noticed if it was there."

Sigrid looked around the large attic and saw that Mrs. Beardsley had rejoined the docents who, with Pascal Grant's help, were still laboriously checking the attic's inventory. She carried the embroidered satin envelope over to the senior docent.

"Have you ever seen this?" she asked.

"It's Sophie Breul's glove case," said Mrs. Beardsley. "How did it get up here?"

"Where's it normally kept?"

"Why, down in her dressing room, of course."

She led the three police detectives down to the second floor, to the dressing room that connected Sophie Breul's bedroom to her bath. With barely a moment's hesitation,

Mrs. Beardsley went straight to a chest of drawers and opened the second one from the top.

A whiff of lavender drifted toward them as a puzzled Mrs. Beardsley said, "But *here's* her glove case!" and drew out an identical envelope of embroidered pink satin. "I didn't realize there were two."

Sigrid reached for the new one. Inside were several pairs of kid gloves, all imbued with the scent of lavender. She lifted the first satin case to her nose. It was musty and smelled like an old bookstore.

"This didn't come from that drawer," she told the others.

Matt Eberstadt and Bernie Peters finished up at the New York Center for the Fine Arts before noon, grabbed a sandwich in a nearby bar and grill on York Avenue, then headed over to the Guggenheim Museum on Fifth Avenue.

Afternoon sunlight shone through the barebranched trees of Central Park and slanted on the luxurious apartment buildings on the other side of Fifth Avenue. There, uniformed and gloved doormen opened their doors for residents who emerged from double-parked limos with piles of beautifully gift-wrapped boxes. Santa's little helpers.

"What're you getting Frances for Christmas?" asked Bernie as they passed a nursemaid wheeling an enormous English pram, its tiny occupant buried in a nest of pale pink wool.

'I don't know. Maybe a fancy new robe."

"Didn't you give her that last year?"

"Did I?" They paused for a light and the big detective sighed. "Yeah, I guess I did. I don't know. What're you giving Pam?"

"Diamond earrings," Bernie said happily. "Soon as she got pregnant this last time, I just knew it was going to be a boy, so I put them on lay-away and I've been paying on 'em all along. Next week, they're mine."

"Diamond earrings! God, I hope Frances doesn't hear about them," groaned Eberstadt as they neared the Guggenheim.

Their visit to the Fine Arts Center had added little to their knowledge of the dead man. Tuesday had been the last day of classes until after New Year's, so the only colleagues to be found were some instructors who hadn't turned in all their grade cards.

Dr. Aaron Prawn, head of nineteenth-century American studies, summed up Shambley's career through tightly clenched, pipe-gripping teeth. "Ambitious. Perhaps a bit too. But definitely on his way. A bit of a barracuda? Yes. But one has to be to get anywhere in the nineteenth century these days. Junior colleagues loathed him, of course. Goes with the territory."

Unfortunately, Shambley had been on leave this semester so no one had seen enough of him lately to report on his last movements. The divisional secretary remembered that he'd been in Wednesday morning to pick up his mail, but she'd been busy with a student and had merely exchanged season's greetings with him.

They were luckier at the Guggenheim. Among the scraps of paper in Shambley's pocket had been a receipt from the museum's bookstore and one of the clerks there remembered Dr. Shambley.

"I was in one of his classes at the center last spring," said the girl, a part-time student who worked full-time during the holiday break. "I knew who he was, but he didn't remember me."

Eberstadt found that hard to believe. His own hairline had receded to the very top of his head where wiry gray curls ran from ear to ear across his bald dome like some sort of steel-wool tiara. He was half bald by necessity; the girl must have paid a hair stylist good money to clip that same area of her platinum white hair to a flat half-inch stubble while the rest of her hair fell to her shoulders.

How many of Shambley's students could have had hairstyles like that?

Bernie Peters was more interested in whether she was wearing a bra beneath that turquoise silk shirt. "Do you remember what he bought?"

She looked at the sales slip and nodded. "Two Léger posters at fourteen ninety-eight each, plus tax."

"Léger?" asked Eberstadt, stumbling over the pronunciation. He pulled out his notebook and pen. "How do you spell that?"

"Fernand Léger," she said, spelling it over her silky

shoulder as she led them through aisles crowded with artsy souvenirs and art books—some of them heavy enough to give you a hernia, thought Peters—to the Guggenheim's collection of posters. "French painter. I thought it was kinda strange that Dr. Shambley would want cubist posters when his field's nineteenth-century American. Of course, he *did* want early Léger and not the mechanistic things from the twenties and thirties that he's really famous for."

She pulled a plastic-wrapped cylinder from one of the bins. "This is it. I'm not supposed to open it though unless you're going to buy it."

There was a small reproduction of the artwork on the outer wrap. To the detectives' untutored eyes, it looked like a picture of two faceless mannequins constructed of Dixie cups and paper chains. They were drawn in heavy black lines. One figure was red, the other bright blue.

"He bought *two* of 'em, just alike?" asked Peters.

"Uh-huh. He got kinda pissed when we didn't have two different examples from that period. It was like maybe he was doing his Christmas shopping or something. But then he kinda laughed and said it didn't matter; that he'd just hang one of them upside down. Weird, right?"

Her loose shirt fell forward as she bent to return the poster to its proper slot, but Bernie Peters noted with only half his attention that she wasn't wearing a bra. The other half recalled the search he'd helped conduct yesterday.

"I think I saw those posters in the Breul House basement," he told Matt Eberstadt.

Seated across the library table from the two female detectives, Mrs. Beardsley had grown weary of the way one had to say the same thing three different ways before the police moved on to a different question. Beyond the possibility of a trunk in the attic, she had no idea where Sophie Breul's extra glove case had spent the last seventy years, nor what that satin case had held, and she had told them so. At length.

This was rapidly becoming, she decided, a delicate question of etiquette.

On the one hand, police officers were, by their very calling, of a lower socioeconomic order. One must, of course, treat everyone—even one's inferiors—graciously although a certain distance was allowed.

On the other hand, Miss Harald—*Lieutenant* Harald, Mrs. Beardsley reminded herself sharply—had been met on a social level and she was, after all, a personal friend of the famous Oscar Nauman.

So one could hardly snub her with impunity. Not even when she made gross insinuations.

"Now *really*, Lieutenant Harald!" She stiffened in one of the leather library chairs. "I don't know with whom you've been gossiping, nor do I wish to be told. Under the circumstances, I suppose everyone becomes suspect. Nevertheless, it's simply ridiculous to suppose that one—that *I*—would resort to violence."

"But Dr. Shambley did fill a vacancy on the board of trustees which you had hoped for, didn't he?" asked the lieutenant.

"I let it be known that my name could be considered," Mrs. Beardsley admitted. "One is seldom chosen immediately. It is quite usual to be passed over the first time or two."

"Will you ask to be considered now that the seat is vacant again?"

"Certainly," said Mrs. Beardsley firmly. "Why not? Everyone knows my devotion to the Erich Breul House is unchanged."

"Yes," agreed the police officer. "We've heard that you're often the first to arrive in the mornings and the last to leave at night."

Her tone sounded more conciliatory and Mrs. Beardsley unbent slightly. "One can't claim too much credit for that when it's merely a matter of walking across the square."

"And you do have a key," mused Lieutenant Harald.

Mrs. Beardsley looked at her sharply. Such a drab-looking person today in that dark gray suit and no makeup. On Wednesday night she'd been rather striking in an odd way. Or was that only because one linked her with Oscar Nauman?

"Tell us again, please, what you did after the others left?" she was saying.

Mrs. Beardsley sighed and went through it all again: how all the guests had gone by eight-thirty, how she'd sent Dr.

Peake on his way, how she'd overseen the caterers' departure. She did not try to describe how she loved being alone in this house, how she could almost imagine herself a member of the Breul family, or how alive they often seemed to her. Never mind if Pascal were in the basement or Dr. Shambley in the attic. As long as one didn't see or hear either man, one's imagination was free to see and hear the Breuls.

"No," she said again. "I didn't go down to the basement because I thought Pascal was still out; and Dr. Shambley had made it quite clear more than once that he did not wish to be disturbed when he was working. I ascertained that all the candles were snuffed, then I unplugged the Christmas tree and went home without seeing either of them."

Mrs. Beardsley braced herself for more questions on that point. Instead, the Harald woman sat back in her chair with a trousered knee propped against the edge of the gleaming table top and asked, "Why did Pascal Grant dislike Dr. Shambley? Some of the other docents have told us that he avoided the man whenever he could."

"Dr. Shambley made him feel uncomfortable," she hedged.

"How?"

Protective maternalism surged in Mrs. Beardsley's breast. "Pascal Grant couldn't hurt a fly," she told them. "Surely you see what a sweet gentle boy he is."

"That's why we don't understand what he had against Dr. Shambley," said the younger detective, smiling at her across the table.

Mrs. Beardsley approved of the blonde's tailored femininity, her coral lipstick and modest eye shadow, her Cuban-heeled boots and brown tweed jacket worn over beige-and-peach plaid slacks. So much easier to talk to, she decided. And really, weren't policewomen rather like nurses? One could discuss anything with nurses.

"It was painful for Pascal to speak of it," she said, bravely ignoring her own embarrassment, "but it seems there was a man at the sheltered workshop where Pascal trained when he was twelve or thirteen." Her voice lowered. "A *sexual deviant*, if you please! And he took advantage of his position to force himself on some of the boys."

"And Shambley—?" asked Detective Albee.

"Oh, no!" exclaimed Mrs. Beardsley. "When I realized how uneasy Pascal was, I cross-questioned him quite thoroughly, for I would have denounced Dr. Shambley had that been the case. No, no, I'm quite certain he did not approach the boy; but evidently, there was some physical resemblance between Dr. Shambley and the man who had once abused him. Something about their eyes, I believe. Poor Pascal. His reactions are emotional rather than reasoned. But you must surely see from this that his instinct is to retreat, not attack. He simply avoided the man whenever he could."

The other two women were silent for a moment, then, absently tapping her pen against her knee, Lieutenant Harald said, "Getting back to your own movements, Mrs. Beardsley: you saw no one after the caterers left?"

"Not even," added the other officer, "Mr. Thorvaldsen when you crossed the square?"

"I'm sorry, Detective Albee, but when it's that cold, one doesn't linger outside to pass the time of night with casual pedestrians whom one may or may not know. I simply didn't notice."

"So when you say that you went home shortly after nine and didn't return," said Lieutenant Harald, "there's no one who can confirm your statement?"

Mrs. Beardsley inclined her head. "No one."

Once more they asked her about seeing Thorvaldsen leave the house at midnight and then they thanked her for her cooperation.

One with a completely clear conscience did not register relief at having done one's civic duty, Mrs. Beardsley reminded herself, and walked with quiet dignity from the library.

Sigrid glanced at Albee. "Well?"

"Oh yes," said Elaine. "I could see her deciding that he was a bug that needed to be squashed and just doing it. But only if he was hurting her precious house. And he wasn't."

"That we're aware of," Sigrid told her. "We still don't know where he found that glove case or what he took from it."

"And we may never know," sighed Jim Lowry, returning from the attic at the end of her comments. "The docents say there're more than a dozen trunks and wardrobe boxes full of

Mrs. Breul's stuff up there and the inventory sheets don't go into much detail. Just 'apparel' or 'accessories.' And the case might have held a jeweler's box, but they don't think there was anything valuable still in it because all her good stuff was sold when the house became a museum."

Out in the long marble hall, there was a sudden babble and chatter of excited female voices and through the open doorway, they saw a bearded professor with a harried air as he shepherded his charges past the ticket table.

The art students from that Raleigh women's college, no doubt.

"This might be a good time to break for lunch," Sigrid said judiciously.

At the gallery off Fifth Avenue, Rick Evans mechanically set another painting on the easel, readjusted the two flood-lights on either side, took a reading with his light meter, then focused his camera and clicked the shutter.

When he first came up from Louisiana in September, it had surprised Rick how strongly the art world depended upon slides. The first cuts in competitions were made by judges who looked at slides; grants were awarded, exhibitions decided, magazine articles written—all very often on the basis of photographic slides alone.

His grandfather spoke of this trend with contempt, but Hester Kohn merely shrugged her shoulders and asked Jacob to consider the cost of shipping fees, not to mention wear and tear on the artwork itself.

Rick set another large oil painting upon the easel. It looked a little topheavy in composition, all those purple slashes at the top and empty unprimed canvas at the bottom, and he checked the label on the back of the stretcher to make sure it was right side up. He no longer tried to understand each picture. All he cared about now was making a technically perfect slide.

In the beginning, his grandfather had brought a chair into the workroom and sat beside him during these photography sessions and talked to him of each work's artistic strengths and weaknesses. "See how the dynamic forces play against the static, Richard," he would say, his words lightly accented with German and the smell of peppermint. Or, "Why do you

161

think the artist placed the yellow so low? Why to buoy up the work and to relieve the dark weights above. Contraction and relaxation, *ja?*"

And if the picture touched a chord, he would go off and rummage through books in his office and come back with illustrations that showed how Vermeer, though a Dutch realist of the seventeenth century, used the same approach; or how Picasso or Matisse had dealt with the same matter differently.

"Do you see?" he would ask. "Do you see?"

"Yes, sir," Rick would reply, wanting to please. And he *did* see when his grandfather pointed it out, but when asked to critique a fresh picture, he always muddled it.

"Mein Gott!" Jacob had exploded one day. "The simplest thing in art and you do not see it!"

That day, he had grabbed Rick by the shoulders and fiercely swung him around to glare into his face. As their eyes locked, the anger had drained from the old man's face.

"Paul's eyes you have," he'd said sadly, "and in you they are blind."

After that, his grandfather continued to sit in on some of the sessions and to instruct as before, but the intensity had gone out of his lectures and he had stopped asking Rick to describe what he saw.

He could stand that, Rick thought, as he snapped the last exposure on the roll of film. What he couldn't stand was the look that had appeared on his grandfather's face when he and Hester had returned from the police station yesterday.

"You were there last night?" Grandfather had asked in a dreadful voice. "In that *Schwachsinnigen's* bedroom?"

"In his *room*," Rick had said, reddening under the scornful implication. "And he's not an idiot, Grandfather, just a little slow. We're friends."

"Ja, sure," his grandfather muttered wearily, and suddenly he looked his full eighty-two years, old and frail and utterly defeated by what fate had given him. He had touched the picture of his dead son, then sighed and laid it face down among the papers on his desk, swivelled in his chair, and turned his back on Rick. "Tell Hester to come in," he'd said stonily.

He would stay until after Christmas, Rick thought, sliding a fresh roll of film into his camera. After that, he would go home and let his mother pull strings for a job with one of the state bureaus in Baton Rouge. He would walk back-country lanes again and take pictures of pelicans and swamps for wildlife calendars or tourist brochures.

And he would stop trying to deny to himself that he was what he was.

Next to a rent-controlled apartment, Zeki's, just west of Third Avenue, was that most precious urban find: an as-yet-undiscovered, good, midtown restaurant. Even Gael Greene was unaware of its existence. Although celebrities often lunched there, knowing they would not be bothered by gawkers, New Yorkers came for the Turco-Croatian cuisine of delicately spiced lamb and indescribable breads, not to see and be seen.

It was nearly two and the outer room was still crowded as Oscar Nauman passed through. He spoke to a couple of friends, nodded when the barman said, "The usual?" and found Jacob Munson at his corner table in the back.

"Sorry I'm late," he said, sliding into the chair opposite his dealer. "The garage down the block was full. You order yet?"

"*Nein.*"

Oscar looked across the snowy white tablecloth and frowned. "You feeling all right, Jacob?"

The old man shrugged. He looked shrunken today. His face was nearly as gray as his thin beard and his brown eyes had lost their elfin luster.

"Not coming down with something, are you?"

"It's nothing. A little cough. What are you? Nurse Nightingale?" Jacob asked irritably.

"That's better," Oscar grinned.

But as his glass of ale arrived accompanied by a martini, the grin faded; and when the waiter had taken their orders, he said, "What's with the drink? I thought your doctors said—"

"They did. Lean closer, my friend, and I'll tell you a secret: Jacob Munson is not going to live forever. Tomorrow he could drop dead; so why not a martini today?"

He lifted the glass and sipped long.

"Then who'll take care of my show?" Oscar asked lightly, determined to shake Jacob out of this puzzling mood.

"Elliott Buntrock will." He caught the waiter's eye across the room and signaled for another martini. "There's a Buntrock under every rock," he said bitterly.

"Jacob?"

"You're a lucky man, Oscar Nauman. When *you* go, you will leave behind you good work that will honor your name."

"What the hell's going on?" Oscar demanded.

Munson sank back in his chair. "Roger Shambley was killed Wednesday night." He twirled the stem of his empty martini glass back and forth between his wrinkled fingers.

The silence stretched between them. "So?" Oscar finally asked.

"So your lady policeman thinks my grandson Richard did it."

"*What?*"

"She's wrong, though. You will tell her this?"

"Jacob—"

"It was Benjamin or Hester or maybe both together," he said heavily. "I don't know."

As the waiter brought their food and another martini, a paroxysm of coughing shook his small frame and Oscar told the waiter to take away the drink and bring his friend club soda with a twist of lemon.

When Jacob was breathing normally again, Oscar said, "Talk to me, Jacob. What's happening at the gallery?"

"You know what Horace Kohn and I tried to build." Jacob stared at the savory chicken stew before him. "We never said *caveat emptor*. Never! What we sold we backed with our reputation and for better than a half century, Kohn and Munson Gallery has been trusted. Never a stain on its name."

"Yes."

"You remember Paul?" he asked abruptly.

Oscar remembered Paul Munson as a handsome, sweet-natured kid. Bright enough, but not the flaming meteor he'd become to his father since his plane had crashed sixteen years ago. Odd to think Paul would be nearing forty if he'd lived. "Rick reminds me of Paul," he said as he buttered a piece of crusty bread. "Same eyes."

"They are nothing alike," said Jacob, anger in every syllable. "Paul had an eye for art."

"I meant in looks," Oscar said mildly. "Same shade of brown. Besides, aren't you being a little hard on the boy? He's only been here three months."

"Three months, three years, it wouldn't matter. It's his mother's fault. Suzanne turned her back on the gallery."

Oscar occasionally had trouble remembering that there were two older daughters, Suzanne and Marta. He vaguely recalled that both had earned doctorates in other fields, but Jacob almost never spoke of them. All his pride had been bound up in Paul and when Paul died, Paul's friend, Benjamin Peake, had become his surrogate.

"She made him a photographer. She made him a—" His voice dropped lower—"a *Schwulen*."

"A what?" asked Oscar.

The old man's face twisted with shame. "A faggot."

Oscar ate silently. There were so many different sexual proclivities in the art world that he was surprised that Jacob could still be homophobic. Or did tolerance stop when it touched him personally?

"He was with the janitor that night. In his bedroom."

"So what's the big deal, Jacob? It's not the end of the world."

"Only the end of my line," Munson said bleakly, drawing his fork through the sauce on his plate. "The end of the gallery."

"Oh, come on, Jacob. If the boy doesn't work out, Hester will keep things going. And it's crazy to think she had anything to do with Shambley's death. When Sigrid and I left Wednesday night, you and Hester were planning to share a cab back uptown."

"She got out at East Forty-ninth. Said she was meeting someone at the Waldorf. Yesterday when she came back from the police station, I made her tell me who. It was Benjamin."

Oscar stopped cutting his lamb and started to wonder if Jacob were experiencing the beginnings of senility. His voice was gentle as he asked if Jacob had forgotten that Hester and Ben—?

The art dealer interrupted with an impatient wave of his hand. "It wasn't about sex, Oscar. Wednesday night, Roger

Shambley accused Hester and Ben of passing a piece of forged art through the gallery. Yesterday I asked Hester of this. First she said no; then she said there was no way Shambley could have proved it."

He pushed his plate aside with most of the food still untasted. "She may be a woman, but she isn't that stupid, Oscar. Shambley wouldn't have had to prove anything. A gallery's word is its bond and if that word becomes a lie—"

He gave a palms-up gesture of hopelessness.

Sigrid arrived at the gallery with Jim Lowry shortly before three. The soft-voiced receptionist informed them that Mr. Munson had not returned from lunch and that Miss Kohn, as they could see, was busy at the moment but if they wished to wait?

"Yes," Sigrid said and Lowry took a guide sheet from a nearby stand.

"Notebook pages?" he asked sotto voce. "Twenty-three hundred a sheet? Who's Ardù Screnii? Never heard of him."

Stunned, he began to circle the airy showroom, peering first at each matted and framed drawing and then at the price Kohn and Munson was asking for it.

Sigrid pretended to study the drawings, but she chose those that would give her reflected views of Hester Kohn, presently occupied with two customers. The dealer wore hot pink today and a chunky pearl-and-gold necklace.

From the conversation which floated through the nearly deserted gallery, Sigrid soon gathered that the man and woman were a husband and wife from Chicago and that he was a commodities trader. She also gathered that they expected more from an Ardù Screnii drawing than pure aesthetics.

"Of course," she heard Hester Kohn say, "you have to realize that the bottom line is whether you *like* a work. I mean *I* can't tell you something's going to go up."

"Yes," the man nodded sagely. "Yes, I know that but—"

"I can tell you how some things *have* gone up, but if you're buying one of these purely as an investment—"

"Oh, no, we *love* art," said his wife, a dark, intense woman in her early thirties. "Of course, my decorator's going to *kill* me. My taste is changing. Growing. I was always so—um—traditional, you know? And here I came home with

166

this huge modern canvas and my decorator wouldn't let me hang it in the bedroom. Said it defeminized the room—it's all traditional antiques, you know? So I put it in storage. But if I get one of these Screniis, then it's coming out of storage. I don't care *what* the decorator says."

She was struck by a sudden thought. "I forget. Screnii was Albanian, wasn't he?"

"Bulgarian," said Hester Kohn.

"Oh, good!" said the woman. "I've always believed in the Bulgarians."

By way of the reflective glass, Sigrid saw Hester Kohn smile politely.

The man chuckled, even though he wasn't quite ready to give up the practical. "Still, a Screnii *is* an investment, isn't it? And a lot more fun than soybean futures."

There was a contemplative pause.

"Not that I'd even know what a soybean looked like if I came face to face with one."

"Aren't they like guyva peas?" the woman asked brightly.

Hester Kohn shrugged.

"Ah well," said the man, "what does it matter as long as I can buy low and sell them high? Now, I think my wife and I are going to have to do a little commodities trading on which one of these Screniis we want."

Ardù Screnii had died in the midsixties, Sigrid knew. He had eked out a living by teaching an occasional course at Vanderlyn, and Nauman was a little bitter that Screnii had never been able to sell one of his major paintings for more than fifteen hundred dollars during his lifetime.

As the two clients left, promising to come back the next day with their minds made up, Sigrid and Lowry approached Jacob Munson's partner. "Miss Kohn? We have a few more questions."

Hester Kohn sighed. "Yes. I was afraid you might."

When Matt Eberstadt and Bernie Peters returned to the Breul House, the docent on duty at the door informed them that Detective Albee could be found in the attic.

"Where's Lowry and the lieutenant?" they asked after they'd climbed to the top of the house and heard about Dr.

Ridgway's discovery of the satin glove case in Shambley's briefcase.

"Over at Kohn and Munson Gallery," Elaine told them. "What's up?"

The two women listened intently as the men described how Shambley had bought two posters at the Guggenheim on Wednesday morning, posters Bernie Peters thought he remembered seeing.

"I haven't found any references to Léger in his papers," said Dr. Ridgway, "but I'll keep it in mind."

The three detectives went down the back stairs, avoiding a group of twenty or so young women to whom Mrs. Beardsley was giving a tour of the house.

In the basement, it took Peters a few minutes to regain his bearings, but he soon went to a box in one of the storage rooms and plucked out the rolled posters, still in their plastic wrap. He slit the paper on one of them and backrolled it so that it would hang straight.

It was just as the small illustration promised: a cubist depiction of two figures that, except for their vivid red and blue colors, reminded Elaine of the Tin Woodman in *The Wizard of Oz*.

They carried it upstairs and asked Dr. Peake if he or Miss Ruffton could speculate why Shambley should buy two identical Léger posters and stash them in the basement.

"Beats me," Peaks said, lounging indolently in a chair beside Hope Ruffton's desk. "Léger's too modern. Clean out of Shambley's period. Most of his work was done in the thirties and forties. He died in the midfifties, if I'm not mistaken."

His secretary was equally puzzled. "This looks familiar though. Now where have I seen—?"

The young janitor passed near by on his way down to the basement and he gave them a shy smile as he skirted the mannequin dressed like Erich Breul.

"Just a minute, Grant," Dr. Peake said. "These detectives found some posters Dr. Shambley left in the basement. Do you know anything about them?"

Pascal Grant looked at the cubist poster and his face lit up. "I have pictures like that in my room."

"What?" exclaimed Peake, coming erect in his chair.

"*That's* where I saw it," said Hope Ruffton. "Those posters Dr. Kimmelshue had. The ones you told Pascal he could put up."

"Oh," said Peake. "Those."

He sank back lazily into the chair again. "For a minute there—" He smiled to himself at the absurdity of what he'd almost thought for a minute.

"Want to see them?" Pascal Grant asked the detectives. Golden curls spilled over his fair brow and he brushed them back as he looked up at Eberstadt with a friendly air.

"Naw, that's okay," said Peters.

He and Eberstadt started toward the front door. "We've still got a couple of alibis to check. Drop you somewhere, Lainey?"

"No, thanks," she said, remembering Mrs. Beardsley's explanation of Grant's unease with Shambley. "One thing though—when you were checking out Shambley's background, did anybody happen to mention if he was gay?"

"No," Eberstadt said slowly, "but when we asked if he was living with anybody . . . remember, Bern?"

"Yeah. They said no. That Shambley couldn't decide if he was AC or DC, so he wound up being no-C."

"Interesting," Albee said. "I'll hang on to the poster and bring it back to the office later. The lieutenant'll probably want to see it."

By the time Matt Eberstadt and Bernie Peters reached the sidewalk, Elaine Albee was already halfway down the basement steps to talk with Pascal Grant again.

"I suppose I may as well tell you," said Hester Kohn. "If I don't, Jacob will."

She led them to the small sitting room she'd created around the window corner of the large office that had once belonged to her father, and Sigrid and Jim Lowry were invited to take the blue-and-turquoise chairs opposite her plum-colored love seat. The upholstery seemed impregnated with her gardenia perfume, which, coupled with a pair of highly chromatic red and orange abstract pictures on dark green walls, gave the office a sensual, subtropical atmosphere.

She loosened her pink jacket button by button and a

languid smile touched her lips when she saw how Lowry's eyes followed her fingers.

As an interested spectator, Sigrid usually enjoyed watching other women operate, but it was almost three and she didn't feel like wasting more time. "What would Mr. Munson tell us?" she asked crisply.

"That he didn't drop me at my apartment near Lincoln Center Wednesday night," Hester replied. "I met Ben Peake after the party. We talked about an hour, then I went home. Alone. And before you ask, no, I can't prove it."

"You'd just seen Dr. Peake," said Sigrid. "Why did you meet again so quickly?"

"There were private things we needed to discuss."

"Things Shambley had brought up in the library?" Sigrid asked.

"Ben told you about that?"

"He gave us his version—" Sigrid said carefully.

Hester Kohn interrupted with a ladylike snort and ran her fingers through her short black hair. "I'll bet he did!"

"—and no doubt, Mr. Munson will have his own version of what he overheard Shambley say," Sigrid finished smoothly.

The seductive languor disappeared from Hester Kohn's body and she became wary and all business. "There's no need to question Jacob about this."

"No?"

"No." She cast a speculative woman-to-woman look at Sigrid. "Oscar and Jacob have been friends for as long as I can remember. Even since I was a little girl. Oscar could tell you how much this gallery means to Jacob."

Her words contained a not-too-subtle threat, which Sigrid coldly ignored. "And not to you, too?"

"Of course to me," she answered impatiently. "But it's different for Jacob. He's old-world with a capital O and that means things like honor and *mano*. It's going to kill him to admit there's ever been anything a little under-the-table with the gallery, but to admit it to a *woman*—!"

Her hazel eyes slid over Jim Lowry's muscular body. "He might talk to you," she told him.

"He's chauvinistic?" asked Sigrid.

"He's a gentleman," Hester Kohn corrected with a grimace. "That means women are ladies. You charm ladies, you

170

marry them, you have sons with them, but you don't take them too seriously or admit them to power. Look around the gallery, Lieutenant Harald: We represent two female artists. And both of them are dead.

"Jacob used to think that Paul and I would marry and Paul would run the business. Then when Paul died, and it was too late to rope in Suzanne or Marta, he half adopted Ben Peake and tried to make *him* marry me. Thank God, *my* father had a different attitude about daughters."

Bright spots of angry red flamed in her cheeks. "Every time I really think about it, I feel like screaming. Men made the tax laws, Ben Peake and his friend came up with the figures, and all I did was sign the appraisal, but who does Jacob blame the most? Three guesses."

"I'm sorry, Miss Kohn," said Jim Lowry, "but I don't understand. Tax laws? Appraisal?"

"It's absolutely routine," she said defensively. "Anyhow, half the galleries in the country are doing it, too."

Abruptly, it dawned on her that neither detective knew what she was talking about. "I thought you said Ben told you."

"I said he gave us his version," Sigrid reminded her. "And we still have to hear Mr. Munson's."

With an angry sigh, Hester Kohn sank back into the cushions of the plum love seat. "This happened a couple of years ago while Ben was still at the Friedinger. One of the patrons there was in serious need of a large tax write-off. Basically, the way it works is that a donor gives a nonprofit institution a work of art. An independent appraiser estimates how much the work is worth and the donor then lists that figure in his tax returns as a charitable donation."

"The appraiser—you, in fact—inflates the figure?" Sigrid asked.

Hester Kohn nodded.

"But why would the institution that's getting the artwork go along with that?" asked Lowry.

"What do they care?" Her voice was cynical. "They're getting a donation they otherwise wouldn't and next time, it might be a really important gift. Besides, if they decide to deaccess, it's usually worth at least half the appraised price."

Sigrid looked at her inquiringly. "Only in this particular case—"

"In this particular case, it was worth about a quarter of what Jacob Munson said it was worth."

"You signed his name to an appraisal statement?" asked Lowry.

"He's the judge of artistic merit in this firm," Hester Kohn said with bitterness. "I'm just the business and financial side. My signature wouldn't have sufficed. See, Jacob isn't asked to appraise things very often because everyone in the business knows he's so goddamned straight-arrow. He might come down on the high side, but his figures are usually within two or three thousand of the true value. The tax people know this, too, and they haven't bothered to question him in years."

"So how much kickback did you and Peake get?" Sigrid asked.

"I had a pool put in at my house in Riverhead," she said candidly. "I believe Ben bought a car."

"And Shambley threatened to blow the whistle on you?" asked Jim Lowry.

Hester Kohn shrugged and plucked a piece of lint from the dark purple upholstery. "Ben thought so, but I wasn't that sure. Roger Shambley was so effing devious. He never came straight out and said what he meant. It was all hypothetical and insinuating. Frankly, I thought he was sounding us out to see if we'd go along with some scheme he was hatching."

"Oh?"

She nodded. "Sort of as if he were saying he knew we'd bent the rules once before and got away with it and maybe we could do something for him. Or with him. It wasn't clear."

"So you and Dr. Peake didn't feel threatened by him?"

"Not really. *I* certainly didn't." She crossed her shapely legs and adjusted the hem of her short pink skirt. "Neither of us wanted Jacob to find out about that tax scam, of course, but it's not like we were going to go to jail or anything if it came out. Appraisals are subjective judgments, right?"

"You forged your partner's name," Lowry pointed out.

"Ye-s," she admitted, "but if it came right down to it,

172

Jacob would claim it was his signature. He'd rather hush it up and say he'd made an honest mistake than let the gallery's name be dragged through the mud with one of its owners up for forgery."

She stood up and walked over to stare through the window at the buildings of midtown Manhattan. A wave of gardenia reached the two police officers as she turned back to face them. "Look, I know I've been rather flip about it and Jacob really does make me furious at times, but go easy on him about what Ben and I did, okay? He's an old man and the gallery's all he has now."

"What about his grandson?" asked Lowry.

She shook her dark head. "He's a sweet kid, but Richard Evans doesn't know art from artichokes. Wouldn't surprise me if he went home for Christmas and never came back."

"One moment, *acushla*," said Francesca Leeds from her suite high in the Hotel Maintenon. She removed a heavy gold-and-amber earring and then returned the receiver to her ear. When she spoke, her voice was like warm melted syrup, so pleased was she to hear Oscar's voice on her private line again.

"It's been almost two years. How many people did you have to call to find my number?"

"None," Nauman replied, making her pulse quicken before he added, "It was on the gallery's Rolodex."

"Beast! You're supposed to say it's engraved on your heart."

He laughed. "Elliott Buntrock just called. He wants to have a short meeting here at the gallery tomorrow afternoon. 'Talk turkey' was how he put it. Think you and Thorvaldsen can make it?"

Francesca looked at the calendar on her desk. "What time?"

"Three-thirty?"

"Four would probably be better for Søren."

"Four it is. See you."

"Ta."

She replaced the receiver and tilted her head so that the thick coppery hair fell away from her face as she slipped the stud of her earring through the lobe again.

The nice thing about parting amicably with someone, she thought, was the free and easy friendship that often continued afterwards. The rotten thing was when the parting was more amicable on *his* part than yours. And the rottenest thing of all was feeling jealous of your replacement when you knew that if you both walked into a room together, nine out of ten wouldn't notice her.

Except that the tenth man would be Oscar.

The interview with Jacob Munson was as difficult as Hester Kohn had predicted.

It began awkwardly when Sigrid, trailed by Jim Lowry, walked down the hall to Munson's open door and found Nauman there, too, just hanging up the phone on Munson's desk. At least Nauman hadn't said anything flippant when she introduced Lowry, and Lowry gave no sign that the artist's name had special curiosity value for him. But when Nauman heaved his tall frame up from the chair, Munson had underlined the personal aspects of the case by insisting that Oscar should stay.

"You *und* Miss Harald, you have no secrets."

"Just the same, I'll wait outside," Nauman said and took himself off.

Munson sat behind his cluttered desk looking like an elderly elf who'd just learned that Santa's workshop was jobbing out its toy production to Korea. He went through the motions of hospitality halfheartedly, offering them drinks, which they refused, and peppermints, which Lowry accepted.

"Wow!" he breathed as the pungent minty oils peppered his tastebuds.

Normally, Jacob Munson would have beamed and offered to share the name of the candy company who imported these particular mints, but not today.

His answers to their questions were monosyllabic. Yes, he and Hester had left the party together. Yes, Hester had gotten out near the Waldorf and he'd gone on home alone. No, there was no one to say what time he'd arrived at his upper West Side apartment, nor could he say when his grandson had come home, as he'd already gone to sleep.

"Besides," he added, twisting the thin strands of his gray

beard, "you know where my grandson was and what he was doing."

"Yes," Sigrid said wryly, thinking how busy Rick Evans and Pascal Grant must have been hauling Shambley's body all over the Breul House.

Munson adamantly refused to discuss what he'd heard Shambley say to Benjamin Peake or Hester Kohn. "You must ask them," he said, drawing his small frame up with Prussian militancy.

"Miss Kohn has told us about the forgery," Sigrid said.

She had thought it was impossible for his stiff shoulders to become more rigid. She was wrong.

"Then you know all there is to know," he said. "I will not discuss this further without my lawyer."

And from that position, he would not budge.

Nauman was still waiting out in the main part of the gallery when they emerged from Munson's office, and he looked up expectantly.

Sigrid glanced at her watch, saw it was almost five-thirty, and sent Lowry to the phone to check in.

"Ready to call it a day?" Nauman asked.

"Unless something's come up," she said.

They watched while Lowry spoke to headquarters on the receptionist's telephone.

"Nothing that can't wait till tomorrow," he reported.

As she dismissed him, she caught the look of hesitation on his face. "Something, Lowry?"

"Just that—well, ma'am, Eberstadt and Peters have checked out all the stories we've been given."

"Yes?"

Her gray eyes were like granite and Jim Lowry lost his nerve. Let someone else ask her, he decided.

"Nothing, ma'am. See you tomorrow?"

"What was that about?" asked Nauman, watching the younger man step out into the cold night air and pull his collar up to his ears.

"I think he wanted to ask if you had a proper alibi." She smiled as she put on her heavy coat and gloves.

"Me?"

"I suppose I'll have to go on record tomorrow and tell them that all your movements are accounted for."

"*All* my movements?" he laughed.

"Well," she emended. "Enough of them anyhow."

They browsed through a few stores along Fifth Avenue, not really intent on Christmas shopping, but open to felicitous suggestions. Sigrid bought a new camera case for her mother. Anne Harald was a photojournalist and her old case had banged around all over the world so much that it was ratty and frayed.

A cutlery store reminded her that Roman Tramegra had recently grumbled about his need for proper boning knives. She found a set with wicked-looking thin blades.

Nauman saw a delicate cloisonné pin enameled to look like a zebra swallowtail and immediately bought it for Jill Gill, an entomologist friend who raised butterflies.

By seven their arms were laden with packages, so they walked to the garage west of Fifth Avenue, dumped everything into Nauman's bright yellow sports car, and drove down to the Village for an early dinner.

Over their wine, Nauman brought up Shambley's death and Jacob Munson's reaction. "He told me everything," he said.

Sigrid held up a warning hand. "Nauman, wait. You do understand that anything you tell me—"

"—can and will be used against me?"

"Yes."

"I know. It's okay."

"I know he's your friend," Sigrid said. "And he seemed like a nice old man Wednesday night, but he wasn't very cooperative today."

"You might be uncooperative, too, if you were eighty-two years old and just found out that your only grandson's gay and your business partner's a partner in murder."

"What?"

In short terse sentences, Nauman repeated the things Munson had said at lunch.

"He doesn't have trouble hearing, does he?" Sigrid asked.

"No, why?"

"I just wonder if he misheard what Shambley actually

176

said. Hester Kohn didn't pass forged paintings; she forged Munson's name on an inflated appraisal so someone could get a big tax write-off for a charitable donation."

Sigrid swirled the red wine in her glass thoughtfully. "Or at least that's what she told me this afternoon."

As the waiter brought their check, she glanced at him in sudden mischief. "By the way, Nauman, what are fungible formulations?"

"Oh, God!" he groaned. "Buntrock's been at you, hasn't he?"

She smiled.

"Elliott's all right as far as this new breed of *helden*-curators goes," Nauman warned, "but aesthetic sensibility is only a meager compensation for the lost wonder of innocence."

In his office at the Erich Breul House, Benjamin Peake sat in the deepest concentration he'd attained since assuming the directorship. Shambley's Léger poster had touched off such an unlikely train of speculation. All the same . . .

He found one of the house's brochures and scanned it, but the information he sought wasn't there; so he swivelled in his chair and took down a copy of *Erich Breul—The Man and His Dream*, that fulsome confection whipped up by the first director sixty years ago. He'd skimmed through it when he took over the house, but it seemed like so much puffery that he'd never bothered to read it carefully. He thought he recalled, though, that the book held a chronology.

Yes, there it was. Erich Breul's life laid out from birth to death. And there was Erich Jr.'s birth in 1890, his graduation from Harvard in 1911, his departure for Europe in the fall, and his fatal accident in 1912.

Peake turned to the section on Erich Jr., but it was sketchy and, except when describing the youth's Christmas visit with his Fürst relatives in Zurich, lacked necessary details. He had arrived in Paris in September of 1912 and died in mid-November.

1912, thought Peake. Just before the Armory Show of 1913 blasted the American art world into modernism. Picasso was in Paris then. Picasso, Braque, Derain, Matisse, Juan Gris and, yes, Léger, too. All the iconographers of modern art poised on the brink of greatness. Nothing in the book suggested that the dutiful young Erich Jr. harbored bohemian leanings, but he was his father's son so surely it wasn't outside the realm of possibility that he'd seen an avant-garde exhibit in that brief two and a half months before he'd died.

Could that be why Shambley had ransacked the house? wondered Peake. Was that why he wanted the inventory sheets and why he accused me of being too lazy to see what was under my nose?

Peake replaced the book and turned back to the inventory file. Not the attic, he thought, the basement. He ran his finger down the itemized list and there it was: "*B.8.4. Steamer trunk. EB Jr.*"

It was really too absurd, he told himself as he got up and walked through the inner door to the butler's pantry. On the other hand, Shambley *had* been on his way down to the basement Wednesday night, right?

Twenty minutes later, he closed Erich Jr.'s trunk in disappointment and brushed the dust of the storage room from his trousers knees. *Well, you knew it was a million-to-one chance*, he thought wryly.

Nauman drove Sigrid home and when they carried in her packages, they found Roman Tramegra positively radiant.

"Come and have some champagne!" he boomed. "I ordered a case for the holidays, but we must celebrate *tonight!* I did it, I *did* it, *I DID IT!*"

"Did what?" asked Sigrid, disentangling herself from his effusive bear hug.

"Sold my very first *mystery* story!" He waved a long blue check at them. "*Mostly Male* magazine bought it—five hundred dollars for fifteen hundred words. What a glorious, *glorious* Christmas present!"

He shepherded them into the living room and filled two more crystal champagne flutes from a bottle that was by now nearly empty. On the table beside the ice bucket was an ornate and expensive-looking arrangement of blue spruce and white poinsettias.

"You *are* celebrating," said Sigrid, clinking glasses with Roman and Nauman.

"Oh, those aren't *my* flowers," Roman told her. He

fumbled through the greenery and located a small white envelope. "They came for you."

Puzzled, Sigrid opened the envelope and found one of Søren Thorvaldsen's personal cards. On the reverse, he'd written, *Please accept my apology*.

"Thorvaldsen?" Nauman growled, shamelessly reading the card over her shoulder. "What'd he do? Why's he apologizing?"

In creating from his own home "A Museum for the edification and pleasure of the public so long as its stones shall endure," it was Mr. Breul's sincerest wish that he might refute those cynics who hold that life has become squalid and ignoble in this new century of ours. Instead of the weariness and boredom induced by more formal museums, visitors to the Erich Breul House are charmed and refreshed by the air of peace and dignity and beauty throughout. Every room invites, every room welcomes the visitor as if he were a cherished guest in the private home of a gentleman of taste and discrimination.

And so he is!

Erich Breul—the Man and His Dream, privately published 1924 by The Friends and Trustees of the Erich Breul House

IX

The day dawned gray and freezing and Sigrid's mood wasn't helped when she reached work and found that Mick Cluett had called in sick again and that Bernie Peters was taking a half day of personal leave.

"One of his daughters fell off her bike this morning and knocked out a tooth," said Matt Eberstadt.

"I thought kids watched cartoons on Saturday morning," Sigrid said, diverted by the thought that the Peters children might be part of a healthier national trend.

"Their TV's in the shop," said Eberstadt.

He described to her what they had learned of Shambley at the New York Center for the Fine Arts and how they'd found the posters he'd purchased at the Guggenheim.

"Matt thinks Shambley might have been bisexual," Elaine Albee chimed in. "And you remember what Mrs. Beardsley said about Pascal Grant feeling uneasy around him?"

Sigrid nodded.

"Well, I decided to have another talk with him. He's got all these reproductions of modern art up in his room—says they remind him of jazz. He's really a nice kid and so good-looking, I wondered if maybe Shambley was trying to lay him."

"And instead of flowers and candy," jeered Lowry, "he brought art posters?"

"It could fit," Eberstadt contended. "Shambley told the girl at the museum shop that he could hang one of the posters upside down and it wouldn't matter. Sounds like he was talking about somebody two cards shy of a full deck, doesn't it?"

181

"A love triangle?" Sigrid said. "Is that what this is all about?"

"Rick Evans said he and Grant were together when Shambley was killed," Lowry nodded judiciously. "And we know what *that* means, but what if Evans knew Shambley was going to try to cut him out and—"

"No way," said Elaine Albee. "Oh, there might be some latent adolescent stirrings, but Pascal Grant says he and Evans were listening to jazz and I don't think he was lying. I don't think he knows *how* to lie. He's such an innocent. Look how quickly he fell apart when we questioned him Thursday."

"You may be right about Grant," Sigrid said, "but Jacob Munson is convinced that his grandson's gay and he's not happy about it."

She repeated the pertinent things Nauman had told her about his lunch conversation with Munson.

"Oh," said Lowry. "So that's what he meant when he said we knew where his grandson was when Shambley was killed. And what he was doing there. I thought he was talking about them moving the body."

"I did, too," Sigrid admitted.

"I asked Grant about that again," said Elaine. "He said Rick didn't want anyone to know he'd been spending the night there because, and I quote, 'People would say it was sex.' "

"And you're sure that it wasn't?" asked Sigrid.

"Not on Pascal Grant's part," Elaine said sturdily.

They moved on to the possibility that Shambley might have tried to blackmail Hester Kohn and Benjamin Peake over Munson's forged signature on an inflated tax appraisal, and considered that relatively minor crime in the light of Munson's assertion that they had instead authenticated and sold forged paintings through the gallery.

It was hard to know which was true, they decided, when everyone who'd known Dr. Roger Shambley agreed that he insinuated, suggested, and implied but very seldom said precisely what was on his mind.

"Look at Thorvaldsen," said Lowry. "A self-made millionaire like him, he has to be sharp, right? Yet, according to him, he went sneaking back to the Breul House Wednesday night and cooled his heels for an hour, all because Shambley offered him a deal. At least he *thinks* Shambley offered him a deal. But he doesn't know what and he doesn't know why."

"Or so he says," Sigrid cautioned. "Don't forget he also hinted to me that Shambley might have caused him a problem if he stirred up trouble right now. He might have gone there expecting to pay blackmail for all we know."

"We checked out Lady Francesca Leeds' story," Matt Eberstadt reported. "And Hope Ruffton's. Both were where they said they were unless a lot of people are lying."

"That takes care of all the checkable stories," said Lowry in his capacity as recorder for this case. He read from his notes, "Of the people there that night, the ones in the clear are Leeds, Ruffton, the Hymans, the Herzogs, Buntrock, that pianist and the caterer's people. Munson, Hester Kohn, Thorvaldsen, Mrs. Beardsley, Peake and Mr. Reinicke can't prove their movements."

Lowry paused and Sigrid said dryly, "You've omitted two people: Oscar Nauman and me."

There was an interested silence.

"For the record, Professor Nauman and I were together during the pertinent time period. If it becomes necessary, I can supply corroboration. Question?"

"No, ma'am," said Lowry.

"Moving on then." Sigrid laid out the blowups Paula Guidry had made of the great hall on Thursday morning. "As you see, the mannequin's cane is missing. Until we have reason to think otherwise, I think it's safe to say that's our weapon. So who's place is worth a search warrant?" she asked them.

They went down Lowry's list, from Jacob Munson—"That old guy?" said Elaine. "He may be old, but he's feisty," Jim told her—to Winston Reinicke. "Lainey has a theory about him," Jim grinned.

Lieutenant Harald was not amused by their byplay. This was where she missed Tillie the most. By this time, he would have provided a timetable with each suspect's movements and motives carefully logged.

"Has anyone heard when Tildon's expected back?" she asked abruptly.

"They keep saying sometime after New Year's," said Matt. "I talked to him two days ago. He was supposed to go to Chuckie's Christmas play last night, his first time out except to see the doctor."

Elaine Albee gave Sigrid a sympathetic glance. "You miss him, too, right?"

"I miss his thoroughness," she answered, with a pointed look at Eberstadt. "I don't suppose Peters remembered that he was supposed to interview the Zajdowicz woman this morning."

Eberstadt patted his pockets. "Yeah, he gave me the name of the place and the time. I wrote it down."

He found the scrap of paper. "Haven Rock on Staten Island. They told him to come after eleven o'clock. That's when the priest finishes confession. Want me to go?"

"No," Sigrid decided. "I'll do it."

The rest home was in West New Brighton on the north side of Staten Island, so she took the ferry instead of driving to Brooklyn and crossing the Verrazano Bridge.

The sun had burned through the earlier clouds and even on this cold December day, the open rear deck of the boat held many camera-snapping tourists. The ferry still offered one of the most spectacular views of lower Manhattan; and although city lights made it much more breathtaking after dark, daytime wasn't bad either, thought Sigrid. She stood close to a bulkhead out of the wind and watched the stretch of choppy gray water widen between boat and shore.

As the ferry moved out into upper New York Bay, away from the shelter of land, several passengers who had burbled about the smell of clean salty air abruptly fled inside to search for hot coffee.

Most cameras were pointed back toward the twin towers of the World Trade Center, but a few telephoto lenses were already focussing on the Statue of Liberty off to starboard. No one was paying attention to Brooklyn on the port side of the boat and Sigrid was stirred by a sudden memory of her Great-uncle Lars. He had often treated her and cousin Hilda to rides on the ferry that once ran between Brooklyn and Staten Island before the Verrazano Bridge was built.

If Albee or Lowry had been with her, she would have kept silent; but since she was alone, Sigrid turned to a nearby tourist and pointed toward what would still be the country's fourth largest city if it hadn't been annexed back in 1898.

"Brooklyn," she said.

The Japanese woman smiled and nodded and a couple of her friends looked up at the thin woman with inquiring faces.

"That tall building is the Williamsburgh Bank," she said, imitating Great-uncle Lars's clear didactic tone. "Five hundred and twelve feet high. The tallest four-sided clock in the world."

"Ah!" said the women. They spoke to their men. A ripple went through the group, then fourteen cameras swung toward Brooklyn.

When Sigrid was escorted to the correct building, a priest was still working his way down Barbara Zajdowicz's corridor, offering to hear those who wanted to confess and bestowing a quiet blessing on those who did not.

The guide with whom a receptionist at the main office had provided her was a white-haired resident, gossipy and plump and proud of his continued mobility into his ninth decade of life. As loquaciously proud of Haven Rock as if he were a majority stockholder and she a prospective customer, Mr. Hogarty described the various facilities: how residents usually began with an apartment, moved into a comfortable single room in this building when they needed medical monitoring and could no longer manage alone, and, if necessary, finished up in a medical ward for the totally bedridden.

"Me, I'm still in my own apartment," Mr. Hogarty bragged, "but a lot of my friends are over here."

"Here" was a clean-lined series of interlocking squares. The residential rooms reminded Sigrid of a solid block set down inside a square greenhouse. Each room opened onto the wide window-lined corridor, a common area hung with flowering baskets and green plants and made homey with clusters of sofas and easy chairs all along its length. It was a pleasant area and one that invited residents and their guests to sit and converse and look out at the small courtyard garden. The clear glass windows were curved to catch every ray of winter sun, and several of the people basking in the bright sunlight exchanged greetings with Sigrid's guide when they passed.

185

As they found two unoccupied easy chairs and sat down to wait for the priest to emerge from Mrs. Zajdowicz's room, Sigrid asked Mr. Hogarty if he knew the woman personally.

"Barb? Oh sure. See, she used to be in me and the wife's canasta club, but then she had that first little stroke a couple of years ago and got religion and—" He broke off and gave a humorous shrug. "I mean, we're all religious here. Me and the wife, that's why we picked Haven Rock. Because it's run by the Catholics, see? But when Barb had her stroke, even though it wasn't a big one—well, you probably know how that can turn things on in your head that weren't there before?"

Sigrid murmured noncommittally.

"Well, that's what happened with Barb, see? So she quit playing cards and started going to confession every week and to mass every time it was offered. The wife said to me it was like being on retreat with the nuns, the way she talked; but the wife and her'd been friends ever since the beginning—we moved into our place the same week Barb did, see, in the next apartment—and they stayed friends. The wife passed away last spring and Barb kept having more of these little strokes, see, so they moved her over here. I try to get over a couple of times a week even though she don't know me half the time."

He shook his head. "Bad when the mind goes. The wife, she was sharp as a tack right up to the day she passed away. Beat me in cribbage that very morning, but Barb— Well, you'll see. Although she's usually pretty good after Father Francis has been here. You a friend of the family or something?"

"I didn't think she had any family," Sigrid parried.

"Well, she didn't, far as I ever heard. Me and the wife, we both come from big families but we only had the two boys. Dick, he's the oldest, he lives right here on Staten Island. Got grandchildren of his own, even. But not Barb. She just had a sister and brother and none of 'em ever had kids. None that lived anyhow."

Sigrid's mental antennae quivered. "She had children that died?"

"Not her. She told the wife her and her husband couldn't have babies. But seems like the sister had a couple of miscarriages or the baby died getting born or some female trouble like that. She never talked about it till after her first stroke. Least that's when the wife first mentioned it to me, see, 'cause Barb'd get on these crying jags about those poor innocent babies and how the sister oughtn't to have done it." He lowered his voice. "See, the sister wasn't married."

The door of Barbara Zajdowicz's room opened and a middle-aged priest came out.

"How's she doing today, Father?" asked Mr. Hogarty as he and Sigrid walked toward him.

"Much as usual, Harry," said the priest. He smiled and nodded at others across the corridor, but did not break his progress to the next room.

As Sigrid started to follow Mr. Hogarty into his friend's room, she saw an unwanted sight. At the far end of the corridor, a tall red-headed man in sheepskin jacket and cowboy boots with a camera case slung over his shoulder paused to compare a room number on the nearest door with something scribbled on his notepad. He saw her at almost the same instant and his homely face took on the look of an excited terrier spotting its prey.

"Yo! Lieutenant Harald," he cried and loped around a passing wheelchair. William "Rusty" Guillory of the *Post*.

"Two minds with but a single thought." His free hand fumbled with the zipper on his camera case. "Didja talk to her yet? Does she know anything about the babies? What've you got for me?"

"What're you doing here, Guillory?" she stalled.

"Same as you." He took two quick pictures of her before she could protest. "Got her name off the deed and ran it by a snitch in Social Security."

Mr. Hogarty's curious face appeared in the doorway behind her and the reporter craned for a view of the interior. "Who're you?" Guillory asked.

"Hold it, Guillory," Sigrid said firmly. "You'll have to wait out here. I was just going in to interview Mrs. Zajdowicz now."

"Talk fast, huh, Lieutenant? If she's got anything good, I can still make the second edition."

Without promising, Sigrid stepped inside the room and closed the door on Rusty Guillory.

"Here she is now, Barb." Mr. Hogarty's gossipy nature was clearly piqued by the appearance of yet a second visitor for his old acquaintance.

Sigrid stretched out her hand to the woman in the wheelchair. "Mrs. Zajdowicz? I'm Lieutenant Harald of the New York City Police Department."

"Police?" breathed Mr. Hogarty.

Barbara Jurczyk Zajdowicz bore the ravages of her age and her illness. Her short straight hair was completely white, her blue eyes were faded, and the years had cut deep grooves in her gray face, but time could not efface the basic structure of her rangy frame and there was a residual impression of strength in her prominent jaw and broad brow. She wore a maroon skirt and cardigan, a white blouse that was pinned at the collar with a lovely cameo, and sturdy black lace-up oxfords. The footrests of her chair were folded up so that her feet touched the floor as she walked herself forward to give Sigrid her left hand.

Her hand was considerably larger than Sigrid's and bare of rings, except for a wide gold band that hung loosely on her fourth finger, trapped forever by the enlarged knuckle. Her right hand held a rosary and lay curled in her lap in what Sigrid recognized as stroke-induced weakness; and when she spoke, her words were so slurred that it was difficult to understand.

"She says did Angelika send you?" interpreted Mr. Hogarty, who'd had more practice. "That's her sister."

"I know," said Sigrid. "No, Mrs. Zajdowicz. I came because a trunk was found in the attic of your old house a few days ago. Can you remember? Do you know anything about it?"

The old woman looked at Sigrid for a long moment, then made a gesture with her left hand. "Go 'way, Harry," she said thickly.

"But, Barb—" he protested, his face dropping.

Again came that dismissive shooing wave of her hand. "Out."

Sigrid detained him for a moment as he neared the door. "There's a reporter out there, Mr. Hogarty. He'll probably ask you questions, try to make you to speculate about certain things which he may later twist for his own purposes. I'd caution you to choose your words carefully."

Mr. Hogarty brightened immediately and bounded through the door with such eagerness that Sigrid realized she should have saved her breath.

She sat down beside Mrs. Zajdowicz.

"Angelika?" asked the woman.

"Your sister's dead, Mrs. Zajdowicz. Like the babies."

"Ah." She closed her eyes and her rawboned fingers began to tell the beads of the rosary. A moment later, Sigrid saw tears seep from beneath those wrinkled lids.

"Mrs. Zajdowicz. Barbara," she said gently. "Were they your sister's babies?"

The old woman nodded. Her eyes opened. "Sister. Sorry. So sorry, Sister. Father . . . bless me, Father, for she has sinned—" She crossed herself with her left hand and her words became unintelligible.

"Who sinned, Barbara?" Sigrid asked urgently. "Angelika? What happened to Angelika's babies?"

"Died," Barbara Zajdowicz said, enunciating as clearly as she could. "Wrong . . . but we . . . couldn't let . . . anyone know. Gregor. He kill her."

"Your brother Gregor killed the babies?"

Mrs. Zajdowicz twitched her rosary beads impatiently. "No. Gregor. Such shame . . . on family. We said . . . woman troubles. Gregor . . . stayed downstairs."

"You're saying Gregor would have killed Angelika if he'd known she was pregnant? So you kept it from him? How?"

"She . . . fat like me."

Too much newsprint had been devoted to stories of large women suddenly surprised to find themselves giving birth for Sigrid to doubt that a sister built like Mrs. Zajdowicz could have gotten away with illicit pregnancy.

"Who was the father?" Sigrid asked. "Was it your husband? Karol?"

"Karol . . . he cried . . . babies for you, he said. But every time . . . died."

Her words were still badly slurred, but Sigrid was becoming used to her speech patterns.

"How did the babies die, Barbara?"

"Sin . . . she sinned . . . Karol . . ."

"Did Angelika kill her own babies?" Sigrid asked.

"They should been . . . *mine!* Not . . . Angelika's." Her rheumy blue eyes glared out at Sigrid, then they filled with tears. "Poor . . . little babies. So little. The shame . . . Sister—"

She held out her rosary to Sigrid. "Pray me, Sister," she pleaded and Sigrid wasn't sure if Mrs. Zajdowicz had confused her with Angelika or a nun, since she was dressed today in navy slacks and a boxy black jacket.

"Who put those babies in the attic?" Sigrid asked. "You or Angelika?"

"Pray me, Sister," Mrs. Zajdowicz wept. "Pray me."

Sigrid looked around helplessly, then saw the call bell on the wall beside the woman's bed. She went over and pushed it. While she waited, she took a shiny white card from her purse and gently pressed it against Barbara's fingers; first the left hand, then her curled right hand. After the card was carefully tucked into her notebook, she sat holding the sobbing woman's hands until the nurse came.

"What's going on?" said Rusty Guillory, when Sigrid emerged. He had managed a couple of hasty pictures of the distrait Barbara Zajdowicz before the nurse closed the door again. "Didja give her a heart attack or something?"

A small crowd had gathered in that section of the corridor and as Sigrid's eyes fell upon Mr. Hogarty, the plump little man looked embarrassed and scuttled away.

"Hey, wait a minute!" called Guillory. "We didn't finish."

"Yes, you did," said Sigrid. "Come on, Guillory. Give it a rest."

"Then give me a statement," he countered. "What'd she tell you?"

"She's confused and unhappy," Sigrid told him. "She's had several strokes, her speech is badly slurred and her mind's not very clear."

"But you got something out of her. I know you, Lieutenant."

Sigrid looked at the circle of avid faces that ringed them. Resigned, she said, "Put your coat on and let's go. You want to make your deadline, don't you?"

They walked through the now-buzzing corridor. "It's not much of a story and we'll probably never know what really happened," she warned.

"That's okay," Guillory said cynically. "Feel free to speculate. I'm going to."

"She and her husband lived there with her unmarried sister Angelika and their bachelor brother Gregor. She says the babies were Angelika's and that they all died at birth. That's all I could get out of her."

"Was it incest, adultery, or good old-fashioned fornication?" Guillory went right to the tabloid heart of things.

"She says her brother would have killed Angelika if he'd known she was bringing shame on the family name," Sigrid said. "I believe her."

"What about the husband?" he persisted.

"I can't go on record about that. She wasn't clear enough."

"So who killed the babies?"

"Fifty years ago, no prenatal care, unattended birth, they could have just died," said Sigrid. "Why does it always have to be murder?"

"Murder sells more papers. You know that, Lieutenant. Besides, didn't the M.E.'s office say the mummified one was born alive?"

"But there's still nothing to say it wasn't a natural death." She pushed open an outer door and walked toward the parking lot. Despite the noontime sun, the wind was biting.

"So who put them in the attic?" asked Guillory, looking at his watch. "Santa Claus?"

Sigrid shrugged. "Sorry, Guillory. I'm all out of speculations."

Rusty Guillory slung his camera case inside the car. "If I make the next ferry, I'll just squeeze in under the next deadline. Need a lift?"

"No, thanks, I have a car."

She waited until Guillory's car was out of the lot before walking back to the dark-clad man who lingered indecisively near an evergreen tree beside the gate. "Father Francis, isn't it?"

"Yes. They say you're a police officer."

"Lieutenant Harald," she said, reaching into her shoulder bag for her gold shield.

"They say you're here because of those poor baby skeletons found over in New York. That it was Barbara Zajdowicz's old house?"

191

"Yes."

The priest was perhaps half an inch shorter than she and his troubled eyes were nearly level with hers.

"Father Francis, did she ever discuss this with you? About her sister? Or the infants?"

He drew back. "I can't answer that."

"I'm not asking you to break the sanctity of confession," Sigrid assured him. "I meant outside confession."

He hesitated. "I really never talked with her until after her first stroke. You have to understand, Lieutenant. Strokes, Alzheimer's, hardening of the arteries—sometimes it's hard for them to keep in touch with reality. Or for me to know where fantasy begins. Everything's so different today. People have babies out of wedlock all the time—actresses, singers, career women—no one hides it anymore. Sometimes we forget what it was like fifty years ago."

"Some things haven't changed though, have they, Father Francis?" Sigrid said. "Things like jealousy and spite?"

"No," he sighed.

"She killed them, didn't she? They weren't born dead, no matter what she told Angelika."

"I'm sorry, Lieutenant." He moved away. "I can't talk to you about this."

Back at the office, Sigrid gave Bernie Peters the card she'd used to take Barbara Zajdowicz's fingerprints. Peters stopped talking about his daughter's newly reimplanted front tooth and developed the latents with special emphasis on the old woman's right fingers, which he then compared to the prints found on the old newspapers.

At a little after two, he brought them into Sigrid's office, where she was going over the case with Lowry's records.

"We wouldn't go to court without finding more characteristics," he said, "but see the double bifurcation at one o'clock on both of these latents and the delta at high noon?"

Sigrid looked through the magnifying glass and agreed they seemed identical. "So what do we have? Evidence that in 1938, Barbara Zajdowicz put one of the bodies in that attic trunk. A woman who's now eighty-seven, mentally confused, and confined to a wheelchair." She sighed. "Write it up as soon as you can, Peters, and we'll send it along to the DA's office. Let them decide what to do about it."

Elaine Albee and Matt Eberstadt breezed in at two-thirty from their interview with Søren Thorvaldsen, flushed and excited by a brief taste of life aboard a Caribbean cruise ship.

"It was getting ready to sail when we caught up with him—the *Sea Dancer*," Albee reported. "And he invited us to ride out into the bay and take his launch back with him. He wanted to hear how the engines ran or something."

"They'd just installed a new generator," said Eberstadt.

"So he gave us a pass and we got to stand on deck and throw confetti and streamers and listen to the band play 'Anchors Aweigh' with a reggae beat."

"They had a buffet already set out like you wouldn't believe," Eberstadt told Peters, who was listening enviously. "Frances would put me on lettuce and water till Christmas if she ever heard about the salmon and—"

"Oh, and those luscious chocolate-dipped strawberries and pineapple slices!" Albee interrupted him.

"Then we went up to the bridge—what a view!—and Thorvaldsen gave us a tour of the owner's suite, one flight down with its own private deck. Talk about luxury!"

"We saw one of Oscar Nauman's paintings," said Elaine Albee, with a wary glance at Sigrid. She wondered how the lieutenant would react if they told her that Thorvaldsen had tried to pump them about her. "It was very colorful."

"Did you happen to remember why you were there?" Sigrid asked coldly.

Eberstadt virtuously produced Thorvaldsen's typed and signed statement. "He had a stenographer come up to his suite and went through the whole evening again, but it doesn't add doodly to what he told you Thursday night."

He read from Thorvaldsen's statement, " 'Dr. Shambley implied that it could be to my benefit if I met with him again that night at the Erich Breul House. I assumed he meant to offer me the private opportunity to add something choice to my art collection. As I have occasionally bought works of art under similar circumstances, this did not strike me as an unusual request. I cannot say positively that this is what he meant. I saw no such piece of art that night, nor did I see Dr.

Shambley. I went in through the unlocked front door, waited in the library for approximately one hour, and left at midnight without seeing or speaking to anyone.' "

Sigrid had listened silently with her elbows and forearms folded flatly on the desk.

"When we first got there," said Albee, "we talked with Thorvaldsen's secretary, a Miss Kristensen. She gave us the name of a security guard who was on outside duty Wednesday night, Leon Washington. She says Washington saw Thorvaldsen enter his office building around ten-thirty and then leave again about fifteen minutes later."

"Convenient," Sigrid said.

Elaine Albee shrugged. "Who knows? We stopped by his place on our way back here and woke him up. He wasn't happy about telling us, but he says he'd stashed a coffee thermos in an empty warehouse across the street and was taking an unauthorized coffee break—"

"Coffee, my ass," Eberstadt interjected.

"—so he saw Thorvaldsen but Thorvaldsen didn't see him. And yeah, he may be lying, but he seemed too worried about the possibility of losing his job to be acting."

Matt Eberstadt nodded. "He said Miss Kristensen promised she wouldn't let it get back to Thorvaldsen and that's all he really seemed to care about."

Bernie Peters sighed. "If the guard's telling the truth, that definitely puts Thorvaldsen out."

"Whether or not he's lying, it's still hard to put Thorvaldsen there." Sigrid leaned back in her chair with her left knee braced against the edge of the desk. "Francesca Leeds said she left him between ten and ten-fifteen; Evans and Grant said they found Shambley's body between ten-fifteen and ten-thirty. Even if he had the full half hour to get back there from the restaurant four blocks away, get inside, kill Shambley and then leave by the basement door, it'd be awfully tight."

"And why would he hang around there for another hour and a half?" asked Elaine Albee.

"Looking for the picture Shambley promised him?" Lowry guessed.

"With Grant and Evans running all over the place?"

"Up and down the *back* stairs," Lowry reminded her. "They never said they were in the main rooms."

Despite Lowry's reservations, the others were willing to strike the Danish ship owner from their dwindling list.

"Reinicke, Munson, Kohn, Beardsley and Peake," said Lowry. "I move to strike Reinicke, too. I can't see him tying the dog up somewhere while he goes in and bops Shambley over the head just because the guy sneered at his taste in art. He didn't seem to be that thin-skinned."

Sigrid listened with only half an ear as they bounced theories off each other. "That's probably all it really was," she told them.

"Ma'am?" said Eberstadt.

"What Lowry said about a bop over the head. A simple whack with a weighted cane that happened to be handy. One blow, not a shower of them. If Shambley's skull had been half as thick as his skin, he might not have suffered anything other than a simple concussion."

"Unpremeditated," mused Albee.

"He was at the party for less than an hour," Sigrid said, "but in those few minutes, he insulted Reinicke and Thorvaldsen and half threatened Kohn and Peake with public disgrace. He didn't seem to care what he said; but at a party, of course, he could get away with it. Although," she added, "Thorvaldsen almost threw a punch at him."

"So," Peters said, "if he mouthed off to the wrong person—"

"Bop!" Lowry grinned.

"If we eliminate Reinicke," said Sigrid, "I could see Benjamin Peake or Hester Kohn flying off the handle. And even Mrs. Beardsley or Jacob Munson might be pushed. But why then and there?"

They didn't see her point.

"Look," she said. "Assume that Shambley says something that so enrages or scares the killer that he or she grabs up the cane and starts after him. At that point, Shambley's already passed through the door under the main staircase and started down the basement stairs when the blow lands on his head. Why? His study was in the attic. Elliott Buntrock went through the paintings stored down there and he's certain that none of them are worth much more than the canvas they're painted on. So why was Shambley going to the basement?"

"Oh, crap!" said Albee. "You don't think it's simple B and E, do you? That he left the door open for Thorvaldsen and a burglar came in? In that case, he could have been trying to get help."

"Great," Peters groaned. "So instead of four suspects, you just widened the field to half a million."

"I don't know." Eberstadt shook his head. "I've got a gut feeling about those two kids down there—Rick Evans and Pascal Grant. You sure that janitor's not stringing you along with that innocent look, Lainey?"

"And what about that empty glove case in Shambley's briefcase?" asked Lowry. "That's got to mean something, doesn't it?"

In a half-empty coffee shop on Fourth Avenue, Pascal Grant savored a forkful of fruitcake and drank from his glass of milk as he listened to Rick Evans talk about Louisiana.

"You'd love it out there in the country, Pasc. No subways or drug pushers every ten feet, no crowds of people hassling you all the time. We could go camping and fishing back in the swamps."

"Yeah, but Rick—" He carefully speared two green cherries and a piece of citron with his fork and ate them one by one.

Christmas carols drifted down from a speaker high on the wall overhead.

"Is it money? You don't need much in Louisiana," Rick said earnestly.

"Yeah, but you'll be taking pictures. What'll I do?"

"You'll help me. Or you can do what you do here. In my town, people are always griping because they can't find anybody to do chores or odd jobs. You can be a gardener. Work outdoors all day long if that's what you want."

"I'd like that," Pascal said, smiling at Rick across the scarred Formica table.

"Great!" said Rick. "Then you'll come with me next Saturday? The day after Christmas?"

Pascal's smile faded and his fork explored a raisin. "Mrs. Beardsley won't like it."

"Mrs. Beardsley doesn't own you, Pasc. You own yourself. Just like I own myself."

"But you're not a dummy," Pascal blurted, his blue eyes miserable. "People may not like me in your town. Your mother won't like me."

"Sure she will. And you'll like her. I called her last night and told her all about you and she said I could bring anybody home I wanted to. And besides, as soon as we're earning enough money, we could move into a place of our own. Maybe even out in the middle of nowhere where nobody'll bother us and you can play your jazz tapes as loud as you want."

The thought of open country was bewildering to someone who'd only known the city, but Pascal had never had a friend like this, someone who did not merely put up with him but actually seemed to like him unconditionally and as he was. The lure of that friendship and the fear of losing it were irresistible and outweighed any nebulous fears about Louisiana's alien landscape.

Pascal put out his hand and shyly touched Rick's. "Okay," he said.

When Sigrid got home at five-thirty, she was surprised to find Nauman and Elliott Buntrock wrestling with an eight-foot Christmas tree in her living room.

"I thought you had a summit meeting at the gallery," she said.

"You didn't hear what happened with Thorvaldsen?" asked Nauman, holding the tree perpendicular while Buntrock crawled around under the lower branches, tightening the screws of the stand.

"No," said Sigrid.

"One of his ships sailed today."

She nodded. "I know. Two of my detectives rode out into the bay and then came back with him in his launch."

"They should have stayed on a little longer," said Nauman. With his foot he nudged aside a large, much-taped cardboard box so that Buntrock would have more space for his flying elbows. "The Coast Guard was waiting for it just beyond the Verrazano Bridge."

"*What?*"

"They took down some of the bulkheads in the engine room and found over six million dollars in fifty- and hundred-dollar bills. A lot of them marked so they could be traced, according to the news bulletins we heard at the gallery. Drug money. On its way to buy a fresh shipment in the Caribbean."

"They confiscate speedboats and fishing boats when they're involved in drug deals," said Buntrock from somewhere beneath the tree. "Do you suppose they'll confiscate the *Sea Dancer*?"

The telephone rang out in the kitchen and Roman Tramegra stuck his head around the corner a moment later. "Ah, Sigrid, my dear. I *thought* I heard you come in. Telephone."

"Lieutenant!" came Albee's breathless voice. "Did you hear about Thorvaldsen? The feds have arrested him."

"So I just heard," said Sigrid.

"This must be what he meant when he said he went back to the Breul House because he didn't want Shambley to cause any controversy right now. Wow!"

Sigrid waited until Albee ran out of steam, then observed, "It's certainly interesting, but I don't see that it affects Shambley's murder. Do you?"

There was a moment of silence, then Albee admitted that she was probably right and rang off.

As Sigrid hung up the kitchen phone, it finally registered on her that Roman was surrounded by take-out cartons, plastic containers, and green-and-white grocery bags from Balducci's. He seemed to be arranging a long snakelike creature on his largest platter.

"What in God's name is that?" she asked.

"Smoked eel. Neapolitans *always* have eel at Christmas, but I wasn't sure what to do with a fresh one, so I got smoked. Isn't it *sumptuous*? I know it should be skinned and cut it into perfect little ovals, but then we'd lose the *effect*." He straightened the tail. "I thought a bed of red lettuce with strands of alfalfa sprouts for seaweed? What do you think?"

"Roman, are we having a party tonight?" she asked.

"A tree-trimming party. Didn't I *tell* you?"

"No," she said mildly.

"Oh, my dear!" he rumbled. "I'm *so* sorry. I was *certain*—" He curved the eel around a mound of tortellini salad and paused to consider the result. "It's such a *little* party—hardly worth calling it a party at all—but we *do* want to celebrate our first Christmas tree, don't we? I'm such a *child* about Christmas! See what you think of my wassail."

He filled a glass from a nearby bowl and passed it to her across the cluttered counter. Sigrid sipped cautiously. Roman might be a child about Christmas but this was no child's drink. She tasted tart lemon juice tamed by sugar, rum, and some sort of fruity flavor. "Peach brandy?"

"Do you like it?"

Sigrid nodded, beginning to feel slightly more festive. "Who's coming?"

"Just family, so to speak. Oscar, of course. And, as you see, he brought along his friend. Amusing chap. A bit too fey though."

Sigrid almost choked on her drink at this pot calling the kettle black.

"And Jill Gill and—"

"What about ornaments?" Sigrid interrupted. "I don't have any. Do you?"

"I bought new lights and fresh tinsel." He smeared two crackers with pate and handed one to her. "Goose liver."

"Umm."

"And your mother sent down that *enormous* box out by the tree. She said it hadn't been unpacked in her last eight moves, but she's sure it's tree ornaments."

Since Anne Harald averaged three moves per every two years, no amount of unopened boxes would surprise Sigrid. She refilled her glass and wandered back out to the living room, where Elliott Buntrock had emerged from the shubbery. He wore black jeans and a black shirt topped by a white sweatshirt that bore the picture of a large yellow bulldozer and the words "Heavy Equipment Is My Life."

"My glass is empty," he complained and headed for the kitchen.

Roman had decked their halls with bayberry candles but he hadn't yet lit them, so the woodsy smell of the fresh pine tree filled the room as Nauman turned to her and, with a flat, deadpan Brooklyn accent, said, "Hey, lady, where's yer mistletoe?"

She smiled and went into his arms.

Even without mistletoe, it was a very satisfactory kiss.

"What happens to your show now that Thorvaldsen won't be underwriting it?" she asked.

"Elliott had already decided I'm not postmodern enough for the Breul House. He's talking about using Blinky Palermo or someone like that to put the place back on New York's cultural map."

"Blinky *who*?"

"Don't ask."

"But what about you?"

"I let Jacob and Elliott talk me into a three-gallery midtown extravaganza," he admitted, "and Francesca's going to line up a new set of sponsors. It's starting to sound like a cross between Busby Berkeley and Pee-wee's Playhouse. I may go to Australia for the year. Want to come?"

She laughed as the buzzer went off in the entry hall announcing the arrival of Anne Harald and Jill Gill at her outer gate.

The next hour was a happy jumble of untangling light cords, testing bulbs, and running extension cords from badly placed outlets, helped along with generous servings of Roman's wassail.

Jill Gill had brought with her a selection of Christmas records ranging from Alvin and the Chipmunks and the Norman Luboff Choir to Gregorian chants; and Sigrid took a bittersweet trip down memory lane when Anne opened the carton of ornaments and lifted out a crumpled tinsel star. All at once she was three years old again and her father was holding her up in his strong young arms to place that same star on the very top of their Christmas tree.

She had been so young when he was killed that her memories of him were fragmentary, and suddenly here was a new one that she hadn't even known she possessed.

Anne leaned over and a faint mist of familiar jasmine followed as her lips brushed Sigrid's cheek. "I know, honey," she whispered.

Candles glowed from a dozen different clusters around the warm room. Nauman struggled to relight his pipe, Buntrock and Roman were debating the aesthetics of icicles slung on in clumps (Buntrock's method) or carefully draped one by one

(Roman's), and Jill brought a fresh platter of canapés hot from the oven.

Elliott Buntrock beamed as he savored the ambience. "How utterly postmodern this is!"

"Late postmodern," Nauman corrected.

Later, when everyone else had left and Roman had stumbled off to bed, Sigrid walked out to Oscar's disreputable yellow sports car with him. It was midnight and the temperature was frigid, but for once the air was so clear that the brighter constellations shone through the city's reflected glow.

At the car, Nauman unlocked the passenger door, but Sigrid touched his arm regretfully. "I can't go home with you. I promised Roman I'd help him clean up before work in the morning."

"I know," he said. "But I have something for you and it's too cold to stand out here on the sidewalk."

As soon as they were inside, Oscar switched on the engine and started the powerful heater; then he turned and gently traced the contours of her chilled face with gentle fingers. In this dim light, for a fleeting moment, the memory of other faces flickered between his hands—women he had known, women he had slept with, women he had even loved for a little space of time.

And now this woman.

For the first time, he had admitted to himself that she had it within her to be the last. And for the first time he was both awed and apprehensive by what he felt for her.

Half angered by the powerful emotions she aroused in him, he reached into the space behind her seat and drew out a flat package wrapped in brown paper. "Here," he rasped. "Merry Christmas."

"Nauman?" She looked at him, puzzled by his sudden belligerence.

He shrugged and stared through the windshield.

Bewildered, Sigrid undid the paper and found a cardboard folder approximately ten inches wide by eighteen inches tall. Inside was a drawing.

Silently, Oscar turned on the interior light so that she could see, and he heard the sharp intake of her breath as she realized what she held.

It was a sheet of light gray paper with a textured surface that was exquisite to touch; and on it was her own portrait, drawn in delicate silver point and highlighted with touches of white.

A taxi lumbered past, an ambulance wailed in the distance, and from the river a block away came the lonesome hoot of a tugboat's horn; but Nauman's small car was a pool of silence.

At last Sigrid turned to him. "It's like something Dürer would have done," she whispered brokenly. "Is that how you see me?"

"Just like Dürer," he said and leaned forward to touch the tear that glistened on her cheek.

Paris.

. . . add my condolences to the Ambassador's and hope it may somehow comfort you to know that it was not a cold, indifferent stranger that personally supervised the packing of your son's possessions, but a father like yourself; moreover, one who has also had to submit to the heaviest burden Providence may lay upon the shoulders of any father.

As a pen more gifted than mine has written, "What is the price of a thousand horses against a son where there is one son only?"

I pray God may strengthen you in this hour of darkness.

Letter to Erich Breul Sr., dated 12.15.1912, from Mr. Leonard White, personal assistant to The Honorable Myron T. Herrick, Ambassador to France.
(From the Erich Breul House Collection)

X

Sunday, December 20

Conscience, duty and sheer willpower kept Sigrid from burying her groggy head back under the pillow when her alarm clock went off ninety minutes early the next morning. Getting up at any hour was always a chore, but she had promised Roman that if he'd leave the mess, she would help him clean up before she went to work; so she dragged herself out of bed and into the shower.

After so much wassail the night before, Roman had professed himself uninterested in doing anything other than putting away the leftovers and trundling off to his bed in what had once been the maid's quarters beyond the kitchen.

Ten minutes in the shower restored the outer woman and Sigrid headed toward the kitchen to see what hot black coffee could do for the inner. As she passed through the living room, she gathered up a handful of dirty glasses and plates and carried them out to the sink.

Roman had cleared himself space on the green-and-white tiled counter and was seated there with newspapers and coffee. His miniature countertop television was tuned to the morning news.

"There's your friend," he said, pouring her a cup of coffee by way of greeting.

She paused to watch Søren Thorvaldsen arrive in handcuffs at the federal courthouse. A moment later, cameras panned over the *Sea Dancer* tied up in custody as belligerent vacationers streamed down her gangways. While the camera lingered lovingly on the stacks of paper money uncovered in the engine rooms, Sigrid opened the refrigerator for juice, encountered the glassy eyes of the Saran-Wrapped eel, and closed the door again, all desire for juice abruptly gone.

When the program moved on to another story, Roman clicked it off and rose with a sigh. "How art the mighty fallen," he said portentously. "I'll begin on the dishes if you'll bring in the rest."

"Deal," she said and carried a large tray out to the living room for the demitasse cups and saucers that had accompanied Roman's *bûche de Noël*. Christmas trees with their lights extinguished always looked vaguely forlorn to Sigrid. There was something sad about shimmering tinsel when it reflected only cold winter daylight.

Two trips with the tray cleared out most of the disorder and five minutes with the vacuum took care of cracker crumbs, stray tinsel, and a crushed glass ball. Afterwards, she poured herself a second cup of coffee and began to dry the pots and pans while Roman continued to wash by hand the things he couldn't fit into the dishwasher.

An unquenchable optimist, he announced that his sale of that short mystery story had finally convinced him that he was ready to begin writing the full-length murder mystery he'd been planning since the first day they met back in April.

"In fact," he said, scouring vigorously with steel wool, "I finished the first chapter yesterday morning. Now if I were to average three pages a day, I could be finished by Easter."

"Three months?" Sigrid asked dubiously. "I thought book took at least a year."

"That's for serious writers," he told her.

"And you're not?"

"My dear, I'm forty-three years old. I have a certain flair for the English language, a certain facility, but *depth*? I fear not."

He rinsed a copper saucepot and handed it to her. "Writers with something profound to say write poetry, writers with something serious to say write novels, but writers with nothing to say write genre fiction. *I* shall become a mystery writer."

He handed her another wet pot. "Don't look so sad. I shall try to be a very *good* mystery writer."

Sigrid smiled. "Tell me about your plot."

"Actually, I don't have one yet," he confessed. "That's

the one drawback. I don't want to write suspense or thrillers or, God *forbid*, one of those dreary down-these-mean-streets-a-man-must-go sort of social tracts. No, *I* want to write classic whodunits, elegantly contrived puzzles, and for that you need a cast of several characters who all have equally good motives to kill the same person. But that's almost impossible anymore. I've been doing some research and there are no *good* motives left."

"No good motives for murder?" Sigrid snorted. "Roman, I'm a homicide detective. Believe me, people kill for a thousand different reasons."

"And most of your cases, dear child, are open-and-shut, no? Domestic violence. The husband enraged at his wife's nagging; the wife who simply *refuses* to be battered any more; addicts killing for drug money. I've been *so* disappointed to see how really ordinary most of your work has been. Oh, I won't say you haven't *occasionally* had interesting puzzles, but usually, it's for money or power, is it not?"

He finished with the pots and pans and began to wipe down the stove and surrounding countertops.

"Well, yes," Sigrid admitted. "But—"

"And most of the time, as soon as you find *one* person with a solid motive, that's the killer, isn't it?"

"So what's your definition of a good motive?" she asked, nettled.

"One that would work for more than two or three people," he said promptly. "Like your babies in the attic in last night's *Post*. Even though that was a dreadful picture of *you*, the story itself would make a *smashing* murder mystery. Just *think*: everyone connected with those babies had a reason to kill them—both sisters, the brother, even the husband. If I were using them in a book, I should probably add in a grandmother and a crazy nurse or priest."

Roman paused with the wet dishcloth in his hands. "Illegitimacy used to be such a *wonderful* reason for murder! Along with miscegenation and incest. Nowadays, if it's not drugs or mere lust, it's for something as pointless and bizarre as a parking place or a pair of designer sunglasses.

"People used to kill for *noble* reasons—for revenge or honor or to usurp a throne. Today, everyone lets it 'all hang out.'" His lip curled around the phrase disdainfully. "You can't build a believable mystery around simple *scandal* for its own sake anymore. Can you *imagine* trying to write *A Scandal in Bohemia* today? Instead of hiring Sherlock Holmes to retrieve that picture of himself with Irene Adler, the king would probably be trying to peddle the negatives to *The National Enquirer*."

Sigrid laughed. "And would probably be turned down because both parties in the picture were fully clothed."

As she dressed for work, Sigrid thought about the remaining suspects in Roger Shambley's death in light of Roman's insistence that most contemporary homicides were committed for gain. She had to admit that Shambley's shadowy threats carried little weight in today's tolerant atmosphere. And yet . . .

She brushed her hair, put on lipstick and eyeshadow, and even rooted out a red-and-gold silk scarf to add color to her charcoal gray suit, but all the time, her mind kept switching back and forth between Matt Eberstadt's reservations about Rick Evans and Pascal Grant, and her own unanswered question of why Shambley had been killed on the basement steps.

She put on the shoulder holster she'd begun using when her wounded arm made a purse impractical back in October; and her subconscious threw up something that she'd overlooked till then: what had Rick Evans done in those few minutes between the time he left Pascal Grant's room and the time young Grant met him over Roger Shambley's body?

The more she thought of it, the surer she became. She glanced at her clock. Still a little early but Albee was usually an early bird, thought Sigrid, and began punching in numbers on her phone.

Elaine Albee answered on the second ring. She sounded a little dubious when Sigrid outlined her theory, but she procured the address Sigrid wanted.

"You're the boss," said Albee, and promised to meet her there as soon as she could get the search warrant.

When Sigrid arrived at the apartment building in the West Eighties, she discovered that Jim Lowry had come along, too.

"I'm the recorder on this case, aren't I?" he grinned.

The building was one of those solid old brick co-ops with a daytime doorman and a well-tended elevator that rose smoothly to the eighteenth floor.

It was only a few minutes before ten when they rang the bell, but soon there was a flicker of movement behind the peephole, then the door was opened by Jacob Munson, still in his robe and slippers and holding the art section of the *New York Times*.

"Lieutenant Harald?" he said, surprised to find them on his threshold.

"May we come in?" she asked. "This is Detective Lowry, whom you met on Friday, and Detective Albee. We'd like to talk to your grandson."

"Richard? *Ja*, sure." He led them down a dim hall lined with framed black-and-white drawings into a large sitting room bright with a half-dozen modern paintings on the walls and numerous small sculptures and art objects atop cabinets, tables, and window sills. The bookcases were filled to overflowing with art books of all eras and a Mozart sonata cascaded in a ripple of crisp harmonics through the room.

It was a room of culture, a room that had filled up slowly and judiciously over the long years with objects and pictures that represented careful winnowing, a room that had probably been familiar to the adult Nauman while she was still a child in grade school. Imagining Nauman here made Sigrid sad for what she now must do.

"Please sit," said Munson, gesturing to comfortably shabby couches and chairs. "My grandson is asleep, but—"

"No, I'm awake, Grandfather," said Rick Evans from the doorway. "What's up?"

He wore jeans and an LSU sweatshirt and he looked very young and vulnerable with his bare feet and sleep-tousled hair.

"We'd like to talk to you again, Mr. Evans," Sigrid said. "About the statement you signed Thursday."

Rick glanced at Munson. "The lawyer said I wasn't supposed to talk to you without her."

"You may call her if you wish, but this is only to clarify things you already told us."

"Should I, Grandfather?" he asked.

Jacob Munson fingered his thin gray beard. "No tricks?" he asked.

"No tricks," Sigrid promised. "If at any time he wants to stop, then he can say so. We'll take him downtown and you can invite your lawyer to be present."

Rick's eyes were apprehensive as he sat down upon a near-by leather hassock.

Munson folded his paper, placed it neatly on the morning pile beside his chair, and prepared to listen.

Sigrid turned to the young man. "You've told us that on Wednesday night at approximately ten-fifteen, you were visiting Pascal Grant in his room in the basement of the Erich Breul House when you heard a strange noise. Is this correct?"

"Yes, ma'am," he said in his soft Southern voice.

"You said that you went outside to investigate, carrying a softball bat; that you heard a noise which you identified as footsteps in the passage to the service door; that someone unknown to you left by that door; and that when you returned to the main kitchen, you saw Pascal Grant bending over Shambley's body. Correct?"

"Yes, ma'am," he repeated.

"Who did you think had gone down that passageway, Mr. Evans?"

"I told you. I don't know," he said. His brown eyes met her steady gaze and then darted away.

"How long would you say that you were out of Pascal Grant's sight?"

"I-I'm not sure. Two minutes, maybe three."

She sat silently, then held out her hand to Albee, who gave her the legal document.

"This is a search warrant, Mr. Munson. It gives us the authority to search your apartment. If you've no objection, we'll begin with your grandson's room."

"No!" cried Rick, springing to his feet.

Munson looked up at his daughter's son and his face was terrible in its aged, pitiless intensity. "Why not, Richard?"

The youth made a hopeless gesture and sank back down on the hassock.

Sigrid nodded to Albee and Lowry.

"That your room through there?" asked Lowry.

"Yes, sir." His shoulders slumped in defeat.

As the other two detectives disappeared down the hall, Munson asked Sigrid if she would like coffee or tea.

"Nothing, thank you."

"I assume you've heard about Thorvaldsen?"

She nodded.

"Shocking," he said and sat back in his leather chair with a weary air.

The Mozart sonata came to an end and was replaced by Handel. Otherwise the room was silent.

She did not expect Lowry and Albee to be gone for more than a few minutes and she was right. After all, how many places were there to hide something as long as a gold-headed walking stick?

"Mein Gott!" Munson exclaimed, when Lowry returned, carrying the cane carefully by the handkerchief-wrapped tip. "Richard, *was ist das?*"

Rick Evans swallowed hard, then stood up manfully and said, "I guess I'd better put my shoes on. And maybe you could call Miss Difranco, sir, and tell her I've been arrested for killing Dr. Shambley?"

"Oh, don't be an ass," Sigrid told him. She turned to Munson. "You'd let him do it, wouldn't you? Your own grandson."

Munson glared back at her, his small frame rigid with anger. "I disown him!" he said. "He is a disgrace to my blood."

Rick was bewildered. "Grandfather—"

"No! I have no grandson who is *ein Schwuler.*"

Rick flushed and drew back as if he'd been struck. "I'm *not!*"

"What did you see when you stepped out of Pascal Grant's room Wednesday night?" Sigrid asked softly.

"Not *see*," Rick quavered, trying to hold back the tears. "I smelled something. Peppermint. All the way down the passageway, the smell of peppermint. And then when I got home, I saw the cane in the umbrella stand and there was blood on the knob."

Grief-stricken, he looked at her and shook his head. "I couldn't believe my eyes. It was just there in the umbrella stand for anyone to walk in and see, and he was in bed sleeping like a baby."

"*Schwul*," growled Munson.

"That's what set you off, wasn't it?" Sigrid asked him. "What did he do? Taunt you that your grandson was a homosexual and that he would prove it to you?"

Jacob Munson gave a short laugh and glared at her defiantly. "Now I'll call Miss Difranco and tell her you've arrested me, *ja*?"

"Yes," Sigrid said, and wondered how she was going to tell Nauman.

No. 14 Sussex Square

Dearest Friend,

We are so sorry you do not feel you can join us for *Götterdämmerung* tomorrow night, but Henry and I do understand. To think of hearing Wagner without Sophie beside me in our box to translate certain of the passages is almost insupportable. How much more unbearable for you!

You are very kind to give me her *Ring* scores. I cannot think of any keepsake of hers I should rather have had, and I shall always treasure the memory of the happy hours we spent pouring over them in her music room, our two voices blending together in the songs of the Rhine maidens.

With affectionate gratitude,
Jean

Letter to Erich Breul Sr., undated, from Mrs. Henry Bigelow (From the Erich Breul House collection)

Epilogue

". . . anybody ask you who I am, who I am, who I am . . ."

The jazz version of an old Southern folk carol floated through the basement room and Pascal Grant sang along as he folded his few clothes into neat bundles and fit them into the canvas bag Mrs. Beardsley had given him for Christmas.

She seemed sorry that he was leaving the Breul House, but had surprised him by saying, "I think you'll make an excellent gardener, Pascal."

"If anybody ask you who I am," he warbled, "Tell 'em I'm a child of God."

He put his tapes in the side pocket because he planned to carry the player in his free hand; his little television was wrapped in a shirt and tucked into the middle compartment.

On the radio, a tenor sax picked up the melody line. *"The little cradle rocks tonight in glo-or-ry, the Christ Child born in glory."*

He and Rick weren't leaving till tomorrow, but he wanted to be ready. So much had happened that sometimes his head got dizzy thinking about it—Rick's grandfather in jail for hitting Dr. Shambley and killing him even though he didn't mean to, then Rick's mom and aunt flying in to look after Rick and Mr. Munson, and Rick's mom saying maybe he and Rick ought to go on down to Louisiana because Mr. Munson was going to pay to get out of jail and since he was mad at Rick somebody had to feed her two dogs and the cat.

Two dogs and a cat! thought Pascal, dazed with happiness. He'd never even thought about having a pet before.

"Mary rocks the cradle, peace on earth . . ."

213

When everything that was his was crammed inside his new suitcase and old knapsack, Pascal looked all around him and suddenly remembered that Mrs. Beardsley had said, "Now, Pascal, you must leave your room *exactly* as you found it."

Well, he knew what that meant.

Very carefully, he took down the posters that Dr. Peake had said he could have and rolled each one tightly, secured them with rubber bands and carried them out to the storage bin in one of the storerooms. He hated to give them back, but there was no room in his cases.

Finally, he took everything out of the trunk with men's clothes and laid on the bottom the paper picture with the funny monkey head. On top of that, he laid the two brightly-colored cloth pictures, then put everything back in the trunk and closed the latch.

Mrs. Beardsley was standing on the stairs as Pascal Grant returned from the storage rooms and her heart melted at the sight of his beautiful face. She was rather sad that he was leaving the Breul House, but the city was becoming so crazy and he was so vulnerable. Surely Louisiana would be better for him.

As joyous music surged through the open door in final chorus, she smiled fondly. "All packed?"

"Yes, Mrs. Beardsley. And I did everything you said, too—put my room back just like I found it."

"That's nice, dear."

"*If anybody ask you who I am, tell him I'm a child of God.*"

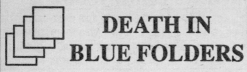